CONNOR WOLF

Let Hunting Dogs Lie

Prologue

Garrett Langford's heart felt like it was going to burst through his chest. He could feel the blood pumping hard and fast through his veins making him queasy. Beads of sweat trickled down his forehead and cheeks. He was breathing deeply, heaving with every inhale and exhale as though each one took a great deal of effort. What had he done? This was all wrong. This was never how it was supposed to go. He was meant to be the one in control, the one calling the shots, but instead, he felt like a puppet on a string being manipulated by forces beyond his understanding.

How had everything turned out so bad and why was he now continuing to dig himself into an even deeper hole, one from which he may never come out of? The events of the last few hours flickered through his mind like a movie played frame-by-frame. Except this was a horror movie, a nightmare unravelling in slow motion. Garrett tried to block out the thoughts but they kept coming no matter how much he wanted them to disappear.

Lights flashed through the trees around him and Garrett raised his head in alarm, eyes flicking frantically from left to right like a wild animal. Was it a nosy torch in the hands of a pedestrian that would just happen to illuminate him and call it in? Then he sighed a sharp breath of relief; it was just a passing car with its full beams on. Nobody could see him of that he felt confident, yet he still felt the panic in the very pit of his stomach that at any moment armed police were going to swarm his location and whisk him away clad in shackles and chains.

How would he answer all of their questions? He had no excuse that wouldn't be crushed by the weight of the lightest scrutiny. He could just imagine them now, marching him into a steely-grey interrogation room and cuffing him to the middle of the table like he'd seen in movies. There would be one officer all aggressive and up in his face trying to scare the truth out of him whilst the other would try and calm him down and take over the questioning. That officer would be nice and would swear he just wanted the truth and how everything would be just fine and dandy if Garrett would give it to them. But of course he couldn't. The truth would put him in a far worse position than any lie.

He couldn't think about that right now; he had to focus. The thick shrubs and trees that surrounded him near the entrance of the footbridge provided a good cover from the motorway beneath him. There were only a few cars that rushed by in the dead of night. Their headlights flickered upwards and glanced about his hiding spot but not enough to expose him. He didn't want to think about what was happening right now, but he was afraid of what would happen to him if he didn't do this right. Everything had to go perfectly like a choreographed dance, except Garrett was dancing with his life and one misplaced step or off-beat action would collapse his entire routine.

"I'm so sorry." Garrett whispered in a croaky voice as he grabbed a fistful of the man's lapel and made to drag him further. He felt himself sob; he wasn't entirely in control of his own emotions. Garrett raised a wrist and drew the cuff of the jacket across his forehead and brow, mopping the sweat that was trickling into his eyes and making them sting. He dropped the man once again and paced nervously on the spot, cold tears of anguish and fear rolling down his face. His hands flew up to his head and he grabbed fistfuls of his own hair. This was not how this whole situation was supposed to turn out; it was just an accident that was all. He should have called the police when he had the chance but that wasn't an option now, he was too far into the lie. The lies. He could hear them all swimming around his head like angry sea creatures just itching to break free. He wanted to yell and scream, belt the truth out for everyone to hear and be free of it all. But he couldn't, he couldn't do anything other than what he was about to.

He cleared his throat and steadied his breathing; there was no point in dwelling on it now, he was committed. The sooner he dumped the body the sooner he could move forward and pretend that it never happened, that's the way it would work. That's the way it *had* to work. The alternative would be to face those police officers and that horrific outcome could not be on the table; he would never survive in prison.

Garrett fumbled with the man's jacket once more and dragged his limp body to the edge of the trees, praying that his plan would work. The body wasn't heavy but after dragging it for a while stuffed into a suitcase, his whole body ached with the effort. It had to work. His whole future now depended on it. He was only a few feet and a short drop away from his new life. The dead man's life.

He wracked his brain, thinking, hoping that he had done all that was necessary to take on the identity of the body before

3

him. The next part was the most crucial; everybody in his own life must think that he was dead. There could be absolutely no chance that anyone would question it. This was the worst part and the thought of it made him feel sick to his stomach, but it was necessary. He couldn't make himself think about it all anymore. He was already disgusted with himself.

A lightbulb moment pinged in his head. The suicide note! He had nearly forgotten to put it in the man's pocket. He quickly fumbled around in his own jeans and withdrew a creased, dirty-looking envelope that contained the confession that he had committed suicide and that he wished to be cremated. That part was essential. No loose ends.

He raised the crumpled letter to his lips and kissed it gingerly. This was it. It was time to say goodbye to his life, he could have no more contact with anyone he knew from this point onwards. He would have no parents to wish him good morning, no friends to hang out with after work, he would be completely and utterly alone. They would all think him dead. That was what hurt the most. He could deal with not seeing these people again but knowing the pain his lies would cause them was almost unbearable and they would blame themselves. He knew they would, they would take it upon themselves and cry at night wondering how they had missed the signs and question if they could've stopped it.

He sobbed quietly to himself. If he were to have even a chance of getting away with this, he knew he had to be strong. Garrett allowed himself one more minute to grieve the loss of his own life and then sucked in a deep, shuddering breath. The cold night air whipped down his throat and into his lungs, it steadied and grounded him. No more delays.

He tucked the letter into the breast pocket of the man's jacket and double checked that his wallet contained all of Garrett's identification and bank cards; he would need to be positively identified on the spot. Once more, he grabbed the man by the lapel and pulled him out of the shrubbery and into the open. Garrett's heart began to race again as he dragged the body towards the footbridge in front of him. He kept low and moved slowly. It was unlikely that any of the speeding cars on the motorway below would be able to pick him out against the background. He was sure to keep his head down and his face averted on the off chance that someone glanced up at him. Carefully, he continued to drag the body until he was almost halfway along the footbridge.

He glanced either side to make sure he was alone and felt a small pinch of relief when he saw that he was. He waited a few more moments for the cars below to continue passing, the passengers completely oblivious to the horror that was about to come. He waited, the adrenaline pulsing through him, for a clear spot on the road. He could feel the sweat beading through his shirt. His clothes clung to him. He watched the road with steady eyes for a space. It was coming. Just past the three cars. He heaved the body up so that the man's torso was hanging limply over the railing. Two cars left; he could see the gap.

He kept himself hidden behind the body as he grabbed the legs and lifted slightly, raising the body up so that it balanced on its midriff. He could discern the make of the last car as it came towards him. One last breath. He lifted a little more on the legs and the body tipped over the edge. He watched it flail for a moment like a rag doll as it fell toward the road. He could hear his heart pounding in his ears, feel it pulsing behind his eyes. A sickening *thud* echoed up to Garrett on the footbridge. He kept low once again, then sprinted back through the shrubs that he had been hiding in. A deafening echo of screeching brakes and honking horns filled the air. By the time the screaming, horrified passengers had gotten out of their vehicles to gawk at the obstruction in the middle of the road, Garrett was nowhere to be seen.

2 Days Earlier

Chapter 1

Garrett was seated at his desk, his eyes focused intently on the phone in his hands.

"Shit, shit, shit." He exclaimed loudly. The black digits on his mobile banking app glared at him like big, bold warning flags telling him that he was now overdrawn. He jabbed a thumb at the dropdown bar to show his recent transactions. The loading symbol twirled round and round for a full minute before he closed it down violently. "Ah, fuck it." He said moodily in his gruff, cockney accent. He ran a hand through his black stubble and waited for the app to reboot.

Garrett drummed his fingers impatiently on his desk as it fired back up. He logged back in and clicked back to his transactions. Of course, he should have remembered. His loan repayment was due on Monday and with another eight days still to go until payday, he'd have to do something he really hated. Ask his boss for another sub of his wages for the third time this year and his boss always made him feel like scum for asking.

Garrett ruffled his short-back-and-sides hair, leant back on his chair, and let out a long, exasperated sigh. He looked up. He was sitting at his desk on the third floor of a large tower block in central London. As much as he wished it were, it was not a flashy skyscraper, it was a copy-and-paste building that looked like an old, disused hostel that nobody wanted to use anymore. There were mouldy patches in the corners of the rooms and the carpets which hadn't been worn away were in desperate need of a clean. The building manager was cheap and would never splash out money for something as trivial as cleaning or mould.

Garrett worked in the 'tech' department as most people who knew nothing about software and computer engineering called it, something that caused a pang of annoyance any time someone mentioned this to him. He particularly hated being tarnished with the same brush as an Apple Genius. He scoffed as he thought about it again. There was nothing genius about unscrewing two tiny screws and clipping a new battery in. But he was sure they probably got paid more than Garrett did to do it. If nothing, he was certain their buildings weren't anywhere near as grotty.

The office was not the sort of office you would find at the Google HQ, either. In fact, it was the most stereotypical, depressing office he could imagine. The room was filled with small, square cubicles, each one home to a desk, a filing cabinet, a few dozen folders and a computer that barely wanted to work at the best of times. The outdated machine worked almost as well as the staff did most of the time and the internet speed was on par with a dial-up connection.

He closed his eyes and pinched the bridge of his nose. He really needed to get out of this place. It was the only job he could find that would pay him enough to live on and it certainly wasn't anything close to his dream career. But at least it was a job. He could have been out on the streets, homeless and begging for money. That thought made him shudder. He may not have had much of a life, but he at least had a roof over his head. Garrett opened his eyes and watched as little stars burst in front of his vision. He heaved himself up from his chair and made his way to the water cooler in the corner of the room. He filled up a plastic cup with lukewarm water and took a long gulp before placing the cup back on top; he needed something stronger. He then made his way to the tiny kitchenette that was tucked away in the corner of the room.

It consisted of a small, portable stove, a sink with a mouldy plug that never seemed to work and constantly drained itself as if it were afraid to hold the water in and do its damn job. There was a mini-fridge that was always empty, except for the one time Garrett found a carton of eggs that had been there so long, they had turned into some sort of science experiment. The final touch to the dingy room was the cockroaches that seemed to thrive in the dirty sink and on the mouldy countertops. Garrett tried not to think about them too much. He made himself a coffee, using the instant powder that made it taste like cardboard. He added two spoons of sugar and stirred it vigorously, almost hard enough to break the chipped mug that was stained brown at the bottom, before taking a sip. It was disgusting, but it was hot and caffeine was a godsend.

He returned to his desk with his coffee and sat down in his chair. The only thing that seemed to be keeping him going was the thought of escape.

Unfortunately for Garrett, at twenty-six years old he was considered the pensioner of the office and it had been that way for over three years. Barely able to scrape a living, Garrett was struggling every day with finances, aided slightly by the fact he paid only minimal rent to his parents who still seemed to be encouraging that he would, one day, afford a place of his own.

He had found himself earning a fraction over minimum wage for a company that offered no benefits except the occasional cheap cup of coffee from the break room, thanks largely to a criminal record he managed to get on his eighteenth birthday party. The record states he was being 'drunk and disorderly' and therefore, had to be detained for the night. Truth be told this may well have been true since he could barely remember anything from that night.

Garrett pushed himself up to standing. He looked at the clock mounted on the central column. It was nearly five O'clock and he was more ready than ever to get out of this depressing building. No one paid him any attention as he slowly made his way through the maze of cream cubicles, putting one brogue covered foot in front of the other and marched quietly to the office at the end of the room. The blinds in the window had been closed and the door was sealed shut in its frame despite the open-door policy that upper management kept banging on about in passive-aggressive emails. The plaque on the door read *Janet Jacobs*. Garrett sighed once more as he smoothed down his creased, white shirt and tucked it into his black suit trousers. He wasn't required to wear a suit to work but he insisted on it, stating he felt more professional in it. He braced himself and tapped softly on the door.

"Come in." A bored voice called from inside. As Garrett opened the door, he was greeted by the familiar sight of the fifty-something year old who he'd been made to endure for the last few years. She was short and squat, her ageing face made to look even worse by the years of smoking and drinking. She pushed her thick-rimmed glasses up her greasy nose only to peer over the top of them at Garrett as he shuffled in.

"Oh good." She exhaled wearily in what Garrett felt sure was supposed to be a quiet voice but had indeed been very audible despite her vague attempt at a mutter under her breath. He said nothing.

"Yes, Gary?" She said in a drawling tone. A twitch of anger flickered over his face as she called him the wrong name yet again. He let it slide, feeling pretty sure it was early the symptoms of some disease that was probably self-inflicted. He hoped it would take the old bat soon and then he might have a chance at getting a promotion one day. He vowed that if he ever got to sit in her seat, he would be far nicer than she was. Her always-on, aggressive attitude brought the morale down and it showed on people's faces who, of late, daren't even crack a smile when she was nearby. She was like an evil overlord that sucked and squeezed the life out her minions until there was nothing left but the robotic carcasses that tapped away on the old keyboards.

"I, err..." He started. He really didn't want to have this conversation again. "I wanted to talk about... about maybe getting a sub?" His tone went high as he reached the end of the sentence, making a fast decision to ensure it sounded like he was asking and not demanding. Janet stood up without answering, which barely made a difference to her height, and shuffled over to a filing cabinet. She riffled through the documents inside.

"Shut the door." She ordered in her husky voice. He felt very wary as he did what he was told, taking as much time as he could to do so in the process. When he turned back, Janet had taken a small, rectangular box out of the drawer and was sitting down in her squashed chair again. She pulled something out of it and stuck it between her crinkled, chapped lips. Garrett realised it was a cigarette.

"I don't think you're supposed to be smoking in a public building." He offered slowly. Before he had finished his sentence, Janet had struck her lighter and had lit the cigarette and was pointing a fat, polished finger at the smoke alarm above her head. Well, what was supposed to be a smoke alarm. She had evidently removed it and had stashed it somewhere to stop it going off. She took a big puff and blew the smoke out engulfing her head in a dense cloud of grey. Garrett coughed slightly and wafted his hand. She didn't seem to care.

"Look, I can't keep doing this, Gary we're a business not a loan company." Garrett gave a small nod. He went to speak but the smoke got caught in his throat and he ended up coughing once more.

"I'll tell you what," She started. A small bubble of hope appeared in his chest. "You stay until nine tonight and I'll give you a two-hundred quid advance on your pay-check." Garrett contemplated this. He was really looking forward to going home on time. It was a Saturday and half the office had already gone but he was stuck at his desk poring over a project that one of his co-workers had screwed up yesterday and then passed to him to take the blame for. He hadn't said anything, of course. He was far too much of a coward to cause any type of drama in the office. That's why he worked in software instead of some customer-facing role where he knew there would be difficult customers who just wanted to take him for a ride. People like Janet. Janet cocked her head and raised an eyebrow into her hair which hung limp and thick as though she'd smothered it in a pot of axle grease.

"Sure." He said, deflated. Janet grinned showing her yellowing teeth that were coated in thick plaque and made a hand gesture as if to shoo him out of the room. Apparently, that was the end of their conversation.

Garrett closed the door behind him and trudged moodily back to his desk. He half-fell into his chair and wiggled the mouse so that the computer monitor blinked back into life. He glanced up at the clock again. Only five minutes past five. Another three hours and fifty-five minutes to go. He groaned and sank into his project once again.

Garrett all but ran out of the building the moment the clock hit nine. Truthfully, he hadn't accomplished much in the extra four hours he'd been forced to work. Instead, he'd spent a great deal of his time scrolling through numerous guys he could hook up with on a dating app that wasn't really interested in people dating so much as meeting them for one night only and never seeing their face again. That was the sort of night he needed after a twelve-hour slog in the world's worst building.

He breathed deeply when the fresh air hit him. Although it wasn't exactly fresh, in fact it was heavily polluted with car fumes and smog, it was a great deal better than Janet's disgusting office.

He climbed atop an old road bike, weathered pale blue by the years of sunlight abuse, that had been chained to the building's bike rack and pushed off into the London traffic. Garrett cycled everywhere he needed to go. He had passed his car test when he was seventeen but had neglected to use his car unless for very long journeys out of the city that were rare enough that it didn't warrant paying the hefty charges for driving a vehicle in the middle of the city. Not to mention the traffic delays which happened not just during rush hour, but seemingly every hour of the day save for the early hours of the morning. Relatively fit, Garrett had no problem cycling and his average build meant he was not overweight but also not in the best shape of his life. Being in tip-top shape required far more commitment and money than he was willing to spare. He ate cheap and greasy foods often as they were quick and abundant in the city where everything was about fast living. Quick loans, fast food and easy gambling. Anything to make life a little more bearable.

It took only twenty minutes for him to pull up at his parents' house and only a minute more for his mother, wearied, grey and slender to begin fussing over him as he chained his bike to the garden fence and slouched into the sofa. He had considered finding someone to hook up with, but he felt gross and tired and not at all ready to pretend to be happy for a few hours.

It was only his mother and father that lived there, his two older sisters, Harriet and Ella had flown the nest many years ago after studying at university and securing well-paid jobs in their respective fields.

He hadn't seen them for over a year and rarely spoke to them, but it was simply the way it was in his family. No one was ever too close and most of the conversations were kept light and surfacy much like making small talk with a plumber whilst he fixed the kitchen sink. This applied to everyone in his family except for his mum who had rushed into the kitchen to boil the kettle and was now trotting back through with a cup and saucer in one hand and a packet of chocolate biscuits in the other. His mother was a pretty woman back in her prime as it was obviously displayed in the many pictures of she and his father before he was born that were dotted all around the room. She was small and looked frail but was as youthful as a woman twenty years her younger.

"How come you're so late back?" His mother asked, curiously. Her tone was soft and empathetic.

"Just work stuff, mum. Don't fuss; I'm fine." He lied casually. Garrett often played his problems down to his parents. There wasn't much they could do even if they did know how far behind his bill payments had been. They would probably offer to support him until he could 'get back on his feet', but he wouldn't take it; he was far too proud, if not a little ashamed to take his parents' money. He was also fairly certain that this was as much 'on his feet' as he was going to be until they passed away and left him the house. They were living off their pension schemes which weren't bad, but it was his duty to care for his parents at their age, not the other way around. His mother sniffed and patted his leg.

"Well, there's steak and kidney pie in the fridge. Help yourself, love." She said. She got up and headed upstairs to bed. Garrett walked through to the kitchen which was decorated as if they still lived in the 80's. The countertops were brown and speckled, the cupboards a dark brown and the kitchen table was apparently an antique but just looked old to Garrett. He opened the fridge and pulled a pie tin from it that was wrapped in cling film and helped himself to some cold pie; heating it up in the microwave was far too much effort. He plated some up and put the rest back in the fridge.

When he sat back down on the sofa, he found a remote and clicked on the TV for a moment. He flicked through the channels. There was something about some corrupt politician, then it was a program about the crime rate in London, then another report about moped gangs in London. He finally settled on a channel that was airing some movie that was half-way through so Garrett didn't quite understand what was happening.

He sank even further into the sofa, the dim light of the lamp illuminating the sparse furniture. A cream sofa with purple cushions, a matching armchair and a small, glass coffee table that he put his empty dish onto only minutes later. His eyelids became heavy, and his head started to nod. His vision went in and out of focus as the sound of guns and explosions from the movie popped and clapped around him, but he was too tired to pay any attention to what the actors were saying. Through his closed eyelids the flashes of light from the TV gently lulled him to sleep and he was very quickly snoring lightly on the sofa, his head lolling over the back.

Garrett had barely been asleep for an hour when he suddenly took a huge gasp for breath and woke up instantly. He rubbed the back of his neck that felt stiff and sore and figured he'd woken up because of the terrible position he had fallen asleep in. He glanced at the TV which was only displaying a black screen with the words *channel off air* written across it; the movie had ended. He slapped his hands around the sofa searching for the remote. When he couldn't find it, he made to kneel down to search underneath it but before he managed to do so, he heard the sound of a loud *rip*. Garrett groaned and reached to feel the crotch of his trousers. His fingers traced over the split seam that was now revealing his black boxer shorts.

"Give me a fucking break!" He hissed as he wrenched his belt and trousers off. Abandoning the search for the TV remote, Garrett headed quietly upstairs and instead of getting into bed as he originally had planned to do, he changed quickly into a casual white shirt and dark blue jeans, swapped out his brogues in favour of trainers and headed back downstairs. He was too worked up to sleep anyway, he might as well go out for a few drinks and doze off later.

He checked his watch. It was nearing 11 O'clock. A few drinks at the local pub might make him feel a bit better, though he knew going out and spending money that he really didn't have was not the answer to his financial problems. He quickly pushed those feelings down, as he often did with negative thoughts, and searched the sofa for his phone that must have fallen out whilst he was sleeping because it wasn't in his ripped trousers that he had thrown in the bin with resentment. He closed his fingers round what he hoped was a phone down the side of one of the cushions. He pulled it free, noticing a fresh scratch across the screen and checked the battery level. It still had over 30 percent left so he shoved it into his pocket along with his wallet and made to leave the room. He stopped at the doorway.

"Great. That's about right." The TV remote that he was hunting for earlier was on the arm of the sofa. He picked it up, pushed the power button and threw the remote back down on the seat cushion.

At half-past 11 Garrett was pulling up a seat at the local pub The Grumbling Goblin. He had no idea who decided to name the pub, but he had heard from the owners that had bought it last year, the original owner was a young man who was very wealthy. Apparently, he had a thing for online gaming and thought it sounded fun.

"A double vodka-coke, please." He said to the lady behind the bar. She was tattooed and had short, spiky hair. She slid the glass towards him and when he glanced down at it, he was pretty sure that was not a double but didn't say anything.

"Four quid." She said bluntly thrusting him the card reader. He tapped his bank card on it and all but downed the drink.

He shook his head as it raced down his throat and gestured for another. When she held out the card reader again without so much as a 'thank you', another card had paid for it before he could even reach for his own. He looked up at the stranger who caught his eye.

"Erm, thanks." Garrett mumbled.

"No problem." The man said with a smile. He was around six feet tall, slim and was dressed in a crisp suit but was not wearing a tie. He had his top button undone and was showing a smoothly waxed chest. Garrett turned back to his drink but evidently the man was not finished talking. He took a seat next to Garrett and took a sip of his own fancy cocktail that was bright yellow.

"I'm David." The guy said in a way that instantly made Garrett aware that he was gay as well. There was a waft of cologne when he took a seat and it smelt expensive. Garrett became acutely aware that he had forgotten to put his own on before leaving the house and prayed that he didn't have any unpleasant odour seeping through. If he did, the man named David did not seem to notice or was not bothered by it. Feeling it would be rude to ignore him after he had just bought Garrett a drink, he decided to introduce himself.

"I'm Garrett." He kept it short with the hopes that he would go away. He was cute and definitely Garrett's type, but he felt so bummed out he just wanted to drink and then go home. Had this been another night and Garrett would have probably made a fool of himself as he attempted to chat David up.

"Come on, you're here on your own and basically downed your first drink without even blinking. What's up, you want to talk?" David smiled and it seemed genuine, and he took another sip of his drink. Garrett, on the other hand did not smile but waved off the invitation a little briskly.

"I was just trying to be nice. Enjoy your drink." David said coldly. He stalked off towards a small group of girls who rubbed his shoulder as he approached them. Great. Now Garrett felt worse. He knew he shouldn't have been so rude to someone that had just bought him a drink. He stewed on it a little longer and decided he would probably regret it if he didn't go at least apologise. He rose from his stool and followed David to the group of girls.

"David... Hey, look I'm really sorry for being an asshole. Can it be my turn to buy you a drink?" David turned around and smiled again. This time, Garrett smiled back. He was pretty hot, Garrett thought, maybe this night would turn out better than he'd anticipated. David and Garrett took it in turns over the next hour buying each other drinks. Garrett was surprised at how easy it seemed to talk to him and how completely understanding he seemed to be. It also turned out that David happened to work in IT, too, though he worked freelance and always over email to create websites for big companies. Garrett fawned over how he would love to do that instead of working for Janet. It seemed they had an awful lot in common. David was currently on business for a potential client meeting that he had in two days' time, which was rare as most of his clients only spoke to him on the phone but this one had insisted on a face-to-face meeting.

"So anyway," David had said after the conversation had turned away from Garrett and onto the topic of how David had come out as gay to his parents back when he was a teenager, "once I'd finally plucked up the courage to actually talk to my parents about it, they decided they would hear absolutely nothing of it and said that if I choose to not marry a girl and give them grandkids then there's no point me being part of the family. So that night I packed up and moved out. I ended up working freelance as a photographer for a bit staying in hostels and the like until I finished my degree. Once I'd graduated, without my parents even attending I'd like to add, I ended up landing a big job for some agency which went really well, and I then went about setting up my own business. I've been extremely lucky, actually. After that job I've had a steady workflow and now I've been doing it about five years now and it's bought me a gorgeous yacht which I keep in Margate." He finished. Garrett sipped his fifth (or was it sixth?) drink. Part of him was envious but mostly he felt excited at the possibilities if he had the opportunity.

"That's insane, I've been on a ferry, but I don't think it's really comparable!" He laughed and David joined him, "I'm really fortunate that my parents are super understanding about my coming out as gay, and I was barely able to get the words out when they already told me that they'd guessed." Garrett said without thinking. After seeing a solemn expression cross David's face, he quickly changed the subject.

"But I've had rotten luck with work, and I can't believe how far you've come. Where do you normally live if you're only in London for a business meeting?" He asked.

"I actually live in Spain mostly but I'm rarely there – I don't even know my neighbours; I'm all over the place most of the time but I've been in London quite a bit recently." Garrett couldn't believe how much he'd been missing out on working at a dead-end company when he, too, could have been earning a fortune and living the dream instead of living in his parents' spare room.

"That's crazy. Man, I can't believe that we basically do the same thing! Let me get you another drink." The next hour passed this way. Drinks, more drinks, shots and then when the bar owner rang the bell for last call, they stumbled out of the pub together singing the National Anthem loudly both sporting matching cocktail umbrellas behind their ears.

"Why don't you stay with me tonight?" David asked eagerly as they walked and stumbled down the lit-up street.

"Will the hotel even be open at this time?" Garrett responded taking out his phone to check the time despite the fact it had died earlier in the evening.

"Hotel?" Came David's response as a puzzled look crossed his face, "Who said anything about a hotel? I own the place!" They both burst into guffaws and steadily dragged their feet for another twenty minutes. They stopped outside a high-rise complex. David plunged a hand into the inside pocket of a red leather jacket that Garrett did not recall seeing him with and fumbled for a moment before he finally managed to pull out a piece of chewing gum which he threw into his mouth.

They both stood and stared at the revolving door in front of them, trying to time it just right so that they stepped in without it hitting them both. They giggled loudly as they stepped out of the doorway and almost tripped on the floor as they did so despite the fact there was no obstruction at all.

"Shh!" He whispered to Garrett at a volume that was almost definitely louder than an actual shout. As they made their way to the lift at the end of the foyer, Garrett stumbled and slipped on the shiny floor and fell forward. David caught him before he hit the floor and they stood laughing about it whilst they waited for the lift to arrive. The lobby was large and clean with cream tiled floors and a reception desk toward the back with a door right behind it.

When the lift arrived, David and Garrett stumbled into it and David pressed the number 13 and they watched the doors close. They barely spoke in the lift for fear of being too loud and awakening the neighbours. The doors pinged open and ejected its passengers into the corridor.

Once David had successfully managed to win the fight against his door, Garrett inhaled sharply as he took in the flat. The first thing that caught his eye was the view. From this height, the floor-to-ceiling wall of windows looked like a backdrop on a computer screen. The lights that glistened from thousands of windows, the tiny pin pricks that were the headlights of cars and taxis on the street. The luminous glow of city lights in the sky that could be mistaken for daybreak. David grabbed his hand and lead him through the spacious, modern lounge and onto the long, graphite-grey sofa.

They began to kiss and fumble, the only light coming from London's city as it spilled into the room casting odd shadows and pools of light that slowly moved around the walls like a gently spinning disco ball. Though they were both inebriated beyond belief, the sexual tension was positively electric. Garrett didn't get to see much more of the flat after that moment; all he saw were the clothes that were thrown haphazardly to the floor and the lush king-size bed that was dressed in thick, white pillows and cushions. The rest of the night became a blur of body parts and pillows, followed by a near-comatose sleep that offered little respite to his severely dehydrated body.

Chapter 2

A thumping headache kicked Garrett awake as the usual honking of traffic from the street below floated up to the high-rise complex and drifted in through the open window.

"Argh!" He exclaimed, raising his hands to his temples. He half fell out the bed with his eyes pressed as tightly shut as he could manage to block out the light but allow him to see where he was going. He crossed the bedroom quickly and went straight to the kitchen. He wrenched the door of a glass cabinet open and took out a tumbler which he filled with water. He drained it in a few seconds and turned back to the sink to refill it again. This time he sipped the water gently. He opened and closed his mouth a couple of times wishing he had a toothbrush to hand; his mouth had the stale taste of old beer and his teeth felt fuzzy under his tongue.

He blinked slowly and cast his eyes around the room. The kitchen was large with granite work-tops and an island which separated it from the lounge. It would not look out of place at a stately home or celebrity house. The whole flat, minus the clothes, was completely spotless and decorated in simple, but modern colours that made it look even more like a show-home from a magazine advertising the 'high life' of the rich and successful. He looked down and realised he was completely naked. He glanced quickly at the bedroom door from which he had just emerged and, though he couldn't remember seeing him when he got up, checked to see that David was not yet awake. Garrett skirted across the kitchen and scooped up his underwear from the floor and hastily put them on. He was not ashamed of his body but the thought of standing completely naked in a random stranger's expensive suite made him feel a little uneasy. It was far easier to be naked when he was blind drunk. The pounding in his head subsided slightly but a particularly painful throb made him squint and his vision pulse around his periphery.

He walked slowly over to the gigantic television that was mounted on the wall and, underneath on a sleek unit, was an assortment of painkillers. Garrett mouthed the words 'thank you' as he pushed two paracetamol and two ibuprofen tablets into his hand and swallowed them gratefully, chasing it with more water. He let out a long sigh.

"Morning, you." Came a voice from a door that was between the bedroom and the kitchen. Garrett started and turned quickly. He flushed red. David was standing in the doorway, fully dressed in tight jeans and an oversized jumper that made him look every bit as if he belonged in a flat like this and making Garrett feel even more exposed. It was one thing to be undressed with another person but being undressed alone just felt wrong.

"Oh, erm... Morning," Garrett replied nervously, "I'm sorry, I just took some painkillers... My head." He pointed to his skull that was still thumping and groaned once more. David waved him off.

"No problem, that's why they're there!" He smiled, "Oh I charged your phone for you, we have the same, snap!"

25

He walked over and passed Garrett his phone who took it gratefully.

"Thank you so much." He replied as he tapped the screen and unlocked it with his fingerprint. Four missed calls from his parents, two texts from his boss asking where he was and another six messages on his hook-up app. He rolled his eyes and put his phone on the side.

"I'm sorry I ended up crashing here, I must've just passed out." Again, David waved him off,

"No drama, it's cool. You want something to eat?" He opened up the door of a tall, high-tech fridge with a tablet built into it. Garrett never understood why a person would need excessive technology on something as simple as a fridge. As long as it keeps food cold, it's doing everything it needs to. Why on earth would anybody need to send a text from a fridge? Maybe he was just bitter because he couldn't afford one but the whole idea seemed ludicrous as he would happily tell anyone that asked his opinion on it.

"Sure." He replied, hiding his aversion to the fridge. He realised he was indeed very hungry. As if to second that decision, his stomach gave a loud gurgle. David pulled out some cream cheese and smoked salmon and put them on the counter. He pulled some fresh bagels from the cupboard and made enough food up for them both. He turned to make coffee and Garrett noticed this was also excessively high-tech. It was a professional-grade coffee maker complete with milk steamer. Garrett fought hard not to roll his eyes; his breakfast usually consisted of a bowl of corn flakes, or mini Weetabix if he was feeling flush, if he remembered breakfast at all.

After a light breakfast of bagels and coffee, something Garrett wasn't sure people actually ate, assuming it was just one of those movie clichés, he went to take a long shower, exploring the fancy options of David's high-tech bathroom. This was one piece of technology he loved. There were fifteen jets in the shower and there was a whole control panel to adjust all the settings. He tried them all out for a minute, it was the fanciest shower he had ever used, and he doubted whether he would get to use one again unless he paid an extortionate price to stay in a five-star hotel that most likely cost in the thousands per night.

David had left him a fresh, sealed toothbrush on the edge of the sink with a travel-sized toothpaste which was easily the best thing all morning. David really was every bit a gentleman and host as he could have hoped which only made Garrett double-down on the guilt he felt for snapping at him at the pub. When he was washed and his teeth were clean, Garrett wrapped a white towel around himself which had been waiting for him on a hot towel rack.

When Garrett walked into the lounge to pick up his clothes from the floor for wearing once more, he saw they weren't there. Garrett frowned and backtracked, heading for the bedroom. On the bed, which had already been remade to hotel standard, he saw his clothes folded neatly on the corner, a brand-new pack of socks and underwear next to them, labels still attached. Garrett was rather liking David a lot more now his headache was manageable, and he realised he would quite like to see him again. There was a handwritten note on top of his clothes that read:

I had your clothes refreshed whilst you were in the shower. Keep the pants and socks, really, don't give them back.

Garrett chuckled to himself at the note. The whole thing was completely unnecessary. He was very grateful, but he usually jumped back into his clothes and slipped out before he was spotted. This felt almost like a date.

He donned the fresh outfit and looked around the room. Like everywhere else, it was simple, stylish and modern. The curtains were controlled by a remote and most of the electronics were all connected to a voice activation system that Garrett vaguely remembered David using last night. He had a feeling that if he asked aloud for the lights to be turned off, they would be. Garrett chuckled again. It was all very James Bond. He sat on the edge of the bed for a few minutes, just enjoying the comfortable feel of the sheets and mattress beneath him. The bedding was Egyptian Cotton and felt soft under his fingers. It was one of those little things that he would never have the chance to enjoy again.

Garrett checked his phone; he had already admitted to himself that he was not going into work and decided to make it official by calling in sick, to which he received an earful from Janet about him calling in over three hours past his scheduled start time, but he didn't care. He had also given his parents a phone call to stop them worrying, too. When he finished the round of updates, he checked his phone once more and saw his screen was blank with no new notifications.

He found David in the extra room that Garrett hadn't yet been in, besides the closet. He sat at a long glass desk with his back facing the door, looking intently at three monitors and then tapping away steadily on a keyboard and didn't turn around when he heard Garrett enter the room.

"You all good?" He asked him.

"Much better. Thanks so much for everything, the breakfast, the…" Garrett hunted for a word that would suit David's generosity, "hospitality." He settled on though he still didn't feel like this was strong enough.

"I think I'm going to head out if that's cool?" He always felt awkward leaving after a one-night stand if he failed to slip out before they woke up.

"Sure," David turned around on his swivel chair, "thanks for last night, I had fun." He winked. Garrett smiled back,

"So did I. Do you want to maybe meet up again before you leave?" Garrett asked before he could stop himself. David nodded.

"Absolutely, I have a meeting this afternoon at lunch, but I'll be free after that?" Garrett wracked his brain. What day was it? Sunday. His last workday before he wasn't back in until Wednesday thanks to hastily booking his annual leave that he would otherwise have lost which made Garrett realise why Janet was so angry. His spirits lifted as he thought about it.

"I'd like that. I'll see you later." Garrett scrawled his phone number down on a Post-It note and bade him goodbye.

Garrett left the building and when he reached the street outside, realised that his pushbike was left at the pub. He was in a relatively good mood, so he headed back in the direction of the pub that he left last night hoping some air would do him some good. It didn't take him long to arrive back at the pub where he saw his bike, which was thankfully still leant up against the bike park with no padlock, his last-night's underwear in a carrier bag in his jacket and his headache gone. He slowly cycled back home and spent the next half hour explaining to his parents that he was fine and that he was sorry that it took him so long to call them, promising them that he wouldn't let it happen again. Part of him just couldn't believe he still had to tell his parents where he was going and when as if he were still a 15-year-old boy barely able to grow three hairs on his upper lip.

Trying to kill time for the morning was surprisingly tricky. He didn't want to seem too eager and arrive early, but he was fighting with boredom and the time seemed to trickle ever so slowly. The hours ticked by, and Garrett spent the majority of it scrolling mindlessly through social media. Before long, Garrett's phone buzzed. It was David and the message simply contained an address. It was the location of a fancy restaurant called De Lucia's, a pricey Italian place that he had never been to before but had cycled past a few times. Garrett smiled to himself, a rarity for someone who so rarely smiled at anything and stood up from the sofa. He said goodbye to his parents letting them know he might not be back tonight and left out the front door.

The air was not incredibly fresh, the pollution from the city meant that almost nowhere in central London had clean air, but he breathed in a deep lungful anyway, grateful to be going somewhere different on what would have otherwise been yet another weekend at home with his parents. He didn't mind spending time with them, however, he had often wished he had more of a social life. Garrett hopped back on his pushbike and began pedalling slowly so as not to sweat and turn up looking rough.

De Lucia's was not far, and he soon saw it in the distance. The roads were busy and the paths either side of the main road were crowded with tourists and shoppers as was always the case in such a popular city. In truth, he rather disliked living in the city and with a pang of envy, or maybe it was jealousy, he wished he had David's life. Surely, he deserved that much at least? He frowned as he made towards a Toucan crossing. By the time Garrett arrived and had parked up, he had become sullen, and he was feeling sulky when the staff opened the doors for him. He walked up to the Maître D who was a tall, slender woman in her mid-forties with long, curly blond hair that fell almost to her waist. She was dressed in an elegant, form-fitting black dress with a large bow on her shoulder. She sported a wide smile that looked every bit as fake as she did.

"Good afternoon." She said in a bright, business-like tone, "Do you have a reservation?"

"No, I don't. I'm here to see…" It had just occurred to him that he had no idea what David's surname was. He fumbled for a moment and withdrew his wallet. He was almost certain that he took a business card of David's from a stack on his desk out of idle curiosity intending to check out his website and see where he, Garrett, could improve. He remembered wanting to Google him the second he got out of the flat; no one who had enough money to own an expensive property like his in central London was completely unlisted, he had thought. But he had forgotten all about the business card until this moment and made another mental note to search for him the next chance he got. There was just something about David that intrigued him, yet he couldn't put his finger on quite what it was.

Finally, he pulled out a crisp, light-grey business card with a simple geometric design and bold letters on the front. *David Ellison, Website Designer.* Garrett almost scoffed. David had really made all that money just designing websites? The Maître D cleared her throat softly. Garrett shook his head,

"I'm here to see a David Ellison. He should be expecting me." He then began to wonder whether David had told the lady to expect him or whether he had just made that up and was just acting the way he had seen other people do so. Maybe David wasn't even here anymore. Garrett's stomach plummeted at the thought. The Maître D nodded and took the card from him before making a quick phone call. Garrett drummed his fingers on the counter as he waited, feeling more and more out of place. He had never been in a situation like this before; he was used to being the one that people chased, not doing the chasing himself. The minutes felt like hours and he was just about to ask the Maître D what was taking so long when she finally put the phone down and smiled at him.

"Yes, of course. I'll take you to him now. Please, follow me." She smiled sweetly, her teeth were perfectly straight and white as if she had just stepped off a mouthwash advert. The décor in the restaurant was very refined. Each table was a comfortable few metres apart so as not to disturb any of the guests that were all dressed in nothing less than a three-piece suit or a glittering dress. Garrett felt very self-conscious and made an effort to tuck his short-sleeved shirt into his blue jeans in a poor attempt at fitting in, feeling very uncomfortable in his white trainers. If he was upset before he walked in, he most certainly was even more so now. He silently cursed David for not telling him how to dress for a place like De Lucia's considering he must have realised that Garrett could not afford to eat at a place like this. He could feel judgemental eyes that looked him up and down as he followed the lady through the tables. Garrett felt his face flush with embarrassment, and he was sure he was glowing red.

Hanging from the ceiling were small, glass chandeliers every few metres which cast glittering light onto the diners in a soft, yellow glow. Each table was round and covered with a crisp, white tablecloth topped with a vase of classy flowers that Garrett did not know the name of and sparkling cutlery that he was sure would be spotless and polished to a mirror finish. The Maître D's footsteps clicked softly on the shallow-piled, cream carpet as she led him to the back of the restaurant, toward a secluded booth in the corner. Sat at the table was David, suited in a light grey waistcoat, his jacket placed on the seat beside him. He immediately stood up and kissed Garrett lightly on the cheek when he saw him.

"Hey, you." He said in a flirty tone.

"Hey." Replied Garrett bluntly; the jealousy he had built up on the cycle ride had not entirely worn off and it was now sitting comfortably on top of the annoyance of being dressed completely inappropriately for an establishment of such refinery. The lady whisked off at once and left them both alone in the booth.

"Have a seat!" David exclaimed brightly. Garrett sat down on the comfy, leather seat opposite him.

"Ugh," David breathed, his hands flapping as if to further enhance his point, "I swear, I am so glad that meeting is over; he was such a creep. Wanted me to design a porn website. That was *not* something he mentioned in our emails." David shook his head incredulously and took a swig from a wine glass that half-filled with a sparkling white liquid.

"Oh, that is weird. What did you say?"

"I said hell-to-the-no." David said snapping his fingers and then laughing airily. "Let me get you a drink." He added. Before Garrett could protest, a small, neatly dressed waiter of about 20 came gliding through the tables, a white cloth draped over his left arm. He looked very pretentious, Garrett thought but it would be rude to call him over and not order anything. Thinking quickly, he simply said,

"Can I have a Coke, please?" The waiter nodded sharply without a word and turned on his heel, nimbly wending his way back through the tables toward the bar.

"Thanks." Garrett muttered.

"No problem. Look, I'm sensing that you maybe don't want to be here today. Are you ok?" Garrett began to feel bad again, dredging up the same feelings he had about last night. He was being impolite.

"I'm sorry, I've just been a bit distracted lately. I'm stressing out about my job and, don't get me wrong, last night was fantastic, but I just know I'm going to have to pay for it with my boss." As soon as he had started talking, he found he couldn't stop. The waiter returned with Garrett's drink. He popped a glass bottle of black soda down and cranked the cap off with a bottle-opener. The waiter then decanted half of it into a crystal-clear glass and set the bottle back down next to it. He did all of this without speaking and as soon as he had done so, he left the table.

It seemed that Garrett had been holding a lot in and now he had started talking, the flood gates had opened, and he was spilling all of his problems to a man he had only met just yesterday. David was the perfect listener, which came as no surprise seeing how he was excellent at most things; he reacted in all the right places and asked short, open-ended questions for the next half hour. When Garrett had finished talking, everything about him – coming out as gay, his work, his lack of money, his parents, everything – was laid bare. David reached across the table and gently rubbed his forearm.

"You have nothing to be ashamed about." He started. "I completely understand how you feel; I have been there, and it sucks. You just have to believe in yourself and that it will get better." For some reason, his calm, supportive demeanour did not make him feel better, it irritated him, and he wasn't even sure why.

"Thanks." He muttered. David smiled warmly which was returned reluctantly. As David drained the last of his wine, Garrett was starting to realise why his polite gestures annoyed him so; it was easy for a rich, successful person to say it would be alright when they were wearing a £1,000 suit and living in a £1M suite in a comfortable area of London. The words felt empty and meaningless. He sincerely doubted that David knew what he was going through or how he felt. The mere fact that David was so flippant with money infuriated Garrett even more. Who takes a person home for a one-night stand and ensures they leave with brand new socks and underwear and treating them to salmon for breakfast? It felt like he was showing off.

David pulled his phone out from his pocket and shook his head at whatever he was reading, put it face-down on the table and looked up at Garrett.

"I'm just going to use the loo. I'll be right back and then maybe we can go for a walk?" He asked.

"Sure thing." David rose from his seat and left the table. Garrett drummed his fingers lightly on it as he glanced at the phone on the tabletop. An urge to look at it swept over him. He tried to resist it but found himself glancing around nervously to see if anyone was paying him any attention. There were only a handful of people who could see him tucked away in the booth but all of them were engrossed in their own business. David would be back soon.

The urge was too powerful, and he snatched the phone up and lowered it beneath the tablecloth. It was still unlocked.

The screen was open on a banking app, much like the one he himself had used yesterday. But instead of the negative figures glowering at him from the screen, there were numbers. Many numbers. At a glance, he thought that it was only just over £5,000. But then, as he looked a little closer, he realised that the numbers following it were not the pence, they were the pound. Garrett's mouth fell open in shock and his stomach sank an inch or two. It was over £5M! His heart thrummed in his chest. The insane jealousy rushed through him once more. For a brief moment he considered transferring himself a few hundred. Then the feeling passed, and he felt shocked at the fact he would even consider stealing from one of the nicest people he had ever met. But surely if he were that nice of a person, he would have offered to help him out financially, Garrett mused. But then his logical side immediately told him that they had only met yesterday, why would he give money to a complete stranger?

He glanced across the room and his heart dropped once more; David was walking back. He quickly put the phone back on the tabletop, face-down and sipped his drink as if he hadn't just been considering stealing from him.

"Shall we go? I've settled the check." David told him. Garrett nodded quickly, only too eager to leave. They spent the rest of the day together with Garrett feeling even more ashamed of himself and even more inferior as the hours passed.

When the cold evening drew in and the light began to fade into an orange glow that glittered off the glass buildings, David invited him back, once more to his flat.

"I need a shower so bad." He moaned to Garrett, throwing his keys down onto the kitchen side.

"Go, honestly; I'll be fine."

"Want to join me?" David teased, tugging playfully and his shirt. Garrett laughed softly, but politely declined.

"Later... I promise." He said with a wink.

"I'll hold you to that!" David replied with a grin as he sidled off to the shower.

The moment the door clicked shut, Garrett's mind leapt into action. He had a plan. One that was making his heart race. He was going to steal £1M from David Ellison.

Chapter 3

Rough hands gripped a printout of an old couple. Jake glanced once more at the photo that he had committed to memory. Their faces had been etched into his mind; he had been staring at them for months now and this was the first real lead in some time. It certainly wasn't the lack of money that had stunted his investigation, hell, he'd had more expendable money on this job than any other; it seemed that his client was made of the stuff. Whenever Jake had asked his client for extra funds to see if a hunch panned out, the money was swiftly deposited without so much as a follow-up question. Jake felt something like pity for his client, but a job was a job, and he was compelled to see it through.

Jake considered his military training, oh so long ago, and remembered what his drill sergeant had told him about interviewing. Never go in with an aggressive attitude. It was far more likely a civilian would respond if they did not feel like they were under interrogation. And so that was his plan. He had a name, Wendy, that's who he was looking for. In front of him was a cluster of buildings situated in the middle of a small village in Wales. She must be here; he'd tracked her for days and this was the last place she had stopped. Jake had a knack for finding people, he was good at what he did and that wasn't just boasting. Reconnaissance and surveillance were part of his expertise that he relied on almost daily. It was an essential skill for a PI.

He started with the pub, figuring that was as good a place as any to start. The locals would undoubtedly be in there and they would hopefully be able to point him in the right direction if Wendy had been through recently; in a town this small, he was confident they were all close-knit. He entered the fumy establishment that reeked of old cigar smoke though nobody seemed to smoking, and took a seat at the bar. After ordering a pint and casting his eyes around the room, he still had nothing. The walls were a dingy yellow and were plastered with old, outdated wallpaper that peeled at the edges, curling inwards. The room was alight with the glow of old lamps that occasionally flickered.

The hum of chatter bounced off the hardwood furniture; bare tables with matching stools that were all a dark, oaky brown. Every person inside all looked the same; large men and women clothed in denim and sporting flat caps and wax jackets. Jake felt like he'd walked straight into a bar in the West Country full of farmer folk. He was about to catch the attention of the bartender when a burly man with a thick accent sat down next to him.

"You lost, mate?" The man asked. Jake took another sip of his beer and smiled.

"Just looking for someone, actually." Jake replied. The man's face softened and he nodded.

"I might be able to help you then, what's the name?" He asked. Jake told him the name and watched as the man's face turned from amiable to stony in an instant.

"I know her." The man said with a bit of a growl. Jake wasn't sure whether he was unhappy or if he simply spoke this way all the time.

"You do?" Jake asked. The man nodded.

"Aye, she was through here a few days ago." He said, licking his chapped lips. Jake noticed the lack of teeth beneath his thin, fleshy lips.

"Do you know where I might find her?" The man chewed his tongue for a moment, eyeing the man before him with a mild expression of distrust. He seemed to put it to the back of his mind, however as he proceeded to give Jake exact directions to her house. Jake thanked him and walked out, following the directions he was given with some reservations as he did not put it past the man to give him the wrong address just to get rid of him.

He approached the middle house, on a side road, with a red door and gave it a knock, not too hard, he didn't want her to think somebody was here with an aggressive attitude. After a moment, he saw through the frosted glass a movement, and a figure approached the door. There was a rattle and a *click,* and the door opened, it was a woman, he assumed it was Wendy.

"Can I help you?" she asked, her voice heavy with a Welsh accent.

"Are you Wendy Immerton?" Jake queried, trying to sound as non-threatening as possible. The woman's face softened, and she nodded.

"I'm sorry to bother you, I'm a private investigator working on a case for a client, I wondered if I could have a quick word?" He held up his open hands, palms facing outward, in an attempt to appear harmless despite his broad, muscled figure. She nodded, letting him in.

"Just one," she said warily "I've got a shift soon." She glanced outside as if she were expecting somebody but backed away from the door nonetheless to give way to Jake. She seemed like a kind woman, Jake thought at first glance.

"This shouldn't take long." He reassured her and she led him into the living room of the house that was cluttered with ornaments and books. She motioned for him to sit on an armchair while she sat at the other end of the small sofa.

"My client is very eager to find out what happened to his parents who went missing about a year ago. You see that's why I'm here; my investigation shows they may have disappeared on one of the hikes that you lead through the mountains and I'm just here to ask if you may have seen them at all." Jake produced the old photo from his pocket and handed it to Wendy. She took it gingerly and looked at it for almost a full minute, taking in the details. Her face fell as she looked at the photo and then back up to Jake.

"I'm not sure, it was a long time ago and there were a lot of people. I might have seen them but I can't be sure." Wendy looked so forlorn that Jake felt sorry for her. He tried another tactic.

"What contingency measures do you have in place in the event a person goes missing on one of your hikes?" Wendy perked up a little at this and Jake could almost see the wheels turning in her head like a giant machine with cogs and gears.

"We usually have somebody who stays behind to wait with for the person who got lost while the rest of the group goes to find a safe place until a headcount can be made to ascertain that there is in fact a missing person," she said, "sometimes they might be a little slower than the rest of the group or maybe it was a false alarm, but I don't remember anything of the sort happening on that particular hike; like I said, it was so long ago." Jake nodded thoughtfully and produced a small notebook from his pocket.

"Do you mind if I just make some notes?"

"Am I in trouble?" She asked timidly.

"Ma'am I'm not a detective and I don't work with the police or any other public body, I'm a private investigator. I'm just trying to get some information, anything that you may have could help. Do you keep record logs on who attends the hikes?" Jake added, scrawling down notes. Wendy nodded.

"Yes, I have a list of attendees from every hike I've done in the last year," she said, "I can get it for you if you like." Jake's heart raced, this could be it, the breakthrough he needed.

"That would be fantastic, thank you." He said gratefully. Wendy rose from the sofa and left the room trailing a scent of old perfume behind her. Jake waited until he heard her footsteps on the stairs before he stood, too. He cast his eyes around the room, memorising every detail as best he could. He had a quick look in some of the drawers on the unit and rummaged through the shelves on the bookcase but found nothing out of the ordinary. There were photos of what he assumed were family members, an old letter which was signed off from a past boyfriend and there were many buttons and pins that looked like hiking awards. Above the mantel piece in the centre of the room, nailed to the wall was a photo frame that contained the diploma of a degree she had earnt. It was so dusty that he couldn't make out any of the words.

He heard movement from the stairs and quickly returned to his seat, clasping his hands on his lap as Wendy entered with a small box.

"Here you are." She said, placing the box on the coffee table between them with some difficulty; the table was strewn with gossip magazines. Jake thanked her and began to rummage through the box. It contained old notepads of all different sizes with dates labelling the fronts. It took a few minutes but he eventually found what he was looking for. On one of the pages in an old, green notebook, there was a list of attendees for a hike that had taken place about a year ago. The couple in the photo were listed as participants. Jake's heart leapt with excitement, though he turned to Wendy with an unreadable expression.

"It says here that the couple in this photo," he pointed to the photo he had previously shown her, "had in fact attended on the day they went missing. But it's also written that all bodies were accounted for, do you happen to know why this is or who signs off on these?" Wendy shook her head.

"I'm afraid I don't know, I only collect them at the end of a day. I was working and it was my hike, but if the booklet says they came back, they came back. Each person on the hike ticks off their own name when they return, if all the names have been ticked off at the end then everyone goes home." She shrugged slightly giving a small half-smile. Jake nodded.

"Do you mind if I take a photograph of these names? Maybe one of the participants ticked off their names by accident and I'd like to talk to them."

"Please, by all means, I am sorry that I couldn't be of more help." Wendy said. Jake stood and took a quick photo of the notepad on the coffee table. He thanked Wendy once more and made his way to the door.

"If you do recall anything else that you think might help, or think of someone else who might know more, then please do call." He told her, handing her a slip of paper with his name and phone number scrawled onto it. She promised that she would and as he left, he glanced back and saw Wendy standing in the same spot, watching him leave. There was a part of him that felt she had not given him the full story but it seemed Wendy had told as much as she wished to. For now.

As Jake left the house, he thought now might be a good time to check in with his client. He pulled his phone from his pocket and dialled up the number. When it went to voicemail he gave a brief rundown of the events and that he would be looking to interview the other people on the hike, but finally, there was something. His parents definitely started the hike and someone, at one point, must have seen what had happened and there was a chance one of the other six names on the list was that person. He hung up the phone and walked back to his car which was parked at the end of the road. When he sat down he stared at the names.

"Where are you?" He muttered to them. He was vividly reminded of a similar situation in Afghanistan. There were multiple people he was looking for, civilians but they had knowledge he was told to retrieve. He remembered the way he had looked at a similar list of names. But he wasn't interrogating those people the way he would interrogate the ones on the list in front of him. Still, the methods of information extraction he used would stick with him forever. Something like that could not be forgotten with something as menial as time. It would take years of therapy and counselling to come to terms with what he had seen and what he had done but he wasn't sure he wanted to come to terms with it.

Presently, it could have been someone else and that he was merely observing, once he decided to relive it again, he knew he would never feel the same. The part of him that functioned in a civilian society told him to repress those feelings and that, one day, they would disappear forever. He wasn't entirely sure that was true, but the alternative was too raw and emotional for him to deal with.

Chapter 4

Revelling in his brilliance, Garrett had been brooding on his plan for the entire day and by Monday morning, he had it all figured out down to the nuance and felt ready to execute it. He had redressed once more in the same outfit after crashing Sunday night at his parents and had left early to return to David's flat who greeted him fondly and beckoned him inside.

The plan he had in mind was fairly simple and, if he did it quickly and quietly, by the time David found out, Garrett would be long gone. The first step was one of the most crucial. He had to open a bank account online, using David's passport as identification. He had seen that the bank was now trialling a new way to open an account at home. All that was required was a photograph of a passport and, if successful, that would verify a person's identity. Garrett mused for a while thinking of how dangerous that might be. Dangerous for someone like David, but a blessing for someone like Garrett.

Having quizzed him earlier under the guise of idle curiosity, he now knew where David's passport was which would make this first step quick and easy. This is what he busied himself with the moment he was alone.

Garrett tip-toed silently to the office, wordlessly pitying David for his overly trusting personality. Garrett opened the top drawer of David's bedside table. He pushed aside a notebook, some pens, a nasal spray, and condoms until he found what he was looking for. It was exactly where he was told it would be. He took the burgundy passport and put it swiftly in his pocket and gently closed the drawer. He sat himself down on the leather swivel chair of David's office and double clicked the mouse to wake the screen. The screensaver popped into life and swirled in front of Garrett's eyes. He shook his head; the computer was not password protected. He had no time to ponder why on earth somebody in the 21st Century would not use a password and the only conclusion he could come to was that he did not expect his flat to broken into and for a thief to use his computer. It was probably unlikely to have a break-in at a place like this. There was security hired around the clock and Garrett imagined there was probably a whole security office.

He tapped the button to open the tabs in the right-hand corner and clicked into private browsing mode. His fingers struck quickly over the keyboard as Garrett loaded up the website for NationFirst bank, the most popular one that was trialling the fully automated account opening service. He cocked his head to the side, directing his ears to the doorway. The shower was still running, and he could hear David clattering around in the bathroom. Garrett navigated through to the *open an account online* page which loaded up quickly.

The instructions were simple and clear. He followed them and entered David's name and date of birth and used his email address, too. He was then greeted with a screen asking him to verify his identity online or go into his nearest branch. Praying that this would work as he hoped it would, he held up the passport to the webcam and it took a scan. The page then showed a waiting symbol which went round and round, it was like watching a clock. Garrett put the passport back into his pocket; he would return it to where he found it as soon as he was done.

From the other room he heard the squeak of a tap and the water stopped. Garrett's heart skipped a beat. The page automatically refreshed and told him that his online account was now active and that further information had been sent to his email. Garrett nervously glanced over his shoulder, but David hadn't returned yet. He quickly forwarded himself the emails and deleted them from David's mailboxes. Garrett had just launched himself onto the bed when the bathroom door opened and David walked out. He was still drying his hair with a towel when he sidled into the bedroom, a separate towel wrapped around his waist and tucked in at the hip.

"I just need to nip out. I'll be back later if that's alright?" Garrett asked trying to keep his voice casual and heading to the door nonetheless. He wasn't sure that he had managed to pull this off as David squinted suspiciously.

"I just need the pharmacy, it's nothing major, don't worry." He reassured him.

"Well, I hope it's not STI meds." David joked with a chuckle. "Oh hey – what's this doing out?" He added holding out his arm. David was pointing to the bed which had on it the passport he had stolen. Garrett's stomach sank as he realised it must have fallen out of his pocket having forgotten to put it back in his haste. Garrett swallowed hard, his heart thrumming rapidly in his chest as he frantically thought of an excuse.

"Were you – were you checking my passport picture?" David

groaned embarrassingly and put his head in his hands in feigned shyness. "It's hideous, oh I hate that picture; I had just woken up with a massive hangover-" and David leapt into some story about a night out that Garrett didn't pay attention to. He was sweating nervously, and his hands were trembling. He could feel the prickling of sweat beading across his forehead and down his back. He was always a nervous sweater, and it was one of his obvious tells that he was lying about something. There were so many excuses he could have come up with to explain the passport and Garrett was kicking himself that he almost crumbled at the slightest question that should have been easy to answer. He would have to do better than that going forward if he was hoping to get away with stealing such a large amount of money.

David let out a yelling laugh that swept Garrett back into the conversation. David was holding up the passport photo again.

"I mean," David finished, "what are the chances?" Garrett had no idea what the chances were considering he hadn't paid attention to the majority of the story he had just told but he figured he could probably jump back in without too much difficulty. David's stories, from what he had witnessed, were often able to be condensed into a few sentences at most but he dragged them out, they all seemed to end in a question that really didn't matter what the answer was.

"Yeah, what are the chances?" Garrett parroted back. It seemed that David was satisfied with his answer, however poor and tossed the passport back onto the bed as if were something profoundly disgusting. Oh, to have such simple worries as a bad photograph, thought Garrett bitterly. He, Garrett, had far worse things to consider such as losing his job and having no money. He lived in his parents' house and probably would for a very long time. But hey, having a bad photograph that no one has to see must be horrendous. Garrett felt himself roll his eyes at this thought but he had his back to David who didn't see.

"Anyway, you said you were off out. I'll see you in a bit. Don't forget I'm leaving tomorrow night." David said airily, biting his bottom lip and winking; a clear invitation for one last night of passion before he left.

"I'll be back soon. I'm not going to miss your leaving." Garrett replied as he exited the flat. He didn't lie too much, he would indeed be back soon and he was going to a pharmacist... Of sorts. Garrett pulled out his phone and opened the contacts. He scrolled down and jabbed at the one that said *D*. He started typing a short message,

Need supplies.

Garett hit send and put his phone back in his pocket. He was standing at the lift waiting for it to arrive when an old lady in a smart dress with large earrings stood next to him. She glanced at him in a not-so-subtle way and then turned to face him.

"David, darling, how are you? It's been a terribly long time since I last had you over for dinner. Hiding from me?" She giggled. She spoke with a posh accent that implied she believed she was important. Garrett turned to face her. She looked about mid-seventies and was dolled up as though she were about to meet the Queen or someone at least as important. Her smiled faltered slightly as she took in Garrett's face and then surveyed his clothes.

"So sorry, dear," she said, her tone instantly changing to overtly formal, "I thought you were David. He lives on this floor; gosh you look alike. Brothers?" Garrett did not feel like discussing any part of his relationship with David to this woman.

"Uh, no." He said flatly. The lady merely nodded silently as though she expected him to carry on. When he didn't, she cleared her throat softly and faced the lift again. Garrett felt his phone buzz in pocked but ignored it until he was alone.

"I'm one of David's neighbours." The lady said as the lift dinged, and its doors opened. She strode in confidently but had a bit of a limp that didn't seem to bother her. "Yes, we used to be quite the team. We would always-"

"Sorry, I've just realised I left my wallet." Garrett lied smoothly this time, interrupting whatever boring story she was about to tell. He had absolutely no interest in talking to old ladies. When he was growing up he had a lady just like her for a neighbour who seemed to love him until he came out. Whenever she saw him after that, she would always throw dirty looks at him and make snide comments about how he was a sinner. He often overheard her telling her husband in the garden about 'the queer boy' next door followed by a whole string of ugly insults that had never left him to this day. He often experienced this kind of language and behaviour from the older generation and had taken a staunch disliking to them ever since. Garrett watched the doors close on her and she was gone.

"Silly old cow." He mumbled to himself viciously. When he was sure that she was on a different floor, he pressed the button again and waited once more for the lift. As he did so, Garrett pulled out his phone and opened the text from *D*.

Same place, same time.

Garrett didn't reply, the less communication the better.

51

When Garrett arrived back in the lobby, he made eye contact with no one and hurried out of the building. Standing outside, he leant against the outside of the building to dodge the people that seemed to be walking without any concern to whomever they might take out on the way. He pulled out his phone and called an automated line for a taxi that said it would be with him in six minutes. This was one of the few perks of living in the city. Anything that was ordered online such as fast food and taxis was only ever a maximum of 10 minutes away. He had done a bit of food delivery on his pushbike before which made decent money in tips but took a whole lot of effort and stamina that Garrett did not possess.

The taxi pulled up early and Garrett got in. By the name on the taxi license in front of him he could see the man's name was Carl. He gave Carl the location of an abandoned retail park and, without a word, Carl pulled off into the traffic. Garrett was always amazed that London taxi drivers had to memorise the road names and work through all the streets from memory.

When the taxi pulled up it was almost 11am, and the sunlight was bright and rising rapidly across the sky. Garrett thanked Carl and exited the vehicle feeling very exposed in the almost-empty car park. What cars were there looked like they had been sat there for months; there were deflated tires, grimy windows that could barely be seen through and a few of them even had a smashed window or two. The cars cast small shadows on the ground beneath them and there were small pools of oil or diesel under a particularly rusted blue one.

Garrett walked slowly towards the two large, grey buildings in front of him that were once bustling with customers but were now closed down. The windows were mostly boarded up from the vandalism and broken glass. Between them was a narrow alleyway where the old businesses disposed of their wastage in giant, red bins that was now locally known as being a hot spot for illicit drug activity, and this was where Garrett was heading. The overhead sunlight threw the alley in almost complete darkness thanks to the buildings' sloping, overhanging roofs. Garrett looked around nervously; he hadn't been here in some months and knew that someone could definitely be watching. Maybe he was paranoid, he thought idly, but maybe he was justifiably nervous. The shadows of the alley swallowed him as he stepped reluctantly into it. He could see a figure, hunched in shadow, standing by one of the large bins that had been left overflowing and stinking.

"I need a roofie," Garrett said in a low voice hoping it would come off naturally. He didn't want to be too identifiable and so he also kept his head down and avoided eye contact. If he hadn't come off natural, D made no comment.

"80 quid." Grunted D. That was it. No comment, no warning. Just a price. He didn't care whether someone was going to be raped or who knows what else, thought Garrett. His stomach twisted with disgust. Part of him yearned to just hand over the money and be gone but there was another part which made him want to explain. He wanted to D know that he wasn't that sort of person who was looking for an easy night with some random girl. He wasn't a predator who couldn't care less about a person's age so long as they were to drink from a cup they'd just been handed without so much as a blink. But ultimately it didn't matter. D would not care. In fact D made a profit from those sort of people who wouldn't take kindly to being questioned. He put it out of his mind and shoved the money into D's hand who reached into a small, black leather satchel and withdrew a tiny plastic bag. Garrett pocketed the small pill and turned on his heel without another word.

Another taxi ride later and Garrett was rapping on David's door. When no answer came he noticed a small note sticking out of the crack of the door frame. It told Garrett that the door was unlocked and to make himself at home; David would be back before long.

Garrett strolled slowly over to the sofa and took a seat. He knew the plan but he also knew that he had to execute it perfectly. He started to picture how it would look and mentally walked himself through the plan, matter-of-factly checking an imaginary tick-box as he did so.

First he would be spending a little time with David, that would ensure he knew exactly where he was and what he was planning to do with his day to make sure he didn't have any impromptu meetings scheduled. Plus Garrett actually did like David so it probably wouldn't be a bad day anyway. Then came the action. The moment to physically play out his plan.

The roofie he had in his pocket would hopefully be enough to knock David out for a few hours at least. He had never used a roofie before but he was fairly sure he knew how they worked. Drop it in a drink and wait for it to be consumed, seemed simple enough. If lowlifes in pubs and clubs could manage it, Garrett was sure that he, too could figure it out; it wasn't rocket science. He wasn't sure how long these things took to kick in so he was prepared to spend some time with David waiting for it to hit him, to make sure everything went right and that David was sufficiently comatose. He could not afford to leave this to chance by spiking him and then leaving with the hopes it would work. Garrett had to make sure that David had been affected sufficiently and he had more than one dose in his pocket in case it didn't. He considered whether it affected men differently than women due to having a larger body mass in most cases. To be on the safe side he might just dose him twice; it wouldn't do for him to wake up and call the police.

Garrett continued to muse over his plan until David had returned from wherever he was. Once Garrett was sure that David was incapacitated the clock would start and he would be at the first real hurdle of the plan. He would need to gain access to David's phone and attempt the transfer on the app. That was the best-case scenario. If, however, this wasn't possible for any reason, Garrett was prepared to leave the building and head down to his nearest NationFirst branch which was only a quarter of a mile away. Once he was there, with David's wallet in his pocket and his cards to hand along with his passport, Garrett would need to ask the teller to transfer a million pounds into his new account. He was ready and prepared with an answer should he be questioned why. Garrett would simply say that he is setting up a savings account for himself where he could monitor his own expenditure and leave it at that. He would be careful to keep his answers short and concise. People always got caught when they tripped up on all the details that they'd forgotten to memorise in their monologue of an excuse.

Once it was confirmed that the account was bursting with cash, he would race back to the flat where, if all had worked out fine, he would find David still knocked out and he could replace his wallet, ID and phone in time to hopefully watch David come back round. If David were to ask what happened to him Garrett was ready to explain that he, David had complained of feeling drowsy and needed to lie down and so Garrett had stayed to make sure he was ok. Once David was back on his feet Garrett would make up some excuse and leave, bidding David a final farewell. By which time, if everything went smoothly Garrett would be long gone before David became aware that he was short of a hefty sum. Even if David did come back to look for him, London was a big city and it was highly unlikely that he would ever see Garrett again.

Yes, he thought to himself, the plan was excellent. The best part was that because they were both similar looking, if David did call NationFirst they would calmly explain that he himself had come into branch and transferred his own money to a new account. Garrett had already made a mental note to password-protect the account to give him enough time to withdraw it in cash before David, eventually, regained control of it. Garrett knew that the cash withdrawal would likely take at least a few days and by then, David would almost certainly be aware of the missing money. He also knew that cash was almost untraceable and, with David's identity, no one would suspect him enough to launch any investigation. The teller at the bank would be able to explain to the police that the person they saw in front of them matched David's description and picture on the ID. The CCTV footage would also show the same thing. There wouldn't be a person alive who would believe it wasn't David and there wouldn't be enough evidence to make any charges against anyone else. David would then wind up looking crazy and he would have no choice but to cut his losses or risk appearing like he was trying to commit fraud to steal £1M from a bank after withdrawing it in cash and trying to pass it off as a robbery.

Garrett had prepared himself for the forthcoming before he entered David's flat and it was only the rehashing of his plan that occupied his mind as he looked around with a feeling of satisfaction. The place was large for a London flat, but nice and modern. The furnishings were classy and it smelt like David, which Garrett found to be such a turn on when he first stepped through the door on the early hours of Sunday morning. He knew the memory of David would be with him for a long time to come as he looked at a photo of David at his own graduation that was set atop the coffee table.

Garrett had served his community, worked for them and tried to please them. He had even attempted to live up to their expectations …and now it was time for his reward. He knew he deserved it. After all, David was practically the nicer of what could be his twin and he had managed to reap the rewards of life.

Garrett had been careful not to leave anything behind as clues for after he had left, no lingering emails or receipts from his theft that could give rise to an investigation into Garrett and David seemed far too nice to connect the dots himself. If, on the off-chance Garrett had left something in the flat, or a police investigation somehow went ahead and they found out it who had really taken David's money, he could always say he was high and didn't know what he was doing. He would tell the judge how truly sorry he was for his actions and how they were despicable and wrong and that he would never do something like it again. Maybe he would go into rehabilitation or something like that, perhaps community service, but his current life plan wasn't working out; it was worth the risk.

He looked at his watch whilst sitting on David's sofa and saw he didn't have much time if the plan was to go ahead today. He had needed to be quick so that David wouldn't suspect anything as soon as he came home, but now he could afford to take some more precautions. So he pulled out the two white pills in his inside jacket pocket and tucked them up his sleeve, into his wristwatch strap so as to administer them without any obvious movements. Very soon David would be home and then he had to drug him. He needed David to be completely unconscious, that part was crucial.

It wasn't long before Garrett heard the door handle rattle and it opened slowly. David walked in sighing hard.

"Oh my god!" He exclaimed loudly, seeing Garrett lounging comfortably on the sofa. "I swear if I see another lady today that wants to know the ins and outs of the city as if I'm a bloody tour guide, I might scream. I've never spoken about museums and coffee shops so much in one conversation." David let out a loud *ugh!* as he dropped into the sofa cushion beside Garrett.

"Did you get your STI meds?" David teased with a sly smirk across his face.

"Yep, they said it'll help to diffuse the swelling and the pus, but I'm afflicted for life. They also said I should let all my recent sex partners know as they've probably got it too, so," Garrett slapped David's thigh playfully as he stood up from the sofa, "consider this me telling you." Garrett and David burst into laughter.

"I'm going to miss this when I leave tomorrow." David said as Garrett went to pour out two glasses of water.

"Well, you can always come back, you know." Garrett said across the room in a hopeful tone.

"Yeah, I'm here sometimes but I just rarely get the chance to *live* here." Garrett plopped the pill into one of the glasses that he had filled with sparkling water and watched it dissolve quickly. It made no change to the liquid inside and so Garrett kept the spiked drink in his right hand, intending to keep an eye on which glass was which as if he were playing three-card Monty with a dangerous street gambler. Garrett put the drink down in front of David and felt a small twinge of guilt and regret in his stomach, but he could hardly take the glass away now, it would look far more suspicious if he did that.

"I've got a really odd question." David started. Garrett looked at him quizzically.

"I just don't think I'm ready to get married." He replied in deadpan humour. David laughed heartily once again.

"Darn it!" David exclaimed in a very over-dramatic tone. They both chuckled for a moment before David pulled back his question.

"I just wanted to ask if maybe you'd like to come with me tomorrow?" Garrett's mouth fell open slightly.

"As in, to Spain?" He asked with a blank expression.

"Yes. I rarely find anyone that I actually like and I'm sure this is more than you were expecting. You don't have to decide right now I just want you to think about it." David held up his hands as if surrendering, letting Garrett know there was no pressure. Garrett tried to find a way to say what he was thinking.

"I think it sounds great," and David's face lit up, "but I just don't know that I can. I have my job and my parents. You say you don't come here all too much, so I don't know when I'd be back. I also would have to get a job there and, thanks to Brexit, I can't just go to work, I'd need a visa." David looked a little crestfallen, but Garrett did not feel the same way. Who asked a person to come with them to live in Spain after seeing them for only a few days? Part of Garrett felt a little ashamed for thinking of David that way but the other part was more resilient and that was the part he needed to rely on. Garrett felt his eyes flick unconsciously toward the spiked drink that felt like a bomb on the coffee table, ticking away silently. He imagined that he could almost hear it screaming, whistling, and flashing like a warning siren that shouted *DO NOT DRINK THIS* over and over.

Garrett felt a small bead of sweat form on his right brow, and he hastily wiped it away with the cuff of sleeve. He watched as David muttered that he understood and leant forward to pick up the glass in front of him. Garrett clenched his jaw tight to stop himself from screaming and barely moved a muscle as he watched David drain the glass.

Garrett felt his body seizing in protest to what he had just done. He could not believe that he was capable of something so heinous even though he had no intention of touching David.

He steeled himself against his emotions and pushed them down into the pit in his stomach that consumed all of his unwanted feelings. Garrett wasn't quite sure how long it would take for David to become affected by the pills and so he stood up as if he hadn't just drugged a man who had invited him into his home. Both this one and the one in Spain. Garrett followed David who had walked off looking hurt and upset. Garrett knew he had to watch him and so he followed David who perched on the edge of his bed, his head sagged downwards looking towards the floor. Garrett took a seat beside him and inhaled a steadying breath; his heart was beating fast and he was beginning to feel awful about how he had responded. He knew he should have told David that it was purely logistical reasons why he couldn't go with him. Garrett attempted to rectify his mistake; he didn't think his conscience would allow him to steal from the man if he had also crushed his spirit, too. He wasn't a heartless monster. Garrett put a hand on David's back and rubbed gently.

"David, I really didn't mean it like that." He said in a soft, consoling voice.

"Don't. It's me I do this. I get ahead of myself and I push people. Except I usually end up pushing them away. It's just because I like you." He heard David's voice break slightly but attempted to clear his throat and pass it off as a cough. He turned his face away and Garrett saw him raise a subtle hand to his eyes and wipe away a tear.

"It's not you, honest." Garrett promised, "I'm just in a difficult place with my life and I just don't know if I can commit like that right now. I'm not saying never, just not right now." This did little to comfort David who didn't seem to acknowledge Garrett. He had to try a little harder.

"I like you, David. A lot. I want to give this a go, you and I. I only want a little time to sort out my stuff. My boss is probably about to fire me anyway so let me see what I can do. I want to give us a try." This was stretching the truth to breaking point. Garrett did like David, but he seemed far too needy, and Garrett certainly wasn't ready to take that on. Garrett's words seemed to have broken through David's shell. He turned to look at Garrett and his eyes were closed.

"I... errr..." David slurred and blinked heavily, "I... I just want. I need to..." He tried to speak but struggled forming the words. Garrett could see his mouth trying to formulate a sentence but it looked like a yawn. This was it, the drugs were kicking in and Garrett was watching it play out. He didn't expect it to look so traumatic. David seemed to lose his balance and he fell softly onto the bedding. He was blinking hard as if he were trying to see through thick fog that was obscuring his vision. Garrett watched with horror at what he had done; he couldn't believe there were people that could watch this nightmarish spectacle and spring into action and undress them. It turned his stomach to think of the things that a person could do to someone who was so incapacitated. David was stuttering and slurring as he lay on the bed unable to talk or call for help and Garrett wrenched his eyes away. The clock was ticking.

Garrett crept around David's flat whilst keeping one eye on him for signs of a severe reaction which didn't seem to be the case. He searched frantically in drawers, cupboards and other hidey holes for David's identity documents and located his passport, birth certificate and driver's license. Once he had found them all he laid them out carefully on the kitchen island. He wanted to have everything prepared and ready for when he might need them, leaving nothing up to chance. Running back into the bedroom, he checked on David once more who was definitely not showing signs of waking up. Putting two fingers on his throat, Garrett checked David's vitals and he appeared to be breathing but unconscious. This made Garrett feel a tiny bit better; at least he didn't have to watch David gawking and blinking making him feel dirty inside.

He wasn't quite sure how long it would be until David woke up. It was time to enact the next part of his plan. Putting a hand into David's suit jacket, he withdrew the man's phone which required a thumbprint to access it. Without thinking too much about what he was doing, he grasped one of David's thumbs and held it against the sensor. When it didn't work he tried the other and the home screen flashed into life. Navigating to David's banking app, he launched it and began the process of transferring the money from his account. Marvelling at the ginormous amount of money in David's possession for a split second, he entered the account details of the new one that Garrett had set up. As the transaction attempted to process, Garrett could feel the sweat trickling down his back and permeating his shirt that now clung to him making him feel claustrophobic.

An alert appeared on the screen and Garrett read aloud it in a hoarse whisper.

"Your transaction could not be processed due to our identity fraud measures. Please visit us in branch at your earliest convenience to verify your identity and proceed with the transaction." Garrett paced on the spot and read it to himself once more.

"Fuck!" He shouted angrily. "Ok, ok. I can still do this." He convinced himself. He still had all of David's identity documents ready to go in preparation for such a complication. He had expected he might run into this snag but it was usually a phone call to the bank and Garrett had been ready to recite any of David's personal information to proceed with the transaction. That's how it had usually gone when he himself had attempted to make a large payment. Though, admittedly, it was never anywhere near the region of £1M. Garrett breathed in and then out four times to steady his breath. Could he make it to the bank and back before David awoke? He rationalised it thinking it had only been 30 minutes since he had administered the roofie and usually girls on social media talked about how they didn't remember anything of the night before, only waking up in the morning. Surely he could nip into the city within that time frame.

That was it. It was happening. Garrett had convinced himself that it would be fine and if he really wanted to make sure it would work in time, he had better get moving and fast.

Chapter 5

Early afternoon light glinted on the black paintwork of the taxi as Garrett pulled up in a large car park. He tipped the Uber driver and stood in the bright sun, gazing up the giant, neon sign of NationFirst bank. The task seemed simple enough. With David's identity documents safely tucked inside his jacket pocket, he started walking slowly towards the automatic doors that opened to greet him. He gave himself a mental reminder to walk slowly and act completely normal. Nobody suspected him of any wrongdoing right now and he intended to keep it that way.

The four security guards that stood menacingly around the entrance, each one clothed in navy blue shirts and black jackets were busy watching a homeless man sleep off a wine-induced coma on the welcome mat. Garrett smiled at them as he entered the building, taking note of the radios clipped to their hips like police officers. This thought did not make him feel safer. He looked slowly around the bank and began checking out all the different security measures in place. Everything was going smoothly so far. There were two more security guards at the back of the foyer which was shaped in a giant circle. In the middle of the room, attached to the ceiling was a large, ring-shaped LCD screen that said *Welcome to NationFirst bank, where the customer is at the heart of what we do* in glowing blue lettering that revolved around the circle like the on-board information screen on trains.

There was a large clock above the teller windows which showed the time was 3pm. Garrett headed toward the windows, to the right of the cash machines where four of them were open. He stood behind a tall man in the queue who was called forward almost as soon as Garrett had stopped behind him. The man moved forward and Garrett took his place in the queue. Almost as fast, an automated voice called him forward to window three.

He walked up to the lady who was manning the window, pulling David's wallet out of his jacket.

"I need to verify my identity to proceed with a transfer." He said cheerfully, trying to make it seem like he knew exactly what he wanted.

The teller was very attractive and polite when she spoke.

"And your name is?" She asked, scanning the man in front of her who seemed to be lightly sweating.

"David Ellison." He replied in a beat. She stared at him for a few seconds.

"Thank you. Bear with me whilst I bring your account details up." She said in a perfect trill. Her fingers whipped over the keyboard as she typed in his name.

"That's great, I can see you were trying to make a transfer. For security purposes could you please confirm the amount you were sending, and do you have any relevant identity documents on you?"

"One million." Garrett replied coolly whilst pulling out the passport that he stole from David. Even as he said it he felt a hot flash run across his skin and his heartbeat stammered. As

Garrett raised the passport to the window, the gentleman that was standing in front of him in the queue glanced briefly at him from the booth to Garrett's left.

"That's great. I'll just need to grab the manager, please bear with me once again, I'll be right back." She smiled and stood up from her chair. Before he could say a word she had left the window and sped off to the back.

Garrett began to panic inside, though the teller hadn't seemed to let on that she knew anything was the matter. But then, Garrett wondered, wasn't that what they were trained to do? To not panic in the face of a robbery. Did she think that's what this was? Garrett could feel the light sweat becoming heavier and he flapped the front of his shirt to help cool him down. He wished they would turn on the air conditioner.

"Umm, is something wrong?" He asked, as the teller returned with a tall man hot on her heels. He was dressed in a neat, crisp suit and had a lanyard hanging about his neck that contained a key card.

The teller responded with a smile.

"No, Mr Ellison, everything seems to be in order here. If you could just give me the account number of your savings and payment details that would be great, my manager has to be present to authorise large transactions such as these."

Garrett pulled up his email that confirmed the new account details of David Ellison and repeated the numbers back to her. The lady copied the numbers of the account details and punched them into the system. Garrett stood on the spot, rocking gently on the balls of his feet. He began to panic that they suspected something though the security guards were lazily patrolling and nobody seemed to be acting alarmed. He just needed to stay calm and it would all be over in a few short minutes.

He watched a security guard pull out his phone and type something and then stowed it back into his pocket. He saw the teller talking with the tall, suited manager for a moment but he couldn't hear what they were saying. He was nodding. That was a good sign. Unless it wasn't. Perhaps he was nodding in agreement to the teller suggesting to call the police and then it would be all over.

"Mr Ellison, I'm so sorry to keep you waiting. We won't be much longer." The manager told him in an equally clear voice, though his was deep and sounded much like Garrett imagined a butler at a stately mansion would. He nodded yet again, afraid that anything more would come across too nervous and raise red flags. Another full minute ticked by, Garrett saw from the clock above the windows.

"Sorry for the delay, Mr Ellison, that's all gone through. Thank you for coming into branch. Is there anything else I can help you with?" The lady asked, keeping her sickly-sweet smile hitched on to her face. Garrett felt elated. One more step and he could leave the bank.

"Yes. I'd like to put a security question on the account, please, which would be needed to authorise any access to it." He wasn't even sure whether this was possible but the longer he could delay David and the police gaining access to the account, the longer Garrett had to withdraw it and disappear. The lady clicked her long, polished nails over the keyboard once more.

"Certainly. What would you like the question and answer to be?" Garrett mused silently, thinking hard about the question. He wanted to use something that was memorable to himself only and hard to guess.

"Make the question, 'What was the name of the first holiday

resort you stayed in and where was it?'" Garrett told her confidently. If she was slightly perturbed by the odd question, she didn't let it show on her face. She tapped it into the computer.

"And what would you like the answer to that question to be?"

"Whipstone Resort in Prague." He said confidently. This was a piece of brilliance he had never expected from himself. He himself had never been to Prague, so if for some reason the police were to start investigating him, they would never think to use this password. He had, however, always remembered it from his school days. It was the first day back after the summer holidays and he had not been able to go abroad like most of the other children had in his year. But his mother had told him that if he began to feel embarrassed about it, he could always make up a great story and tell his friends all about the summer he *wished* he had. And that was exactly what he did. It had stuck with him all those years which made it the perfect security answer that nobody would be able to guess.

"That's all sorted for you, Mr Ellison. The next time you visit us or give us a call, we'll ask you to give that answer before we can discuss any information regarding your account. If you would like to deactivate it or change it at all, just let us know once you've gained access to the account. Is that everything today?" She smiled sweetly as she spoke, she was like a robot, Garrett thought and he told her he was finished and turned around to walk out of the bank.

He exited into the cool air feeling like he could fly. He had actually pulled it off. The whole thing seemed too easy, too simple. Did he really look that much like David that people wouldn't even question it? There was, of course, another step to his master plan. He needed to withdraw the money in cash. He intended to take David's driving license to use as identification for the cash withdrawal, so David was still able to leave the country tomorrow as planned, keeping him as far away as possible. It was genius! Garrett smiled to himself on the path outside the bank as he called for yet another taxi. He was prepared to face questions from David when he got back. He felt sure that David would ask him what had happened to him. Garrett knew that the best thing he could say was something short and simple.

Garrett would swear that he had stayed with him to make sure he was ok and if he questioned anything that Garrett told him, he would simply tell him that he must have been hallucinating or dreaming. Yes, he was sure he could convince David that he had imagined anything contradictory. There was no evidence to prove otherwise.

Garrett was already feeling tired of the lying though it had only been a couple of hours and he couldn't wait to be free of it all in just a few short days. It had been almost two hours since he left David's flat and Garrett was worried that he might be awake already. When the taxi pulled up and invited him in, Garrett rushed to give the address.

The journey to David's wasn't long but he felt a knot in the pit of his stomach that kept cinching tighter and tighter making him feel queasy. When the taxi lurched to a stop a few yards away, thanks to one of the infuriating people that liked to text and walk directly into traffic, Garrett thrust a £10 note in the driver's hand and got out.

He sucked in the air to calm himself. Garrett had never had a panic attack before but he felt sure that he must have been about to experience his first. Bolting into the lobby, he careened into the lift, not caring if anybody was watching him and hammered the number 13. The lift felt slow and he cursed himself for not taking the stairs instead. When the doors pinged open he was about to step out when woman with a young baby strapped to her front stepped in on the seventh floor. She pushed the round button that had G etched into it to go to the ground floor and Garrett waited impatiently for the lift to close once more. When it finally did, the lady in the lift began cooing her baby that was on the verge of breaking down into a full tantrum. When Garrett got out at the 13th floor, he walked quickly to David's door. As the lift doors closed once again on the woman, the lingering screech from her baby echoed in the empty hall and rebounded off the bare, white walls.

Garrett hastily opened the door and sprinted through the lounge to the bedroom at the back of the flat, throwing the receipt that the teller gave him on the kitchen counter on his way past. David was lying in the same position he was left in and Garrett breathed a heavy sigh of relief. Turning back around to the kitchen, he waited for another twenty minutes on the sofa for any stirrings in the bedroom. When none came, Garrett checked his watch and saw that it was now almost half-past four. David had been out for a good few hours. Standing once more, he slowly crept into the bedroom. Again, David had not moved. Garrett approached him on the left side of the bed, leering over him.

"David." He said quietly, his voice cracking, "David, are you alright?" He shook him gently but there was no response. With a sinking feeling in his stomach and a lump forming in his throat, Garrett took David's wrist and felt for a pulse; there was not a single beat under the lukewarm skin – it wasn't hot like it should have been. Garrett's heart skipped a beat and he felt his stomach sink. He pinched the bridge of his nose and screwed up his eyes. Fighting against the pounding beneath his rib cage, he exhaled slowly. He was not a paramedic, it was definitely possible that he had not in fact checked for a pulse correctly. So Garrett did it once more. This time he checked both wrists and moved his fingers to different places hoping vaguely he was just feeling in the wrong spot. Each time he did so, he got the same result. When he finally gave up checking, his head now pounding and his ears ringing, he considered the facts. He had drugged a man, much to his reluctance, and that man was now... He couldn't even bring himself to think the word. It seemed to Garrett that he had only recently passed, yes, a much nicer word for Garrett to comprehend. His heart seemed to skip double-time when he found no thumping beneath his fingers, it was only pure desperation that he kept checking. He shook David once more, refusing to believe what he was seeing. He was calling David's name as if calling it louder would wake him up. But of course David didn't move or acknowledge him.

Garrett backed away from the bed, leaving the bedroom door open as if worried that something might lock him in the room if it wasn't left that way.

He felt too nauseous to think clearly so he sat down on the living room sofa and put his head in his hands. He sat like that for a few minutes, with no idea how to handle the situation.

Two options crossed his mind: he could either go back to the bank and try another transfer or call for an ambulance and let them deal with it. A part of him was disgusted with himself for thinking the former and the other part hated the idea of the latter. How could he explain being at the flat? How could he explain the money transfer that would have happened at the same time he died? If he called anyone he would surely be locked up for the rest of his life. His heart hammered in his chest and his head pounded with a sudden headache. He felt dizzy and sick, adrenaline coursing through him making him feel weak. What had he done? This wasn't the way it was supposed to go. He went back over to David who was still lying motionless and spoke to him, hoping he might wake up but knowing deep down he wouldn't.

"You were supposed to wake up and all of this would be over."

As Garrett was thinking, another stroke of genius hit him. He wasn't sure that he could pull it off but he had to do something and going to prison certainly wasn't on the list of priorities. Perhaps he could leave a suicide note. He could pretend that David was actually Garrett. They looked almost identical. Similar enough that he could pass all the checks at a bank and transfer seven figures without being suspected. Maybe he could fake his own death and use David's body as the evidence.

Then... what? What would he do? He would be dead. Garrett thought even more, pacing the room and throwing glances at David's body for inspiration and an idea struck him. He could switch identities with David. He would become David Ellison and David's body would be identified as Garrett Langford. It was perfect. No one would question it, surely. Any brief glimpse into Garrett's life would show he was in debt and didn't turn up for his last shift at work. There were plenty of motivations for Garrett to want to be rid of his own life.

All Garrett had to do was plant his own identity documents

on David's body along with a suicide note. He thought fast but needed to act faster. If someone came round, he would be done for. His chance was now. One last time, Garrett went to check David's pulse, holding on to a faint glimmer of hope, but his own heart almost stopped when he found none again. He had no time left. He had to act.

He started by looking through David's wallet and finding some photo ID. Then he took out a hotel-style notepad from the drawer in the kitchen and wrote a quick note on it:

I am so sorry to my family - I have caused them enough pain in this life. I have too many problems to fix. I hope my last wish can be respected - to be cremated and for my family to forgive me and move on. I love you. Please don't forget me.

He had never disposed of a body and attempted to make it look like a suicide before but he knew he could not allow the body to be discovered in this flat if he were going to take on David's identity. He had to find somewhere open and public, somewhere that couldn't be tied to the real Garrett Langford or David Ellison. He thought for a moment, weighing options in his head. It would have to be dark. Yes. He knew that much from TV shows, never do it in broad daylight. Over a motorway? Perfect. That would cause enough damage with the fall to obscure some of the subtle differences in features between Garrett and David. Then when David was identified by Garrett's identification that was on his body, it would be obvious that the body belonged to Garrett Langford. There would be no inquest due to the suicide note and that would be the end of it. Garrett wouldn't just live off of the £1M he stole from David, he would take on all of David's assets. Better yet, he could continue to do the job that David was already doing, designing websites for high-end clients.

The more Garrett thought about it the better the idea sounded in his head. He remembered David saying that he had no contact with his parents and very few friends thanks to his lifestyle of living between countries. That took care of most of the problems. But first he needed to get the body to a motorway and to add his own thumbprint to the phone so he could access it whenever he needed to, and before David's body was no longer available to let him do so. David had mentioned something about a car he owned in the private underground car park for residents only. Excellent. Garrett just had to find a way of getting David down into the car without being seen. Could he disguise it maybe? No. He was too heavy. He would have to carry him, and Garrett wasn't strong enough to carry him down there on his own. Let alone worrying about how many people might see him and call an ambulance, or worse the police, which would open up the doors for an officer to easily check identification and then connect Garrett Langford with David Ellison and that would be the end of things.

How could he get David out of the flat without being seen? Garrett began to pace the flat looking for inspiration. Garrett found exactly what he was looking for under the bed. It was a huge suitcase that looked like the mother of all suitcases that wouldn't look out place transporting band gear. It was giant and red.

He could not believe what he was about to do. The idea was ludicrous, and the action was even more so. He laid the suitcase down on the floor and opened it up. He looked at David and assessed the size. It should fit. It might be tight but it would go.

Repulsed and degrading though it was, moving David's body was a relatively simple task and Garrett's measuring was almost perfect; he fit.

Before he could close the suitcase, Garrett felt a churning in his stomach and his mouth filled with saliva. He darted to the bathroom just in time to raise the lid of the toilet seat before he expelled the contents of his stomach into the bowl. He retched and heaved until only bile came up. He could feel his eyes streaming and he was gasping for breath, clutching the rim of the toilet for support. He felt cold and clammy. When he was sure he wasn't going to puke anymore, he flushed the toilet and stood up. His legs were shaky and he felt a bit wobbly but he was ok. He breathed a deep lungful of air in and held it for almost a minute. When he let it out he felt calmer. He was almost done now, he thought to himself as he went back to the bedroom and zipped up the suitcase without looking at its contents.

All he needed to do was lift it into the car, drive out of the flat complex and dump him over the edge of a motorway – then this would all be over and he could start his new life as David Ellison.

Chapter 6

Time dragged slowly until 1am, following hours of pacing, checking his watch, checking the news and pacing once again. Garrett up righted the suitcase, feeling the slump of weight fall, and headed to the front door, dragging it with him. He quietly closed the door behind him and locked it, double checking it before he approached the lift. He rode it all the way down to minus one which was where the cars were parked. Walking slowly across the car park which was clean and only half-filled, he was acutely aware of the suitcase he was dragging, feeling every bump in the floor and silently praying no one would see him. He wasn't sure he had it in him to fake being on the way to the airport for a holiday or else delivering something large to a friend.

He made his way to the car that he knew was David's (and being thankful that David had shown him photos of it the day before). When Garrett approached it, he pressed the key fob that he had found in a small dish by the front door, and the car beeped twice. Dragging the suitcase behind him, he opened the boot and with a great heave, he managed to lift the suitcase into it. Garrett then pressed a button in the boot and it closed automatically. When it was latched shut, he glanced around and got into the driver's seat.

A crisp smell of cherry hit his face as he opened the door and entered, taking a seat on the crisp, clean leather seat. He breathed a sigh of relief as he started up the engine with the push of a button and then turned on the navigation – where did he want to go? He had been considering this in the hours that head led up to this moment. There was a footbridge just outside of Leatherhead. It was quiet and nearby a school which would be perfect at this time of night. Garrett felt sure he could quietly park nearby and take the suitcase with him. He entered the details of his destination into the sat-nav and hit the start button which told him it should take him a little over 50 minutes to get there. That was far-enough away to not be involved yet not too far that it would make it impossible to do.

All of a sudden, there was a loud knock on Garrett's window and he screamed loudly, frantically scrambling for the window. It was the parking attendant.

"Hello, sir." He said through the closed window. The old man had a lisp and his voice was soft. "Are you alright? You look a bit pale." Garrett had to get rid of this man and fast. He did not want him to look at his face for too long and risk the man realising he was not in fact David Ellison as he was pretending to be. The man was old with a fedora and crisp suit. It seemed he had the night shift.

Garrett pushed the button and rolled down the tinted window of the BMW and muttered something about him being fine, but he was in a hurry. The man left and Garrett headed for the exit, driving cautiously but with as much speed as he could manage.

By the time Garrett pulled up to the school, he was sweating profusely despite the heavy air conditioning that had been on the whole time. The lights in the windows of the school were all off and the building seemed empty. He turned off his headlights as he approached it, thanking the quiet engine of the electric BMW. Parking up as close to the footbridge entrance as possible, Garrett acted fast. He pulled up and unloaded the heavy suitcase. He locked the car and headed for the bridge just a few yards from his location.

In the pitch dark, under the cover of the night and trees around him, he emptied the suitcase. David's body was ice cold and he panicked as headlights flashed around him from the speeding cars below. After he dragged the man a little further across the bridge he placed the note in David's pocket and checked for the switched wallets and identification that he had planted before he left. There could be no mistakes, not now; it was crucial for his survival.

The whole thing took less than five minutes and as Garrett opened the car door once more and climbed inside, he could just hear the sound of the horns from the motorway below. With the empty suitcase in the boot and the fear pummelling his heart, he winced at the thought of what he had just done and sped off into the night, putting as much distance between himself and David - no, Garrett - as he could.

He was David Ellison now. He had to believe that. Had to embody it with every fibre of his being if he were to make it out of the coming weeks and months.

And with David Ellison's name, Garrett was free to be whomever he wanted. But who did he want to be? That question had been plaguing him for the last few days - ever since his decision that sparked all of this off. Perhaps it was time to focus on something else besides solely working for a terrible company with low pay and figuring out just what

David's life actually meant to the generous man and what it could mean to Garrett.

After all, being someone else would mean never having to face the consequence of his actions again. It would give him a fresh start without any baggage or real obstacles in his way. His decisions may not have worked out so well for him this time, but they sure as hell made things interesting, and if nothing, they had brought him to this very moment! And if there was anything he had learned from being Garrett Langford throughout the years, it was that he needed life to be interesting.

He had been sitting around the house for days as Garrett Langford, staring at the wall and trying to figure out what he would do next or where he was going. He could have gotten a new job - try to get one of those contracts that David had going on, he was smart enough for that - but going back into an office environment? Garrett shuddered at the thought immediately, feeling it ripple down his spine. Not a chance... Plus, with his new-found wealth there were other options available - maybe even more preferable ones too.

Just a few years ago, he had been planning out his next step - the one that would have him rise from mid-level analyst to upper management, not that Janet would have allowed anything of the sort to take place under her rule. He had been thinking about what doing it all over again, but with a different company might look like. Now he could go back to those same plans and actually achieve them, if he wished. He really wasn't sure quite what he wanted to do with his new life but the fact that he now had a choice was elating. The thought of being able to take hold of his future excited him more than anything else.

But before any of that... Was there even a way for Garrett Langford's body to survive long enough for David Ellison's plan? He knew a couple things about this world, sure; after all, who hasn't seen their share of movies and TV shows throughout their life? But that didn't mean he knew enough to prepare himself for everything that he was about to face. There was only so much research you could do on the subject before it started feeling too immersive - too real. After all, he had spent most of his adult years living inside the boundaries of someone else's world, someone like David whom he would never have even rubbed shoulders with if it weren't for happening upon him by chance in a pub.

If only there was someone he could call, someone who would be able to help him get settled into this new life of his and forget what he had done to get it. But that wasn't an option, not with the number of people that could mess this up for him if he spoke. If he were to get any help along the way, it would do nothing but get one more person involved in what Garrett had done; and based on how things went for him... He didn't want anything else tying him back to what he just did.

He looked left and right through the windscreen. He was in some place with nice houses now, almost an hours' drive from the motorway and many thoughts occurred to him but it also left him with more questions than answers.

The nice houses and expensive cars on the driveways gleamed at him. He could have that too. He had money in the bank, a lot of it. But he needed to save that for now in case anyone started snooping or investigating. He couldn't be seen making extravagant purchases that would show up as odd behaviour. He had to look like he fit in, not stand out and that meant copying David until he was out of the woods and then he could slowly merge David with Garrett until he was living the best version of the two of them.

He spent a long time driving around looking at the houses and thinking about his next steps as to what he wanted to do, trying to keep his mind off the body on the M25 that was no doubt national news by now. Dawn began to break over the horizon as Garrett pulled back up to the flat complex and parked in David's space once more. He had to at least play the game for a while. It was time to really become David Ellison. This meant he needed to dress like David, work like David and act like David. Garrett felt the crushing pressure of the work ahead but it was imperative to keep him afloat and ahead of the game. He was now a murderer. There was definitely no way back for Garrett, not if he wanted to live anywhere outside of a four-walled cell, under surveillance every hour of the day.

The only way forward was to take the path of David Ellison. He stepped out of the car and trudged slowly back through the doors of the lift. He left the suitcase in the car covered by the large parcel shelf. He would move it eventually but right now, the police would have to get a warrant to open his boot and they were not on his trail, he felt confident of that.

Garrett ascended the floors and went back into David's – his – flat, eager to get started on his new journey. The first thing he did was take a long shower, enjoying the peace of the water and the pressure of the jets that blasted his skin. He shaved away any remnants of the scruff that had built up over the last 24 hours and scrubbed himself raw.

As soon as he was dry, he headed toward the only door he hadn't yet opened in the flat. The closet. It was easily as large as the bedroom and stocked full. The cupboards were a clean, crisp white with recessed lighting and an island in the middle that had drawers built into it. There was an empty space for extra hangers and each one was velvet coated. The shirts and suits hung in separate parts to the left, which seemed to be the formal side as there were also dinner jackets, tuxedos and smart trousers. On the right had all the casual clothes including short and long-sleeved, casual shirts, chinos, t-shirts, jumpers and hoodies. The shoes were found under each cubby space, the smart, formal shoes on the left and the casual boots and trainers on the right.

Garrett opened one of the left-hand drawers in the island. It lit up when it was pulled out and inside were a dozen expensive watches that rotated on electric swivels making them glitter. There was at least £100,000 worth of watches looking and ticking at him but he closed the drawer; he had all the time in the world to wear each and every one of them. At the back of the closet, to the left of a bevelled full-length mirror, was a thin door, he opened it and pulled out a rack with dozens of hooks. On each one was a tie. There were ties of all sizes and colours, patterns and fabrics. Below the rail was a drawer which contained a matching pocket square for each of the ties.

Garrett was not quite feeling like suite-and-tie attire and stepped over to the right side of the closet. Flicking through the clothes, he pulled a long-sleeve, white shirt from a velvet hanger and laid it on the island. He then chose a simple beige pair of chinos. Opening a similarly thin cupboard door, he located the belts. From the assortment that greeted him, he withdrew a brown leather one and placed it on the island, too. He then picked out a pair of brown suede loafers. In one of the right-hand, island drawers he found casual white socks, and from the other, a simple watch with a leather strap. He also pulled from a hangar, a navy crew-neck jumper.

Garrett dressed slowly, enjoying each article of clothing as he put it on; he had never owned so many nice pieces of clothing before. Before the David fiasco, he had rotated between a handful of t-shirts and jeans that quickly wore out. He had never owned a decent watch in his life, only the digital one his parents had given him five years ago for his birthday, nothing like the ones he now owned, with multiple dials and exposed mechanisms. And there was a whole drawer-full of them ticking quietly.

When Garrett was dressed he took a long look at himself in the mirror. He admired himself for the first time in his life. He looked sharp and clean. He looked every bit as crisp and expensive as David had done. But of course, *he* was now David so looking the part was crucial. He knew he was safe for now, but a few misplaced words or actions could uncover more than just a few lies.

He left the closet and decided he needed to head out into the world again, knowing full well there were people watching him this time around. He didn't want them to see him doing anything strange or different; instead he fell into David's routine.

Although David did indeed have a ticket to fly to Spain later that day, and much to Garrett's fierce regret, he decided now was not a good time to go. The tickets were booked and laid neatly on the desk where David had left them but he was cautious of seeming too suspicious by leaving the country; that's exactly what someone who just committed a crime would do. No, he had to play the part of an emotional, extrovert of a man who was still trying to seek validation from those around him as if his parents hadn't disowned him like

Garrett was told they had and instead, hide his emotions under a pile of money.

Though he hadn't slept in over 24 hours, he knew he had to go about life as if it were completely normal. Something as simple as slipping up because he was tired just simply couldn't happen. So he greeted the man who delivered his mail. He said hello to the old man in the lift on the way out of the building and smiled at the woman who made his coffee to order at 11am that morning. The journey outside left Garrett feeling exposed and jittery. It wasn't like anything had happened at all to make him feel that way - but Garrett couldn't shake off the feeling that someone might realise who he really was. That set him on edge through every interaction he had with strangers. Especially when he sat down to drink his coffee in the coffee shop.

Two tables over, a young couple were viciously discussing something awful that had happened just hours earlier… on a motorway about an hour away. Some man had apparently jumped off the footbridge into the traffic in the early hours of the morning.

"Oh my god, I can't even believe that! Can you imagine how awful those drivers must have felt? I bet that woke them up!" The blonde woman stirred her iced coffee loudly before she took a sip and then continuing, "I wonder what he was thinking? Must have been pretty depressed…"

"I know," the other woman with brunette, short hair replied, "I don't know if I would ever have the guts to throw myself off the bridge like that. Right into cars. No thanks."

Garrett's eyes were slowly widening as he listened in on the conversation. He never would have thought, but it seemed like hearing someone else speak their thoughts out loud was a good thing for him; it meant he knew what they were thinking. They clearly didn't seem to think it was anything more than an awful thing for someone depressed to do. He started thinking about his family and how they were reacting to the news and doubted they would be speaking of it with such nonchalance. Surely the police would have contacted them by now. He felt sick. But he was in this now and he would have to stick it through. The two women continued to chat about it for a few more minutes and then their conversation trailed off to something trivial.

Garrett did not want to sit here drinking his coffee, but this was all part of the charade he had to keep up, at least for a while. He took his phone out of his pocket and did something he had been avoiding. He checked the latest breaking news. There it was. Top story. Suicide on the motorway. He gulped hard. He had to drink something or he was going to choke on his own tongue which he realised he was biting hard. He took a hefty swig of his coffee, slightly enjoying the way it burnt his tongue and his throat as he swallowed it. Just then his phone vibrated. It was a message from David's client, Albert, asking for an update on the website that he was supposed to be creating for a used car dealership in Leicester.

Garrett pondered for a moment and then texted back saying it was in progress and would be done soon. This seemed to pacify Albert for a bit. He had bought himself some time. Looking back, he wished he had considered other alternatives for raising money before leaping into theft such as starting his own business but he shoved that thought out of his head, there was no point in regret now, it would only make him feel worse than he already did.

Garrett went back to pretending as though everything was

normal, but now his eyes darted from person to person as he overheard their conversations.

"I'm thinking of quitting," a bald man spoke to his phone which he was holding to his ear, "I just can't take it. They've cut my commission to five percent which is bullshit. Honestly, what a joke." The man was absentmindedly picking at a muffin he had bought and was leaving the crumbs to fall over the floor around him. There was a small television on one of the walls opposite the counter for the patrons to enjoy but the sound was muted and the subtitles were on instead. The TV was displaying a segment of a news program which was covering the motorway suicide. Garrett tore his eyes away from the screen and began to drink his coffee in large gulps. As soon as he finished his drink, Garrett left tip money on the table and got up from his seat. He needed fresh air again. Even if it was just for a few minutes.

He had on him a laptop which David had mentioned in passing that he used for his work on the go when he was not at home, this was also protected by a thumb print that he was able to bypass by accessing the written password on the mobile that now recognised his own fingerprint. He made his way down the street and casually wandered past a few shops, peering into the glass as he stalked by. He paid no attention to what was in the window but he noticed that most people seemed to glance inside and copied them.

It was cloudy outside and there were people everywhere he looked. They all seemed occupied looking for somewhere to go, or something to buy from one of the various stores that lined the street. There was a niggling feeling inside that he couldn't shake. It was the sinking paranoia that one of them was following him. It felt too surreal to be walking around as if he had not just stolen another man's identity and disposed of his body like he did it every other weekend.

He looked for a quiet place that he could work on David's project - if indeed he could even focus for that long - and spotted a picnic table in Hyde Park. He set himself up and pulled out the laptop.

He hadn't even opened it up or turned it on when he was approached by a man. The man looked about 35 years old and had short dark brown hair was spiked at the front. He was large and muscly wearing a green t-shirt that stretched over his massive arms. He wore camo trousers, secured by a heavy-duty belt, and big working-man's boots.

"Can I help you?" Garrett asked. In his experience, it was best to be suspicious even without committing a crime; this was London after all.

"Well," the man replied, "I think I can help you." His voice was deep and gravelly.

Garrett felt a flicker of alarm but he tried to play it cool. He decided not to comment on how cryptic that sounded and simply asked what the man meant. The brown-haired guy smiled and then pulled up a seat.

"I've been watching you," he said, "you're looking for something."

Garrett did not reply this time either. He kept silent and waited for the stranger to reveal more information. He threw Garrett a quizzical look as if he were trying to communicate something to him.

"It's okay," he continued, "I'm not rabid or anything. You can trust me."

Garrett felt sure that the man would soon be able to see his heart pounding through his shirt. Still he remained silent. He could feel the blood pumping hard in his ears to the point he could hear it.

"You see," the stranger continued, "I could tell you were looking for something... Or someone, maybe multiple someone's. It's why I came over to you."

Even though he was already running scenarios through his head trying to figure out how this was going to end, Garrett still couldn't help but be intrigued by what this man had to say. Surely if he knew, if he really knew, he wouldn't just sit by and casually talk about it as though they were friends having dinner. There was still an air of mystery in his voice, but it felt like he was hinting to something of which Garrett had no idea.

"I mean, I could be wrong." He said, "Maybe *you* are not looking for anyone." He squinted at Garrett as though looking through him or into him.

Garrett felt himself relax a bit. The man saw this and gave him an understanding nod that did not mean anything to Garrett but maybe it wasn't meant for him; he might have been nodding to himself.

"I get it though," he continued, this time dropping the mystical vibes, "travelling is like that sometimes isn't it? You find yourself in strange places but you can't quite put a finger on why. People tell you they know what it feels like but it doesn't seem to fit together for yourself. That's how I felt when I first arrived here. Lost."

Ok, the man thought he was travelling and that's why he looked so confused and not with it at all. Either that or he was drunk. It could well be the latter. Garrett would play along for a minute until he could politely shake the man off. It was not a smart move to overreact and cause a scene. People walked by and paid them no notice or attention and he intended to keep it that way.

"Oh… Yeah, that's right. I'm not hugely familiar with this area." Garrett finally responded. He did not want to commit and say anything too specific such as never having been to London. If he said something like that, he could be easily found out with a short search on the internet. David had branded his laptop with a QR code to his website for potential customers. Though it wasn't an uncommon practice at all to have a chat with a stranger, Garrett was not sure how well he could trust this man.

"I know, I know," the man suggested, "you're here for work right? That is why people travel isn't it?"

Garrett nodded in agreement even though his heart rate had spiked again. This guy just might have been a bit too accurate with his assumptions, that's exactly why David *had* been in London.

"There's a lot of activity here," the man continued, looking around and gesturing to the people and the buildings that surrounded Hyde Park, "and I mean that in both senses. A lot of people coming and going which is normal for this area but also a lot *going on*. You can feel it in the air. The sex, the secrets, the lies."

Garrett frowned to himself. He was not sure what this guy's angle was, but he decided to take a chance.

"What do you mean?" Garrett asked in his best curious-but-polite tone. The man smiled again and Garrett felt more at ease when he noticed that there were no gold teeth or anything like he associated with gangs or mobster bosses.

"Well," he said, "let me put it another way for you."

Before continuing, the man paused to take a sip of his coffee that Garrett hadn't noticed the man was holding until this moment. He made a mental note to be more observant.

"What I mean is that you are clearly not from here," he said, "I can tell by your mannerisms."

This was it, Garrett could feel that the man was finally coming around to what he had wanted to say.

"People watch you. They observe you. They take in what you give out and what you're giving out is very revealing of your character. You act like you do not belong." The man continued.

"Do not belong where?" Asked Garrett.

"Anywhere. Here. There." The man was still being cryptic and it was starting to bother him.

"I know where I belong. Do you have something to say to me?" He asked in a far braver voice than he felt. For all Garrett knew, he could be setting up an attack when there are people around. Garrett felt his legs stiffen as he prepared to leap up from the bench and run as fast as he could if the moment came.

"You've never heard of the Ripper, have you?" he asked. Though Garrett knew exactly what was being discussed, he feigned ignorance so as not to trigger this man who could end up being dangerous.

"The Ripper?" Garrett repeated out loud, "No I haven't."

The man went on to explain about Jack the Ripper and his heinous crimes. Garrett wasn't sure the man had lost track of his original thought and wondered if he was being threatened. He allowed the man to talk for ten minutes before Garrett checked his watch and pretended he had somewhere to be. When the man offered to escort him there, seeing as he didn't know the area that well, Garrett shook him off and gave the excuse of wanting to learn the surroundings a bit better.

The man was gone. Was he actually just a harmless stranger? Garrett wanted to believe it but there was something about the interaction that didn't sit right with him. He thought about this for a long time as he headed back to David's flat. When he reached the lobby he was stopped by the security and Garrett's stomach shrivelled with fear. This was it. He was going to be caught. The security guard pulled him to one side.

"Mr Ellison," he began, "I don't quite know how to tell you this but your flat was the subject of what appears to be a break-in, sir." His voice was slightly squeaky. Garrett swallowed hard.

"What?" He asked, his voice catching in his throat. He felt the terror flood through him and the blood drain from his face. The security guard, an old, greying man put a hand under his elbow and guided him to a chair nearby.

"Don't worry, sir. I called the police as soon as I heard about it. Some gentleman told me about it on his way out of the building earlier, said he noticed the door was ajar and called security when he asked if there was anyone in the flat and got no reply." Garrett thought he was going to faint. The police? The last people of all he wanted to speak to. Ok, he thought to himself, they're not here to make an arrest, they were here to support him, not interrogate. He needed to gather himself and speak to the police as quickly as he could and get them away from his flat. No one, as far as he knew, suspected anything was off with the suicide, not including the odd man in the park whom Garrett wasn't even sure he knew much about anything. Of course, it was still very early days and things could change at the drop of a hat and all it took was a misspoken word.

"I was going to let you know just as soon as the police got here but I saw you coming down the street. They're just

upstairs, I'll phone up and let them know you're on your way."
He told Garrett, who nodded gratefully on the outside but felt
like his organs were burning or shutting down on the inside.

Garrett ascended the floors once more and was greeted by
a lady in police uniform and another officer, male, who was
talking quickly on the phone but Garrett could not hear what
was being said. He took this as a good sign that they did not
send a full squad clad in riot uniform and battering rams.

"Ah, good afternoon, Mr Ellison. I'm sergeant Allison
Brown." She said briskly. Her voice was booming and
professional. Strictly business-like. He immediately got the
feeling that she would not be out of place training military
recruits for the armed forces.

"We understand a break in has taken place on the premises.
Would you mind following me so we can have a look?"

Garrett wanted to shout at them and send them on their
way, telling them to go get a warrant if they wanted to step
foot on his premises. But he couldn't say that and it wasn't as
if they were here to take him in so he allowed himself to be
lead towards David's flat.

They entered and Garrett felt sick just seeing the state of it
again. Had someone gone through his computer? Why had
he decided to hide out at David's place? He thought about this
too late, as ever.

"Looks like you might have been burgled, Mr Ellison. Do
you notice anything missing at all?" Garrett had a look around.
From what he could see there was nothing missing. But this
didn't mean all that much considering he'd only been in the
flat a handful of times.

"Not that I can see. Security said the door was ajar?" Garrett
asked of the police officer who nodded in agreement.

"That's right, one of the residents called security who called us, concerned that someone might have broken in. We were going to see if we could get the security footage from downstairs." She said in an almost bored voice. Maybe this wasn't the most exciting case for the lady who looked like she would be at home in the middle of a deadly shootout or chasing criminals down the motorway at 110mph. Yes, she looked very much like she would love nothing more than a high-speed police chase instead of questioning a man about a burglary where nothing was taken.

"The locks did not appear to have been forced, either which means I do just have to ask, is it worth me checking the security footage or did you leave your door open when you left?" Garrett wanted to laugh, cry, shout and scream all at once but leapt on to her question realising he wasn't sure just how much she would catch on the CCTV footage, maybe his dark secret?

"Yes," he replied, "I suppose it is possible I might have left it open. You're right, if the locks weren't forced and nothing was stolen, it seems the most obvious solution." He could see the lady fighting to restrain herself from rolling her eyes.

"Well... That is a shame." She said. "But if you do find that something was stolen or if you find any other evidence that might suggest something nefarious at work, please do let us know immediately and get yourself out of the flat, find somewhere, a hotel maybe. Just in case, I've got two police officers that will stay here over night." Her tone of voice suggested that she felt it was a huge waste of public resources. Garrett nodded. He did not want to stay here where he might be under scrutiny himself, but he also wanted to make sure he could keep his eye on the police officers in the event that someone had indeed broken in to the flat; he felt almost positive that he recalled locking the door but admitted he was suffering from lack of sleep and there was a possibility, however small, that he did leave the flat unlocked.

"Okay, thank you for your time," the police officer said, "we'll be in touch." She handed Garrett a business card and asked him to call if he had any information that might help. With that they left and once again Garrett was alone in what was now his new flat. He took a bottle of water out of the fridge. He started reeling over in his mind why he might have been burgled. Why now? Did someone know something? Was somebody onto him? Garrett had a lot of questions and no answers. He even considered that maybe somebody didn't break in to take something out but to plant something in. As soon as he considered this, however, he realised it would be pointless to try and find it considering he could only remember a handful of things that belonged in the flat originally. There would be no way he could spot a planted item if his life depended on it. And it just might.

He sat back on the sofa, slouching across the back cushions and tried to relax but it was beyond him. His mind raced at a million miles an hour as he replayed what had just happened that morning in his mind over and over again. It all felt like a jumbled mess. He couldn't piece everything together, he couldn't find a way to make them all fit. It was like looking into a mirror at a funhouse, the ones that stretched and distorted the reflection, sometimes beyond recognition. That's how it felt, beyond recognition, he was struggling with realising what was real and what wasn't, to differentiate the false memories of fear and paranoia from the real ones that were arguably worse than anything he could have made up in his head.

At some point his mind drifted to being back to his home with his parents, back when everything made sense and he felt a part of him that was longing to be there. It was a simpler time and as he succumbed to the memory he could feel his eyes growing heavy as he drifted in and out of consciousness. He didn't want to sleep but his body had other ideas and he was powerless to sleep's calling.

"Garrett… Garrett… GARRETT!" Someone shouted at him, but there was no sound. It was like the sound had been muted and only visible motions could be seen. His mind was swirling with vivid dreams of David's face calling to him.

"Garrett!" David was trying to shake him awake. Garrett felt his body being wracked with pain as he tried to force himself out of the dream and into reality, everything was vibrating, the floor was shaking. It was like an earthquake but in a silent movie.

He opened his eyes and tried to focus on David's face in front of him, which blurred and shifted making his head pound even more than it already was, David's features swam in and out of focus. He could feel himself trying to grab at an invisible rope ladder that would ascend him into the realm of the awake. But he wasn't awake. And neither was David. David was dead. Garrett had seen to that.

Bright sunlight awoke Garrett and he felt himself moan and lean away from it. He sat up and rubbed his tired eyes that itched. It felt like he had hardly slept at all but it was already mid-morning according to the giant, digital clock on the ridiculously techy fridge.

He reached for his phone on the nearby table and unlocked it. On the screen was an image of David's smiling face which he inwardly welcomed. He had come to like David's vibrancy in such a short time considering all of the negative things he had thought about whilst he was alive. David's presence in his life was so short he was stunned that he had started to rely on it. It was only now that he couldn't just call him or meet up for lunch that he started to wish David were here. He was missing him. He shook his head trying to clear the craziness from it but all that did was make him realise how much his head hurt. He was probably dehydrated.

He stood and stretched, stifling a yawn. He hadn't realised how tired he was until he began to move around. His muscles that were stiff and sore protested painfully, as did the crick in his neck that was the obvious consequence of sleeping upright on a sofa that was not intended for such.

It took him a moment to realise he was in David's flat, not his parent's house and that David was not going to come home and walk through the front door. Garrett had taken care of that. Then all the feelings he had been holding in the last couple of days, the anger, jealousy, hatred, grief and guilt burst out of him like a monster rearing its many ugly heads. He was crying, he was sobbing uncontrollably. He collapsed to the floor, his legs refusing to take his weight any longer. His head pounded and throbbed as he cried, but he didn't care; deep down, he knew he deserved every bit of pain and more. He couldn't think or stand, he lost all of his control at pushing down his feelings that were now like giant boulders, making him sag with the weight of it.

He was vaguely aware that his phone started to ring some time later but he couldn't bring himself to do anything about it. He kept holding onto his knees tightly feeling the pain in them ease up slowly, afraid that if he let them go, if he moved at all, he would crumble to the floor and never move again.

Before long, there were no tears left to cry, no energy for him to feel anymore. All he could hear was the sound of his own breathing which was ragged and uneven.

He felt like he was suffocating and struggled for air. He gasped hard but couldn't seem to breathe easier. Desperate for relief, he crawled over to David's dining table and stood on shaky legs before throwing open one of the drawers. Inside he found what he was looking for, something he had stashed when swapping all of his own belongings with David's. It was the only thing of his own that he had kept, though he knew that it was dangerous to. It was a small insignificant object to anyone else but to him it was priceless. It was a small note that he had received inside of a birthday card when he was a child, it was handwritten by his parents that simply told him how much they loved him and how proud of him they were. They had no idea that he had kept it, let alone carried it around in his wallet every day since.

"David... Why did you have to die?" His voice was broken and exhausted. He hated the world that had allowed him to do what he did to David, he wished he could take it all back.

No answer came but then again Garrett knew that no answer would come.

Chapter 7

There was a tickling in the back of Garrett's throat as he sat in the silence for some time until he coughed loudly. It was the first noise he had made in hours. It was only after he coughed, the noise penetrating the silence like a canon, did he notice another sound outside. Sirens. He began to panic and his heart rate quickened. He became lightheaded and he stumbled away from the table.

He glanced around hoping to see a way out, to find an escape route for when the police came blaring through his front door as he was terrified they would. But he saw none and instead his eyes fell upon David's bed which he spied from the open plan living room; it was rumpled up like David had never slept in it at all. Before he could think twice he ran into the bedroom and fell to his knees.

He didn't know what he was doing, why he was doing it or even how he was able to accomplish it with his focus on nothing more than his own panicked breathing, but he changed the bedding and tidied the bedroom. He did this as though he were any other person. He did this as though he was not afraid that his world would come crumbling down around him with every second that passed.

He made the bed as best he could but then found that he was

unable to do anything more intricately. He cursed himself for being careless and not convincing himself to take the odd man in the park to be a more serious threat earlier.

Before he could figure out any next move the door was being knocked on.

"Mr Ellison, it's Graham from security will you please answer the door?" Once more, his heart leapt out of his chest, he began to feel sure that a heart attack was probably right around the corner with this amount of stress. He controlled his breathing, wiped the cuff of his sleeve across his head to mop up the beads of sweat starting to form on his brow and walked over to the door. He took one last deep breath and answered with the most convincing smile he could muster hitched onto his face, terrified that the mask would slip.

"Come in Graham, I was just about to call you." Garrett took another deep breath and tried his best to ignore the way it felt like tiny little needles were trying to drill their way out of his lungs.

This is not what he wanted, and he was most definitely lying when he said he was about to call Graham. He should have known they would come back, and he should have headed them off early by calling. It was too late for that now. He had to act as if everything was fine, but not too fine. His house had been broken into. He was fine, but not fine. He tried to remember that.

As Graham began to ask him his own questions for their supposed security report, he found himself zoning out. His mind was still reeling from what he had just been thinking and now he was trying not to think as well as answer as best as he could without arousing any suspicion. All he could linger on was that someone would soon discover that he was not David and thus unravel his web of lies until he became entangled in them. Graham asked him about the break-in and if he could think of anything that they had taken. He couldn't and told him exactly what he had told the police. Graham's deduction was that there hadn't been much of value to take minus the computer but that was likely too traceable and that the thieves were probably looking for cash or jewellery. Garrett didn't say anything to contrary, but was silently thinking that if that were the case, there was easily a thief's pension scheme worth in watches at the back of the flat, none of which were missing.

Graham advised him to take care and if he saw anything suspicious to call the number on the card he was given yesterday and report it to security.

He said he would and thanked the man though he had done very little. Then he left and Garrett breathed another sigh of relief. He had survived day one. Only the rest of his life to go. David's life. This thought reminded him that Albert would be waiting on the website production. He headed to the office and sat down at the computer which leapt into action with the touch of the mouse.

He got straight to work, opening a folder labelled 'projects' on the desktop and was pleased that Albert's website was almost finished, just some final formatting to do and shifting some images and texts around so that they did not overlap and obscure essential information.

He was getting into a groove when he noticed a flash outside his window. He glanced up at the mirror across from him and saw more blue flashing light down below in the reflection. He ground his teeth together and went back to typing, ignoring them for as long as possible until they finally disappeared. This was London; blue flashing lights were extremely common and would pass by at least every hour. Nothing to worry about, he told himself.

When he had just finished, he began to compose an email to Albert saying the website was ready. As he was typing, a banner flashed across the screen that read, "BREAKING NEWS, GARRETT LANGFORD SUICIDE BEING TREATED AS SUSPICIOUS".

No. This couldn't be true! He had done everything he could to cover himself, what possible basis could the police have to treat it as suspicious? He hesitated for a moment and then clicked the banner. It brought him straight to a landing page with a picture of his own face obscuring most of the screen. He scrolled down and read the news report.

There was a picture of his face and underneath, the blurb:

Garrett Langford was found fatally wounded in the early hours of yesterday morning. The police are calling for any witnesses to the incident and suspect that, although unlikely, the deceased might have been the victim of foul play. Detective Eileen Brannon heading the investigation gave her first statement to the press just minutes ago.

"Good afternoon, thank you for coming here today. I am appealing to the general public as we have evidence to believe the death of Mr Langford was not a suicide but a potential homicide. I understand this will come as shocking news to his family and friends but we urge you all to remain vigilant and consider whether you may have seen or recorded anything *that could be important to help us all make sense of this awful tragedy. Our thoughts and prayers are with his family and friends." Detective Brannon is a recent addition to the London Met police force and her background and success rate in her investigative work will undoubtedly prove useful in solving this horrific crime.*

Garrett stopped reading and pushed himself back slightly in his chair. It didn't make sense. He had done everything he could, and now this. Who said foul play? The article went on to say that while the injuries were mostly the work of the fall, there were some odd markings on his skin that did not seem consistent with the incident. It was because of this minor evidence police suspected some sort of altercation might have taken place and are hoping members of the public might have seen or heard something, though they admit the chances are slim.

He breathed a small sigh of relief at least there was no mention of David. Not yet. He doubted anyone would have seen him on that footbridge. Still, being treated as a suspicious incident was not going to make his nerves settle. He was already feeling the effects of the guilt and secrets. He was constantly feeling ill, like his stomach had twisted and wouldn't untwist. He was having awful nightmares and struggled to sleep which, on top of his lack of appetite made him feel constantly woozy and drowsy.

He clicked off the news page and returned to the email addressed to Albert. Garrett let him know the website was ready and, considering he had paid upfront, there was nothing else he needed to do. If he had any issues he would be more than welcome to email David back and it would be sorted out. Garrett included a reminder to leave a review on his own website and then logged off to go get something to eat that he could hopefully stomach.

He showered and put on something casual, he hadn't seen anyone except the police and security in a while and he wanted to be dressed comfortably, part of him was still reluctant to wear David's clothes though he knew he had no other option. He walked briskly downstairs and out the front of the building, avoiding eye contact with anyone in case they suspected anything now that his face had been plastered over the news. Walking quickly past groups of people on his way, he entered a small coffee shop, choosing a different one than yesterday so as not to establish a connection with anyone that might recognise his face. He had barely touched the hot sandwich that he unwrapped on the street outside, when he once more, felt the familiar feeling of eyes on him and he stopped walking, turned on the spot and looked around. Some people were looking at him but they were probably just annoyed he had suddenly stopped walking on the path in front of them and was now causing a traffic jam. But no, he couldn't see anyone that looked suspicious. He turned back around and carried on walking.

Someone came into view ahead of him, Garrett's eyes widened when he saw it was that man he met yesterday. The one who had asked him about the Ripper. He kept calm for now but quickened his pace slightly so he would pass by him soon enough if need be. He started to think about how to get away without looking suspicious. The last thing he needed was another person prying into his life and making him act suspicious trying to evade it. The police were surely on the lookout for suspicious behaviour in light of the news article they had just seen about his death. But then something strange happened before Garrett got another chance to try and walk past him unnoticed.

"Hello again." The man said, looking up at Garrett. He had stopped walking, but didn't seem to notice he was blocking the path once more. Garrett looked back at him in shock. How did he know? "What's wrong?" The man asked seeing the look

103

of surprise on his face.

"Nothing," Garrett shook his head and managed to gather his thoughts enough to add, "Just in a bit of hurry, do excuse me." And he walked past him. At the end of the street he turned back around, feeling it safe to do so only now. The brown-haired man was still there. He was still watching him, still blocking up the path as Garrett had just done. He did not like this. Yesterday he had a suspicion this man knew something more but today, he was almost certain of it. What he didn't know was why the man insisted on talking to him. If he truly believed that Garrett had killed a person, why on earth would he want to stand and make idle conversation with him instead of reporting him to the police? He wished he knew.

He dug his hand into his pocket and pulled out the card the police officer had given him. He felt he had two choices. Choice number one involved doing what any other sane, inno-cent person would do if they had been the victim of a burglary and call the number and give the officer the description of the man with the hopes it might bring something up. However he was not just an ordinary, sane, innocent man. If this man knew something about what he had done, involving the police would surely put an end to his new life. Which left choice number two. The only choice he had. He needed to find out who this man was and what he wanted. What he really wanted.

Fighting against his survival instincts, Garrett headed back to the man that was still fixing his eyes on him. The man smiled as he saw Garrett come back. His eyes lit up ever so slightly.

"Beautiful day." He said in a placid tone.

"It is. Sorry, I never got your name yesterday." Garrett said politely, hoping he sounded convincing. This man knew something. He had to. Garrett just needed to find out what.

"My name's Robert." The man smiled and held out his hand for Garrett to shake it which he did reluctantly and pulled his hand away quickly as if he had been electrocuted by it, noticing the rough calluses that scratched at Garrett's own soft hands. Robert clearly noticed this and frowned.

"Robert," Garrett repeated, nodding his head slightly, "what do you want?" Garrett tried to sound polite but with a hint of understanding.

"Nothing. Nothing in particular." He mused. "Let's go for a walk." And they did. For about an hour they walked and talked. Robert seemed to interrogate him about his life, which he answered with vague-enough answers that never really landed on an answer. Then it was Garrett's turn to quiz Robert. It was like a verbal duel, each person fighting back until one of them tapped out. There was no winner and it was a tie. Robert, he was sure, had not gleaned anything useful but Garrett noticed him let something slip that he felt he was not meant to. Something about Leicester. This made no sense at all to Garrett but he was determined to investigate it further. Perhaps Robert had indeed meant to say it but assumed that it would mean nothing to Garrett.

Garrett walked Robert to the train station, both of them caught the same train but got off at two different stops. He waited for Robert to get off first, waiting until he saw him walk away down the road into the city centre. Garrett let out a sigh of relief and headed back towards his own flat which was only just visible and hopped on the next train heading in the exactly the way he had just come. As soon as Garrett was back at the flat, he logged back into the computer and with a swift keystroke he searched for a Robert in Leicester. There were thousands of results.

He attempted to narrow it down by searching Robert, in Leicester with brown hair. He wasn't really sure this would bring anything up but he tried it nonetheless. The only useful result was one of a database from a town hall.

Garrett clicked on the link and it brought up a page listing something about land registry fees. He scrolled down the list until he saw an entry for Robert Hanbury. The date at which it was established that Robert Hanbury would have access to this property dated back three years ago.

He then searched for a Robert Hanbury in Leicester. This turned up much more specific results. He found a few news articles of a Robert Hanbury being in the neighbourhood watch, Robert Hanbury helping to raise money for his local food bank and then, a tiny little paragraph no more than a few sentences long tacked onto the end of one of these news articles. It read:

Robert Hanbury, lawyer and friend was found dead in his home on Tuesday January 14th at approximately 9am.

The police had no reason to suspect anything out of the ordinary and the coroner report disclosed the cause of death and natural. Beside this was a picture of Robert Hanbury. A man, mid-thirties with brown hair. This was the man he had been talking to, there was no doubt in Garrett's mind. Robert Hanbury did not, could not, exist, for he was pronounced dead. But if he was dead, then who was the Robert he had been talking to and why did it feel like Robert had been trying to get Garrett to tell him who he really was?

Garrett did not know and he closed the tab leaving him with more questions than answers.

What was Garrett going to do?

How did Robert Hanbury die?

Who was the man speaking to Garrett in the park?

Who was trying to get into the flat and what were they after?

Chapter 8

Listening to the quiet of the flat and focusing on his breathing, Garrett pondered for a while and continued to dredge up as much information as he could on Robert Hanbury with the limited information he had gleaned from the small articles about him. All he really knew was that the real Robert Hanbury had been a decent man who loved helping his community.

He wasn't quite sure what his next move was. There was a part of him that wanted to find out who this man claiming to be Robert was. But there was another part of him that told him he didn't want to find out.

Garrett rocked gently on the desk chair, feeling the familiar sensation of prickling across his forehead that meant he would start sweating any second. He had no idea how he was going to find this man and what would happen if he did. Who the hell was he? What on earth would he do? But he did know that he needed to find out. This could not be a coincidence, surely. A man who had, as far as Garrett could tell, robbed the identity of a good man and paraded his face around, doing the name a staunch disservice. Garrett swallowed hard and tried not to think about the irony of his thoughts. He pushed that ugly idea down into the pit where all emotions went. No, Garrett couldn't believe that bumping into him was pure chance. Coincidences certainly happened, but not that many and not so close together.

He made up his mind. He was going to Leicester, if for nothing more than to get away from the ever-increasing pressure of London. Keeping his very recognisable face away from London police was probably a good thing, too. He fired up the internet once more and searched a little more to see if he could find out which village in Leicester Robert had lived to see if that could turn up any leads.

He searched for the neighbourhood watch article once more and scanned through it. Horninghold. That was where Robert Hanbury lived. Or had lived before this strange man had presumably taken his identity. It took almost no time for Garrett to fill a small hold-all bag with clean clothes and basic necessities and only forty minutes later, he was seated comfortably on a train bound for Market Harborough, the closest station he could get to Horninghold that had the best seating.

Trees of green and yellow whistled past in a blur through the train window of First Class that Garrett was now sat in. He had considered using the car but whilst there were pending investigations, the paranoia inside him was urging him not to use the vehicle that David had been in and that also contained the suitcase he had moved David in. At least if he were out of the city, they would have a much harder job of finding him and his vehicle. The drive would have been quicker but not having to concentrate on driving gave him time to think and come up with a plan.

The train juddered and grumbled under the soft seat that Garrett had taken up and he was beginning to feel the pressure ooze out of him like a deflating balloon when a voice behind his right shoulder made him start.

"Can I get you a drink, sir?" It was an old lady but she was dressed in a crisp, blue jacket and skirt that was perfectly creased in all the right places and looked much different to most uniforms he had seen train staff wear. This one looked cut to perfection, a tailored look that he had always admired in clothing but had never been able to afford thanks to his lack of money. The lady was thin and tall and her voice was the stark opposite of her ageing face; it was loud and booming. Gathering himself quickly, Garrett responded.

"Um… An orange juice would be nice." And the lady nodded briskly and moved with a speed he had not expected of someone who looked so frail. It was clear that her body had long ago forgotten the age it was supposed to be. When the lady returned only a minute later, she set the glass down and turned back around but Garrett could not see where she went. He sank into his chair once more and stared out of the window, sipping gently from the glass of juice that he did not particularly want and only ordered because she had made him jump and it was the first thing that sprang to his mind. He had barely moved in almost an hour when the overhead speakers interrupted his thoughts with a cool, female voice.

"London St Pancras International, now stopping at Kettering." This was his stop, he had one change and from Kettering he would be on the next train straight to Market Harborough. When the train stopped in Kettering, Garrett removed himself from the carriage, hold-all in hand and sped off to find platform number four. The train arrived just as Garrett, panting from running up the steps and wracked with panic for fear of missing it, stumbled onto the platform. The doors opened and several people stepped off the carriage.

Garrett found his way to First Class once more which was empty and sat himself down.

Garrett arrived at Market Harborough only ten minutes later and he got off the train walking just as far out of the station as the car park and gazed around. The buildings looked old and weathered and adorned with Victorian architecture that had not changed in decades and the station itself looked more like a giant house than the stations he was used to. The buildings in the distance were tall and intimidating, like prison walls surrounding the people who were scuttling around the streets like inmates. But the car park was small and there were few cars taking up the spaces out the front.

As he looked around at the quiet station he felt some comfort in the fact that he did not stand out here. He felt an incredible sense of belonging as if he fitted in which was preposterous because he had never been to Leicestershire before. Though he was just as recognisable here as anywhere else, being away from London felt freeing in a way. He looked around. There was nobody that followed him with their gaze as if they knew exactly what he was there to do or what he had just done some 80-odd miles away. Their faces were all angled in different directions, none of them pointed at him or what he was doing, Garrett almost felt alone for the first time since that awful night.

He stood on the edge of the pavement and took in the pleasant sight of not recognising a single place. He walked slowly down the road toward the houses at the end but as he got closer he realised they were not singular houses, they were flats, only a lot smaller but nicer than the ones in London. There was even a car park right below them. Walking further into what he hoped was the town, cars trawled by on the road, their engines grumbling as they swished past. He noticed quickly that the buildings looked the same wherever he looked, brown and square like cut-outs of cookies just copied on to the end of the next building like a tunnel of brown bricks.

Only a short walk later, he was standing in the centre of what he took be a town centre though it looked nothing like the centre of a city he had ever experienced in London. Even the quietest of retail areas in the big city would have appeared larger than this. But even so, he liked it. He could see the tall clock tower in the distance where he was headed now. Market Harborough appeared to be a bustling town despite it being situated outside of the nearest city. He neared the gigantic clock tower that was imposing and attractive in the middle of the high street. He was not sure what he had expected to see when he got here but it certainly was not this. The clock tower seemed so out of place in such an average town; it was like it had been placed there as an afterthought when in reality it was probably one of the oldest things in the town. All around him were buildings and shops with nothing to offer a man like Garrett though others around him seemed to disagree and they entered the shops with greedy smiles on their faces. Garrett walked towards the clock tower knowing full well where his destination lay and yet was still unable to take his eyes away from it.

He stood and stared, watching the minute hand slowly traipse around the clock face. He must have looked silly as when his mind pulled out of his reverie almost ten minutes had passed. He couldn't even recall what he had been thinking during those ten minutes. It was almost as if he had blacked out and had no memory of it. He felt a presence behind him and he slowly turned around to see an old woman staring at him. She looked like she should be baking in someone's kitchen rather than doing anything as energetic as standing on the pavement.

"I know why you're here." The woman said, "You want to take his place don't you?" Garrett stared at her for a few seconds before speaking.

"How do you even know who I am?"

"Oh you think I can't tell? You look just like him but there is something different about your eyes and the way that you walk and talk. Who are you exactly? You're not from round here by any chance?" She asked looking up into Garrett's face with suspicion clear on hers.

Garrett felt tingles on the back of his neck. He hadn't meant to come here at all but now that he was there, now that she knew who he was, what should he do?

The woman continued talking before Garrett could nod in affirmation or deny her claim, "Yes you're just like him. I can tell by your eyes." She repeated with a half-smile and started walking away from him saying over her shoulder as she went, "Don't let me stop you, love." As soon as she turned around and walked off down the street Garrett felt cold inside.

He was still staring at the clock. Twenty minutes had passed by now and he blinked away tears and snapped shut his mouth that had been gaping. He shook his head violently. Was she real? Had he imagined her? Was his guilty conscience playing tricks on him or had he indeed just been spotted by an elderly lady in the middle of a city over 80 miles away? His stomach turned. There was no sign of the woman and he could not think of any other explanation than his mind playing tricks on him.

"Are you alright, sir?" Said a concerned male voice behind

him with a heavy cockney accent. Garrett turned so fast it made him dizzy. There was a police officer stood before him. He opened his mouth to speak but he found himself unable to make his voice work. Fear paralysed him. This was it. They had hunted him down.

"Sir?" Repeated the officer taking a step toward him. He sucked in a sharp breath of air and blurted,

"Yes. I'm fine." And scurried away. As soon as Garrett was out of sight he whipped out his phone from the small bag he had stowed a fresh set of clothes, a toothbrush and toothpaste in and ordered a taxi to take him to Horninghold, not knowing what he would find when he got there but feeling as though this was the only way to find out what had happened.

It was a small town, not much more than a few streets surrounding the occasional pub. The buildings were all different heights and sizes but they were all dark and dirty brown brick with roofs that seemed to be made of the same material or thatch. It was raining, a light misty drizzle that soaked through his clothes almost immediately. He found the address of a small bed and breakfast that he was looking for, having searched for it on the ride about thirty minutes away. It took him about ten minutes to find it, after scouring up and down streets and asking people who stared at him like he had two heads, before someone agreed to tell him where it was.

When he walked through the door that had peeled paint on the front, a small bell signalled to the lady behind the faded, grubby desk that he had entered the building. She looked like she'd been expecting him - which only caused Garrett's stomach to flip again as this place looked like it hadn't seen a patron in many a year. She didn't say anything but her eyes flicked over Garrett's face then down his body before she swept away leaving him stood alone at the desk.

He cleared his throat and continued to look around. There were cobwebs in the corners of the ceiling, the wallpaper was peeling away in places and there was a dark brown stain on one of the walls that looked like it had been there for many years. He slowly turned round when he thought about how long he had stood there with his mouth wide open when suddenly another man appeared behind the desk.

"Can I help you?" Said the old man in a slow, drawling voice that sent prickles up Garrett's spine. He was looming over the counter in front of him, glaring at Garrett from behind thick, dusty spectacles with grey eyes. Garrett reluctantly confirmed his booking - under the name David Ellison which he almost forgot when he booked it - and was given a key that was slightly bent to room number eight. Garrett thanked the old man who merely nodded his greying head and then proceeded to his room. The door was stiff but with a little shove he opened it and took a look around the room. It was dark and cold. The sheets were off-white, probably washed out and the room had a slight smell of cigarette smoke that seemed to be oozing from the upholstery. There was a small TV stand with an old VCR television on it, the screen tinged yellow in the corners and a thick layer of dust clouding the screen. He turned on the light next to his bed as the ceiling light was barely bright enough to fill the room. The bulb flickered slightly and danced across his face as he sat down heavily onto the single bed that lay facing a wall just beside it; the old springs groaned loudly beneath his weight, protesting violently.

He searched deep in his mind for answers but only found questions about how much longer this would go on for - when could he come back? What happened now? Where did he go? He sat like this for some time. Perhaps an hour, perhaps more. He lost track of time once again in his anxious state feeling overwhelmed by the weight and pressure of the lie he had to live and the guilt that seemed to have formed a rock deep down in his stomach. Then he considered something. It had already been a while since he had checked the status of the investigation; perhaps it had been closed as there wasn't enough evidence. He silently prayed that this was the case. Garrett slowly pulled out his phone, wary of the things it might tell him, and searched for the breaking news (surely it was there). The moment he saw the headline his heart sank.

Garrett Langford investigation still underway; London police department press release...

Garrett Langford. He read the words again and again. It was the first time in what felt like ages that he had seen his real name written so casually. As if that name meant nothing to anyone. But it did to him. He was not David Ellison, he knew that but there was a part of him that felt like he was not only assuming the identity of David but that he actually was him. As if David's soul or spirit, or whatever people called it, was inside of him. His head seemed to be full of buzzing and he rolled over, not even bothering to undress and attempted to fall asleep.

Right now Garrett felt like a man under siege. His name was all over the news - apparently the subject of an investigation that he still had no lead as to how well it was going. He couldn't believe this was his reward for only wanting another shot at life, a shot that life seemed very unwilling to surrender without force. As he thought back, most of it seemed like a blur. His memory felt patchy. Had David woken up and caught him? Or was Garrett's subconscious merely blocking some parts out to save himself from the trauma of his own actions? He couldn't remember. He felt his eyes slowly drifting into the back of his head filling his brain with the fogginess of sleep. There was a ticking noise coming from somewhere in the room. The pipes gurgled loudly. It was hot. Much too hot.

Garrett awoke with a start. He was dripping in sweat. His clothes were soaked through with it. He stood up and headed to the bathroom, walking gingerly on his shaky legs; it was about half past four in the morning according to his watch.

"What are you doing here?" Asked David from the grimy shower as he saw Garrett standing over the toilet. Garrett nearly leapt out of his skin. Was he still dreaming? David was still wearing the suit he had on the moment he died... The moment he was killed.

This isn't real; it can't be happening, thought Garrett. He's not going to let me get away with it. Suddenly a wave of dread washed over him as the thought of himself getting arrested and imprisoned came to him with such vivid realism it could have been a memory of something that had only just happened. He could feel the officers' cold hand grabbing at his wrists, he could smell the coffee on their breath and see the disgust and anger etched into every line on their face. Garrett felt like he was going to throw up and bent over the toilet bowl and vomited again and again and again.

Seconds later, David walked out of the bathroom looking more angry than surprised. "What are you doing here?" Said David again in the same tone, lifeless and eery as if calling to him from underwater. When Garrett looked back up from the toilet David was gone. There was no vomit in the toilet. In fact he wasn't even in the bathroom.

He was still in bed, sat bolt upright, shaking with sweat

117

though the temperature felt cool, not boiling hot as he could have sworn it was. Just a dream. When Garrett laid back down, his breathing slowing down gradually and returning to normal, it felt like he had only closed his eyes for a few seconds before he was wrenching them back open, bright sunlight stabbing like daggers through his eyelids from the curtains he had forgotten to close the night before. Garrett's stomach gurgled with the forgotten meals that he had been too preoccupied to think of the day before, but he could ignore the hunger no longer. Changing quickly into something that didn't reek of stale sweat, he brushed his teeth in the grotty sink in the bathroom that had small hairs poking out of the plug hole and limescale coating the base of the taps. Without even looking in the mirror above him, he had seen far too many horror movies that had proven how terrible of an idea that was, he checked his watch. It was seven-thirty in the morning.

He all but sprinted down the stairs to the dining area. Before he knew it, there was a plate of food in front of him that he had no memory of plating up in his haste, but he ate the eggs, bacon, beans and hash browns slowly, turning it all over in his mind. He was scared. He was seeing things that were so clear it was hard to rule them as mere dreams.

Then he felt something, a little spark of memory. It was like trying to catch mist and only being able to get the last word of a sentence before it vanished.

What are you doing here? David had said. It was definitely David but he wasn't sure how David was speaking to him or if he even was. Garrett rubbed his eyes aggressively until white spots started to appear in his vision. He was going mad. There was no other explanation for it. He knew why he was here.

To find Robert Hanbury. And with that, he finished his food and left the dingy establishment to do just that. He had to find out who Robert Hanbury really was, and if he could, find out who the man pretending to be him was and what he wanted with Garrett. The task before him felt even larger than it had yesterday, as if it had grown monumentally over night. Or maybe the realism of what he needed to do had only started to register now that he had eaten and slept.

Outside, the day was a bit brighter and calmer. For some reason this made him feel even more anxious as if it were the calm before the coming of a storm. He wracked his brain to think of where he could glean more information about Robert and the idea hit him. The local library. He had always been obsessed with books and he figured it would be the perfect place to find out more about Robert Hanbury, or at least a good place to start.

Garrett strolled down the street briskly, inhaling deeply, filling his lungs with the clean air that tasted sweeter than the air in London. He enjoyed the feeling as he made towards his destination not to look suspicious as he did so. He wasn't quite sure how a person *could* look suspicious simply by walking to the library, but the truth of his crimes told him how vulnerable and exposed he was.

A small black car passed him driving too slow through the village. It parked up ahead on left exactly where Garrett would shortly be walking. He couldn't make out the driver but it looked like there was someone in the front seat.

Garrett's heart began to beat faster at the idea that he was being followed again. One of Robert Hanbury's friends maybe? Or one of the other people watching him?

His mind was like a pile up on the motorway, one thought

leading to another and then quickly to another. Much like the pile up that he himself had caused but pushed the ugly, intrusive thought from his mind.

"I'm going mad." He said aloud in an effort to rationalize his thoughts and slow his quickening hear rate. He glanced back at the car but it was gone, nowhere to be seen. He must have been imagining it following him; more likely it was nothing to do with him and drove off of its own accord.

Garrett sped up his pace even more, trying to make the journey to the library as short as possible. As he got closer, Garrett saw that there was no car anywhere in sight and he slowed down again, feeling calmer about himself but definitely not safe. He would feel safe when Robert Hanbury was locked up and no longer posing a threat to Garrett's life or sanity.

I have to start acting normal or I'm going to attract attention, he thought. He knew that too much paranoia was not a healthy practice so he tried to be more open, grounding himself to the present with the things he could see, touch, taste and smell.

He took the last turn and the library appeared on his left. He looked up at the quaint building, integrated seamlessly into the countryside and headed in. He was surrounded on all side by shelves and shelves of books though it was mostly empty of people save an old lady who hobbled slowly around tidying up the piles of novels and organising them into neat stacks. She smiled sweetly at Garrett who, having managed to dig up a little more information on Robert as he scrolled through his phone, headed towards the *reference* section in search of the man's biography, self-published and stored in the *local heroes* section. He found it quickly and sat down to read it thanking whomever might be watching over him that Robert had at least led a mildly interesting life. The front matter of the book was dedicated to Robert and explained that this book was mostly finished before he passed and additional information regarding his death and treatments were added by his wife and friends.

The man was born in 1983. That made him thirty-four years old when he passed away. He grew up in Kent on a small piece of land with his parents. Life was simple for Robert until he went to University where he reported that he studied philosophy, history, and law simultaneously. He graduated top of his class from university and then went to work for a small law firm that specialised in human rights cases.

At the age of thirty, Robert was diagnosed with early-onset, aggravated dementia. It made it impossible for him to keep working at the law firm so he became a consultant and acted in the capacity of a specialist advisor on the odd case here and there until his death.

In June of 2018, Robert Hanbury went from being able to talk about his whole life and hold conversations without so much as a stutter to barely being able to order a coffee or remember where he left his phone. In the months leading up to his fast decline, he travelled extensively around Europe and the Caribbean islands on a cruise.

On December 10th, 2019 he fell into a coma and was diagnosed with a brain tumour. He underwent radiation therapy to reduce the size of the tumour but during that time he received his terminal diagnosis from several doctors.

The dramatic decline in condition led Robert's family and friends to think about what they could do for him. It wasn't long after that, a doctor had approached his wife and advised that the kindest thing to do for Robert would be to let him go peacefully. He was taken off of life support in mid 2020 after spending almost six months in a coma. He was surrounded by close friends and family.

That was it. There was no mention of anything that could be exceptionally useful to determine who would want to see him gone and subsequently take his place. Garrett flicked through and skim-read the part about his early life and career before his fall. He needed more information. Something more personal. He put the small book back on the shelf and craned his neck to see if he could see the old librarian. Maybe she had known Robert; it was a small town after all. He looked for a few minutes, trying to find the woman that had been tidying up books. He found her by a shelf focused on tomes about religion and spirituality.

"I need some help," he said politely as he walked over to her, "did you happen to know a Robert Hanbury at all?" The woman nodded in recognition and sort of shuffled over in his direction.

"Robert was my husband." She sniffed. Garrett's eyes widened slightly in shock.

"I'm sorry for your loss." The woman shook her head and waved off his apology.

"It's alright. We had nearly twenty wonderful years together."

"I apologise for being so forward but I'd really appreciate it if you wouldn't mind answering a few questions." The woman nodded in agreement.

"It's alright. Robert would have wanted me to help anyone who needed it, after all."

"What can you tell me about his health decline?" Asked Garrett. The woman looked at him in surprise.

"Are you sure that's what you want to know?" She said with

a confused look.

"Yes." Garrett replied but felt he might circle back and pry at whatever it was she thought he would have wanted to know. She fell silent for a moment before speaking again.

"I don't really know." She began, "After he finished university he took up work with a law firm and was one of their best lawyers. He travelled around a lot and he said it really helped him think once his illness had set in."

"Why did he travel so much?" Garrett wondered aloud. The woman cleared her throat.

"I don't know, really. I always thought that maybe he was looking for something to make himself feel better about the things he saw all over the world. Try to combat the darkness with the light."

"What kind of things did he see?" Asked Garrett. She shook her head with a sigh.

"I don't know that either." She had sadness in her eyes. It seemed to Garrett that he was not entirely honest with his wife. He pressed her for more information hoping to catch something about a possible enemy or someone that wanted him out of the picture.

"When did you realise that he was losing his memory and then his health?" Garrett questioned. The woman looked at him with a kind of vagueness in her eyes.

"I'm afraid I don't really know the answer to that one either." Garrett rubbed his forehead in frustration wondering what usually happened when people became paranoid. She seemed like a nice enough old lady but something about the situation made Garrett feel that she was holding back .

"I'm sorry," said Mrs Hanbury, "It's a shame Robert never told me anything."

Garrett started to consider whether she really did know nothing or whether she was perhaps suffering from Alzheimer's or Dementia herself. He did not feel comfortable enough to ask. Instead he asked her a different question.

"Was there ever anyone in his life that he spoke about, maybe a friend or someone with whom he felt he had a sort of affinity with? A person who was also interested in law or justice?" He asked. She thought for a moment, scratching her head.

"Not really. There were some people that came to the house, but Robert never felt very close to them."

"Did you ever see anyone that looked like him?" Garrett asked curiously.

The woman looked at him with confusion in her eyes.

"No," she said slowly, "I don't think so." She looked down at the floor.

"I'm sorry," said Garrett, "I don't mean to upset you." Mrs Hanbury shook her head.

"It's alright. I can't remember a lot of things but there are some things that will always stay with me. I know he must have had friends." She smiled to herself, "He talked about work a lot." She looked at Garrett in a way that made him feel uncomfortable.

"He was very proud of his work," she said gently, "It's a shame all that hard work wasn't enough."

"What do you mean?" Asked Garrett feeling more and more nervous about what this woman knows. She seemed to notice the change in him.

"Well," she said, "he got sick. His condition was getting worse and the medication wasn't helping. I believe he was most upset, from what I can remember, about a case he was working on at the time. I think there was a man involved

124

who was locked up and..." She scratched her head with a bony finger trying hard to remember, "yes, that was it. The man was going to be released because of something or other and then Robert had to leave the law firm. I think the case ended up being swept aside and if I remember correctly, the man stayed in prison. I don't know why but Robert's input was going to make or break the case - expert testimony or something of the sort." She took a deep breath and it seemed to take some effort to do so in her ageing lungs. Garrett said nothing for fear of putting her off.

"But then he got worse and left to travel in the hopes of finding some peace before the end - which I like to think he managed." She paused for a moment as if reminiscing a fond memory.

"Do you happen to know who this prisoner was?" Garrett asked hopefully but with little confidence.

"I'm afraid I don't, he always kept the details to himself. It was privileged information he would always tell me. The law firm he used to work at might know, though. They have an office here in the village." She pulled a piece of paper and a pen from a pocket at her waistband and scrawled the address down before handing it to him. She admitted she hadn't seen most of the people since they came to pay their respects at Robert's funeral.

"Thank you." Said Garrett as he made to leave, "You've been very helpful." He shook Mrs Hanbury's hand gently and gave her a kind smile. She smiled back and followed him to the door where they paused awkwardly for a moment.

"Are you alright?" Garrett asked after a moment. He didn't know why but he felt an odd surge course through him that made him feel very protective of the old lady whom he had only just met. She nodded.

"Yes thank you." She paused, "Please be careful. I'm afraid to say there are some bad people out there who were very upset that my husband left. Do be careful."

Garrett nodded thankfully, turning her words over in his head as he headed back outside. He made his way to the office following the directions of the librarian.

Chapter 9

A glass, revolving door to the police station admitted Jake into the building. The foyer was clean and spacious, it was white and surprisingly inviting. Jake walked confidently up to the desk and waited for the man behind to finish his phone call.

"Can I help you?" The man asked, setting down the phone a moment after Jake had stopped in front of him.

"Yes, I'm here to see Detective Eileen Brannon." Jake replied. The man looked down at his computer screen and typed something in that he couldn't see. After a few moments he looked back up at Jake, taking in his rugged features and the lines that only war could have etched into his face.

"She's in a meeting at the moment, I can't disturb her." The man said apologetically and somewhat nervously. Jake was not at all surprised at this reaction; most people did this.

"That's okay, I'll wait." Jake replied in a calm, smooth voice. The man picked up the phone and started to dial a number. Jake leaned against the desk and waited. After a few minutes the man hung up the phone once again placing it back into the receiver.

"She'll be out in a few minutes, she asked me to ask you who are and what it's regarding." The man said. Jake thanked the man and told him he would rather keep this between himself and the detective. He was asked to take a seat in the foyer and Jake picked a comfy bucket chair but perched on the very edge and ramrod straight. Several minutes later a door to the right of the desk opened and a woman walked out. She was in her early fifties, with shoulder length brown, curly hair and green eyes that swept the foyer like a searchlight until its beams fell on Jake in the blue chair, waiting patiently. She was dressed in a grey suit, but it did little to hide her bulky frame yet she carried it with confidence and strength and it suited her powerful aura that she was giving off. The woman approached Jake and reached out to shake his hand.

"Eileen Brannon." She introduced herself smartly. Jake accepted her handshake and shook it firmly. Eileen looked at him with an expression of suspicion, she gestured for them both to walk back through the door she had just come from. Once they were inside, Eileen closed the door quickly behind her. She turned around towards Jake.

"So what can I do for you Mr...?" Eileen asked while gesturing him to follow her to his desk where there were files open and strewn across the desktop, presumably concerning Garrett Langford's death. He eyed these jealously feeling like they could help his own investigation.

"Hanbury." Jake replied coolly as she sat down, gesturing him to do the same opposite her.

"What can I do for you?" She repeated. She glanced at her watch.

"I wanted to find out how much your investigation has yielded on Garrett Langford." Detective Brannon eyed him suspiciously once more and Jake wondered whether suspicion happened to be her go-to reaction to most things; the reaction of a clear professional at work.

128

"Well, I can tell you everything that I've told the press. It is still an ongoing investigation, and we no longer believe that it was suicide." Jake leaned back in his chair and crossed his arms.

"We believe that Garrett Langford was murdered." Eileen said evenly and stared at Jake, waiting for a reaction. There was none.

"I see." He finally said after a long pause. "Is there anything else?" Eileen studied him for a few moments before shaking her head.

"No, I don't think so." She replied and got up to walk him out but Jake remained seated.

"Look, I'm a private investigator and I might have a bit more information to add but I'll need something in return." The detective smirked as though this wasn't the first time she'd been shaken down for information. But what other choice did she have? She was at a dead end with her investigation and the overheads were surely pressuring her to make another statement via press conference by the end of the week. She had to be desperate.

"Ok, Mr. Hanbury, I'm interested. Follow me, let's talk somewhere a little quieter." Jake nodded and followed her to an interrogation room. "Would you like a drink?"

"A coffee would be great, thanks."

"Of course, make yourself comfortable, I'll be back in a moment." She gestured him into the room where Jake took a seat. The detective propped the door open as she left and Jake sat thinking, staring into the two-way mirror that only showed him the reflection of a nearly-forty year old man that was at peak physical fitness but glowered at him with eyes that barely shone since his time in Afghanistan.

So far, Jake had learned that David did not appear to be David but so far his investigations had not turned up very much. However, the maître d' of some snooty restaurant claimed to have seen David at a meeting there and that appeared to be the last time his client was seen before the Garrett Langford murder. The problem was that he couldn't be absolutely sure that the two weren't linked in some way; what he needed was evidence that they were tied somehow. But of course to get that information he had to trade something that he did know, something he had stumbled across whilst asking off-the-cuff questions to random people and showing Garrett's face that had been plastered over the news.

The detective came back in holding two cups of coffee and handed one to Jake. He thanked her and took a sip, letting the hot liquid fill him.

"What do you want to know?" She finally asked after a long silence.

"I want to know about Garrett Langford's death." Jake replied evenly. "Specifically, I want to know who your prime suspect is or anything at all that could help." Eileen studied him for a few moments before sighing and leaned back in her chair. She considered whether or not to answer his question for a moment as she stirred in three packets of sugar into her coffee with a wooden skewer.

"Right now, we have no prime suspect. We're still investigating all possibilities."

She placed the rubbish into a waste bin near the door and sat back down.

"Ok, so what about Garrett Langford's family? Do they have any idea who could have killed him?" The detective shook her head.

"No, they're as baffled as we are. Garrett Langford didn't have any enemies that we know of and although not entirely surprised that he could have killed himself, they felt sure it couldn't have been suicide; he had plans for paying off debt. But I'm sure you'll know as well as I do that parents are often blind to these sorts of things and everyone swears that their kid could never do something like that."

Jake nodded hard. He had seen this first-hand when he was deployed. One of the soldiers under his command was displaying severe symptoms of post-traumatic stress disorder and was struggling to integrate back into civilian life after his medical discharge from service. Seven weeks later, the parents called to say he had killed himself in the middle of the night by overdose. Although gutting to hear, Jake was not surprised. The depression and PTSD was the after-war reality for many soldiers. Some people got a little better with the help of therapy and pills, but most people resigned themselves to live with it and it became a sort of passenger in their life. Suicide was always a terrible but, unfortunately, common thing that he had experience with and just as Detective Brannon had said, the soldier's parents were adamant that she couldn't have done it and that their little girl was just not that sort of person.

"So you're sure Garrett couldn't have been killed by someone from his past? Someone he crossed?" Jake asked. Eileen merely shrugged as she chugged the last of her coffee.

"What if I told you there was one person whom I know for a fact had contact with Mr. Langford. Someone of ill repute, let's say?" Eileen stared at him for what seemed like hours before replying.

"I'd ask how you know so much about this case." She rested her hands on the case files in front of her and shook her empty

131

coffee cup. "Third one this morning, I really ought to cut down." She said, but her face was stern.

"I'm sorry, Detective. I can't divulge that information, but as I said, I'm a private investigator and my client has, let's say, very deep pockets." Jake said after a long pause.

"Alright, Mr. Hanbury. I'll bite." Jake smiled, the truth of his statement was not at all an issue, Jake had indeed found out that Garrett had been meeting someone who sold him illicit substances. This might be helpful to the police and so it was not entirely the red herring Jake knew it to be; he could find nothing else that linked the man to Garrett and was almost certain that he had nothing do with Garrett's death. But Jake needed more information and this was the only way to get it. Eileen studied him for a few moments before finally sighing and getting up to walk out.

"I cannot tell you anything, unfortunately it is classified information, but I am going to refill my coffee. When I come back I am going to ask you for the name of this person and I hope that you will agree to divulge any information you have on them."

Jake nodded and watched her leave. Classic move. Her case files were left in front of him so of course she couldn't tell him anything, he had to look at for himself. And that's exactly what he did. As he riffled through the files he found the autopsy report. At the time, nothing was suspected to be out of the ordinary and so no extensive report was made. It was suspected that the injuries sustained to Mr Langford's face and body could have been caused by the fall. But of course they were not looking for anything else. They also did not conduct a tox screen, again Jake was not surprised. With current budget cuts, if they can find any reason to not conduct more tests than necessary, that's exactly what they will do. Interesting. Jake took more photos of the case files, some of these were interviews with potential witnesses or people of interest, family members, colleagues and the like. He'd read through those later when he had the time. He replaced the file where he found it, and no sooner had he done so did Detective Brannon walk back in to the and took the seat opposite him once more. She made no gesture of the secret deal they made but looked at him with the same stern look, mixed with suspicion that she seemed often to regard Jake with.

"So Mr. Hanbury, you say you have information of a suspect."

"A potential suspect, yes. One that supplied certain substances to Mr. Langford."

"And how good is your information?" She asked, business-like, taking out a pen and paper.

"The best." Jake replied simply. He took the paper from Detective Brannon who did not object but offered her pen to him. He took the pen and scrawled the letter D on it and an address. He then slid the paper back to her and she read it.

"Is there anything else I should know?" She asked, looking slightly disappointed.

"Don't spook him or you'll never see him again. Go in quietly." She simply nodded.

Jake nodded and leaned back in his chair.

"Ok, I think that's all for now." He said after a moment and got up to leave. As he walked out of the door, he turned around and looked at the detective. "Just one more thing, I'm working on another case, do you happen to know a David Ellison?" Eileen's eyebrows furrowed in confusion but Jake was careful not to say anything that might give her cause to think the two names were linked in any way.

"David Ellison? I don't know. Let me check." Jake followed her out of the interrogation room and back to her desk where she sat down and opened up a computer file. After a few minutes of silence, she looked back up at him.

"There was a break-in not far from here, at his house."

"When was this?" Jake asked, leaning forward with eagerness.

"Yesterday." She replied noticing his interest pique. "You know something?" She asked him. Jake shook his head.

"No, I just... He's my client, I need to investigate everything related to him; I'm trying to get a bigger picture of what I'm getting into." Jake lied smoothly, a professional and master of manipulation.

"Well you're welcome to speak to the officer on scene at the break-in if that's helpful?" She asked him.

"That would be very helpful, thanks." He replied. He was given the contact information of a Sergeant Allison Brown whom he was told would be coming back to the station within a few hours, which meant he had some time to go over the documents in Garrett's case file. He bade goodbye to the detective and promised he would call her if he had anything further to report on the Garrett Langford case. As he exited the building, he pulled out his phone and dialled a number.

"Hey, it's me. Yeah, I need you to do some digging for me. I need everything you can find on a David Ellison." He paused and listened to the person on the other end of the line before replying. "Yeah, I think he might be involved in Garrett's death." There was another pause before he spoke again. "Alright, thanks man. Oh, make sure this doesn't go anywhere. Strictly confidential." He hung up the phone.

Jake still felt stuck, he had no clue who might have disliked Garrett enough to want him dead, but what he did know was that David Ellison must be somehow involved; his name had cropped up enough times that it could not be a coincidence anymore. Jake would have to take things one step at a time.

The first thought that came to him was David's flat; maybe it held the answers he was looking for. Having already memorised the address on the police report that Detective Brannon had shown him, he knew exactly where it was and this was where he headed with haste.

He almost jumped a red light in his urgency but Jake arrived safely within the hour. The lobby of the building was pristine, the freshly-waxed floor reflecting the light from the bulbs above like a mirror. Jake attempted to blend in and moved with deliberate footsteps to the lift as if he had been here many times. Nobody paid him any attention as he waited for it to arrive and he was careful not to make eye contact with anyone.

Jake exited the lift on the 13th floor and made his way to David's flat. He took notice of the security cameras above him, making sure he walked and looked as natural as possible. When he faced David's door, he made a subtle check to his left and right and, when he was absolutely certain that he was alone, he withdrew from his pocket a small, plastic container no bigger than a credit card.

Opening it up, he pulled out a thin, metal lock pick and a tension rod. He inserted the rod inconspicuously into the keyhole and then did the same with the lock pick. With Jake's skill serving him well, it only took a moment before there was an audible *click* and the tension rod twisted in the barrel like a key, unlocking the door. Jake hastily replaced his lock picking tools back in the container and stowed it away in his pocket.

He turned the handle slowly, feeling sure that he would not meet anybody on the other side of the door, but acting with caution all the same. Once the door was opened most of the way, he slipped inside and closed it softly behind him.

Just as he had expected; the flat was empty. Although 'empty' only referred to the people. The place was a complete mess and it felt overwhelming to be around it all. He trod lightly, careful not to step on anything that might break and leave clues behind that he had been here.

Although, countered Jake's internal monologue, it would be far less likely that someone would notice if an item was out of place in a home this messy. There were countless glasses in the sink, dirty clothes strewn across the floor and there was a funny odour leaking out of the bin in the kitchen.

Though the open-plan flat was spacious, it felt like there was no escape from the untidiness that threatened to suffocate Jake as he took in the living room. It appeared to be playing host to numerous magazines and books on the coffee table and a sofa that all but looked like it had blown up and left its seat cushions everywhere.

Jake moved further into the flat; he was looking for something specific but he did not know what it was. He wanted answers though he had no idea what form those answers might take and if he wanted to have any chance at finding them, he would need to be thorough. Still, he had to be quick. Anything longer than 15 or 20 minutes was dangerous.

He lifted and replaced the cushions, searched the drawers and ruffled the magazines, he even checked the pockets of the clothes on the floor, careful to lay them down exactly where he found them. Through all of his effort he couldn't find anything that might be useful in solving his problem.

The funny smell was clawing at his nose and Jake reluctantly approached the bin. He nearly gagged when he opened the lid; the smell seemed to be coming from a piece of salmon that had been left in the warm flat for what could have been weeks by the smell of it.

Jake pulled a pen from his pocket and sifted through the contents of the bin that was, thankfully, mostly full of dry waste minus the putrid fish. He wasn't sure what might be in here, but past experiences told him that people tended to dispose of incriminating evidence.

Near the bottom, below a small piece of damp card, was a pair of latex gloves. Though it could have easily been completely reasonable for David to have used them himself whilst cleaning, the state of the flat told Jake that no such event had taken place in some time which posed the question, what were the gloves used for?

Hoping to figure out that answer, Jake pulled a large, empty plastic bag from his pocket and opened it. Hooking both gloves on the end of his pen, he deposited them in the bag, sealed it and put the whole thing in his pocket.

With no hesitation, Jake closed the bin lid and took a look at his wristwatch. He had already been in the flat for 12 minutes and was beginning to feel uncomfortable staying any longer. His eyes made one last sweep of the kitchen and, as he turned to leave, something caught his eye.

On the kitchen side, there was a small, white piece of paper all wrinkled and scrunched. He picked it up and smoothed it out on the surface. It was a bank receipt from NationFirst. There appeared to have been an extremely large money transfer made only days ago.

David was rich and Jake was aware of that, however, something about the timing of the transaction made him think there might be more to it than pure coincidence. Following his instincts, he pocketed the receipt, too and made for the door.

Using the same tools as he did to gain entry to the flat, Jake locked the door behind him; he certainly could do without another break-in report and this time, he would be caught on camera.

As Jake left the building, he considered what he should do with the evidence he had discovered and wondered how it all tied in.

Jake's phone buzzed in his pocket as he sat in the driver's seat of his car, considering everything he had uncovered. He withdrew it and saw that it was an email. There was no subject heading or any words in the body of it, only an attachment. This was exactly what he had been expecting. The attachment was an encrypted folder that required a password to open. He tapped it in, knowing that his guy used the same passcode for every document he sent to Jake – the year of the man's first tour of duty.

The file opened and it contained a dozen different documents. Most of them were the usual birth certificate and address history type of information, but there was one that stood out among the rest. Double tapping it, Jake opened the one that contained information about a prior arrest record. It seemed that David had been arrested on suspicion of some minor crime, had his DNA taken and was subsequently acquitted when the police found out he had an alibi. Though it was interesting to read, it wasn't particularly helpful to Jake's investigation, and he moved on. He read over each of the remaining files hoping for something to jump out at him but found nothing of use.

He sighed and closed the folder down, thinking carefully about what it could all mean.

Chapter 10

Nauseous and on the verge of hyperventilation, Garrett left the office of James and Slater feeling even more nervous than he was when he went in. He had spoken with the lawyer, Alfred Winchock, in charge of the case that Robert had to leave early because of his health. Although most of the information was privileged and couldn't be discussed, Garrett was informed that he had only been put on the case a day before trial and had almost no knowledge of it previously. Robert, however, knew the case inside and out and him leaving was undoubtedly the cause of the defendant losing his appeal. In the end the defendant went back to prison and, understandably there was a lot of aggression from him and threats to kill his legal team.

The last time Alfred had seen Robert alive he looked frail and confused. He could barely remember his own name let alone Alfred's. It was only days later that Robert's wife called to tell him that he had passed and how grateful he would have been to see his partners, friends and colleagues at his funeral. But through everything that Garrett was told, he was still so unsure of what to think about the idea that someone could just take this poor man's name and parade it around like a trophy. He knew that there were many strange things that had happened in the last few days, but he couldn't figure out what to do about this one thing that seemed to be niggling away at him. Who was Robert Hanbury?

He moved towards the side of the building and leant against the wall as his head began to spin. Bending down and putting his head between his legs, all he could think about was how he needed to go home, his new home, the one he stole from David, to check both his mail and answering machine and perhaps find a piece of the calm that he had been wishing to find in Leicestershire. Maybe there was something in the city that would set his mind at ease or at the least, make him feel more comfortable in a place he knew well. The paranoia that had been growing in him over the last few days was reaching its peak and he felt like he was being watched constantly. He tried to breathe but it came out fast and ragged. He was hyperventilating, he was surely going to pass out if he didn't calm down. He got his mind off of the situation at hand and thought about what he would do with David's money, his money. That always calmed him down. He would leave the country soon, he just had to make sure that it wouldn't draw unnecessary attention and also that Robert Hanbury was not in fact about to oust him and send him to prison for the rest of his life. He regained his composure shortly afterward and stood up tall once more.

Maybe he ought to sleep on it, he thought to himself. Perhaps there was more to discover of Robert, maybe the prisoner was somehow linked. That was a lot of digging he needed to do. Maybe he could hire someone to do some digging. After consider this for a moment, Garrett figured it would be all well and good, but he wasn't sure he wanted to drag some stranger into his mess who might leak or blackmail him for who knows how long.

He decided that he would try not to think on it anymore for tonight, he couldn't. He was so tired of it all, the plotting, the planning and the conspiracy, it was making him sick, he could feel it. Not to mention the guilt. He'd been trying to push it down because that's what he was good at, but he knew it wouldn't go away. He could remember everything from when David first introduced himself to Robert and everything in between, the details of it kept repeating on him. The money didn't mean as much to him as he was hoping it would at this moment but he was trying to convince himself that it was all because of the guilt. Once that wore off, he'd be fine and after the police stepped off the case and whoever was really wearing Robert's identity like a mask backed off, he could be free.

Before he even realised it, he was facing the door of his room at run-down bed and breakfast that reeked of stale smoke and stagnant water. When he opened it he saw that someone had been inside; his bed clothes were now tucked in, there were extra biscuits and tea bags which was odd considering he hadn't touched the first set, and the bin in the corner of the room had been emptied. His initial thought was to panic but he suppressed it just like he did his guilt. He was certain he would feel better tomorrow and each day after that.

When the morning did eventually arrive, after tossing and turning all night on the uncomfortable mattress, he was only too eager to re-pack his bag and head once more for the train station. His unplanned visit had not yielded the answers he had hoped, only more questions and a deeper hole in which he seemed to be falling into. Garrett could feel himself becoming more anxious as he headed down to the reception desk. He handed over the bent key and the old man looked it over like it was Garrett's fault that it was damaged. The man didn't say anything, however and hung it back up on the rack behind him. Garrett waited for a moment, hesitating on the spot before taking a slow step towards the door. When the old man continued to look at him in silence, he took another step. It was only when he stood right next to the door that he felt confident the man wasn't going to stop him and so he opened it quickly and stepped outside feeling grateful to be out of that wretched place. He considered leaving a bad review but then changed his mind; the type of people that he imagined would usually frequent a place like this most likely didn't use the internet.

The taxi he had called from the ancient phone in his room had arrived and was waiting for him. The driver did not seem to speak English very well and remained silent for the trip back to Market Harborough. Part-way into the drive Garrett began to worry that the man was not a taxi driver at all and that he had been taken hostage and was awaiting the moment that he pulled up to be hurled out the car when he all-but yelled at the driver to pull over and let him out. Garrett fumbled the door handle and almost fell out of the car in his haste. The driver grumbled something under his breath and drove off with a disgruntled expression on his face. Garrett stood for a moment on the path and caught his breath.

The walk back to the train station was slow and he used the maps on his phone to guide him. It appeared that he was nearly at the station and his mind had been running into overdrive creating a highly unlikely scenario and convincing his brain that it was real. He knew he had to get a hold of himself and that he would soon break down if he could not keep his fear and imagination under control. He walked with a steady trudge, his legs moving with little enthusiasm as he made his way down the empty streets. He continued to look around for anything that might hint that he was being followed such as a suspicious black car that he still hadn't forgotten about despite him trying. But there was no such follower and there were no other people that he met along his way. It might have just been his imagination, but the buildings seemed to be more identical than they had when he arrived. He shook his head, hoping the motion would clear his mind. He wasn't sure that he felt any better but he tried to put all the oddness of the village out of his mind as he boarded the train and took a seat in First Class.

The train ride was much the same as his night in the B&B, cold, uncomfortable and long. But he was glad when the train lunged back into the station and his stomach flipped inside him as he imagined a swarm of police waiting right outside ready to take him in. But no such swarm existed and he passed through the barriers invisible.

He made his way to the flat complex on foot, feeling somewhat more comfortable whilst walking down the busy streets than the quiet ones. Though he knew how big London was he didn't often travel without at least two wheels and journeying without the speed of a pushbike meant he could think without it distracting him from the road. He had hoped that by walking he would be able to think a little better and maybe his next move would come to him with more clarity by the time he got back. It seemed a silly thought now but it had given him some comfort at least for a while.

He fished his keys from his pocket and held them ready in his hand. As he turned and entered the building, he could feel something was off, like someone was watching him. He stopped and listened but all he could hear were the distant sounds of a city waking up and the residents of the building collecting post from the lobby. He shrugged it off, employing the self-control he knew he ought to developer and continued into the building, up the stairs to his flat. The door was locked. Just as he left it.

He walked over to the house phone when he was inside, after locking the door hastily once more. Garrett saw a green light signalling him on the phone telling him he had received a message. The lady on the automated system told him that he had three messages. He pressed the number one to listen to the first.

"Hi, this is Jared Bryer calling for Harry McGuire, I am an intern working at–" Garrett pressed delete before he heard anything else. It was probably some kid trying to sell him something or asking for a donation of some kind. He had participated in long-term studies often enough to know how to get rid of them. Message number two was from a recent client.

"David, hi, it's Jackie. Just wanted to say thanks for the effort you put in on the website, works like a dream. Thanks for fixing the checkout button, think I missed out on a few sales whilst it was down but hopefully not anymore. Anyway, I'm sending you something in the post, from my new art collection, I call it The Fixer and I hope you like it." Her voice trilled and rang with enthusiasm.

Having studied up on David's past clients, Jackie was an artist who sold her works online mostly and made good money from what he saw. Her art was a little Marmite-ish; you either loved it or hated it. David had loved it and had bought a few pieces but Garrett didn't like it at all. He very much thought it was something any three-year old kid with a paintbrush could whip up in art class at pre-school. But clearly there were other people who disagreed. There were in fact, at least two other of Jackie's work hanging around the flat and, when he had settled in to David's life, he intended on donating them and making the place feel a little more *his*.

The third message was from a lady that Garrett didn't know, her name was Penny and she sounded scared.

"Hi, this is Penny here from the law firm James and Slater, I hope you're well. Look, I'm sorry to be calling you like this but I think it's important that we talk. I don't know how else to say this but, David, I think you're in danger."

The message cut off abruptly after that. Garrett's heart raced as he tried to remember if he had met Penny or at least recognised the name. He was sure he had seen it on one of Robert's old case files that Alfred had shown him but he just couldn't put his finger on it. He quickly dialled the number back, after a few rings someone picked up.

"Hello? Penny speaking."

"Hi, it's David Ellison calling," rattling David's name off still felt odd and Garrett knew it would be a long time before it felt natural, "I was in your office yesterday and you left me a message saying I might be in danger," Garrett said quickly, "I don't think we've met before, have we?"

"No, I don't think so," Penny said warily, "I have some information about the case you were asking about but I need to ask you first, David can you keep everything I say between us?"

"Yes, absolutely." He replied instantly.

"I could lose my job for this, and that's best-case scenario." She warned him.

"I promise, this goes nowhere."

"Ok," she sighed, "I think there's more to Robert Hanbury's

life than you were told. Now I'm only going to tell you something I overheard once, I don't think it's common knowledge."
Garrett waited for her to continue, biting his lip nervously. "I
don't know if you knew this but, Robert Hanbury has a twin
brother."

Garrett's mouth fell open ever so slightly in surprise. He
hadn't known that Robert had a brother and his wife certainly
hadn't mentioned it either.

"Do you know where I can find him?" Garrett asked after a
beat.

"No, I don't and I've never even met him myself. I'm sorry,
David. I don't know how many people know but my guess is
not many. Robert rarely spoke about his life to anyone. Most
people didn't even know the name of his wife until they met
her at his funeral. He was a very secretive person for a long
time." Garrett could hear the genuine regret in her voice.

He thanked her before hanging up and quickly made his way
to the office and booted up the computer. Firstly he typed
in his own name, his real name, and his finger hovered over
the search button but he quickly deleted out of fear someone
might have bugged his computer and would start to notice how
many times he searched for a Garrett Langford. He deleted it
and replaced it with Robert's name. He hit enter and waited
for the results to load.

What he really wanted was his supposed brother's name.
That would certainly make more sense than a dead man
showing up. Garrett sat back in his chair and stared at the
screen as it loaded. He had a feeling that he was getting closer
to the truth and, for the first time in a long time, he felt the
smallest glimmer of hope bubble up inside him.

He searched what must have been dozens of websites before

he gave up looking. There was barely anything about Robert and nothing at all about a brother. Maybe Penny was wrong. Maybe she didn't hear quite right. He put both hands on his head and sighed heavily. He leapt up from the chair and grabbed the phone from the dock. He punched the *redial* button and listened to it ring. Penny answered once more.

"Penny Whitworth, James and Slater, how may I help you?" Her voice was soft and cool.

"Penny, it's David, we just spoke." He replied quickly.

"Oh, hello. What can I do for you?" She asked, the pleasant tone slipping slightly.

"You said you overheard someone mention Robert's brother, do you know who it was you overheard it from?"

"Let me think," she said and line went silent for a moment before she came back on, "I think it was at his funeral. Yeah that's right, it was his wife." Garrett cursed himself for not asking the wife's name whilst he was in the library talking to her.

"Do you know her name, anything that might help me find her?"

"Yeah, I think her name is Julia from what I remember." She replied, but she said it in almost a whisper like she didn't want anyone to know she was on the phone and talking about Julia. He gave a quick words of thanks to her and hung up the phone once again. He turned back to his computer and searched for Julia Hanbury on the Horninghold Library website. It was still early but Garrett did not feel like he could manage a phone call with the lady and it was likely the library would be busy, so he navigated to the contact page and opened a hyperlink to send them an email. His fingers hovered over the keyboard for a while as he thought about what to write, when the idea came to him he typed it furiously. After a moment, he was sure it was right and read it over once more:

To Julia Hanbury,

I am hoping this message finds you well. I spoke to you recently in person at the library in regard to your late husband. I was hoping we could call and talk a little more. Please do contact me at your earliest convenience.

Sincerely,

David Ellison

He checked it for grammar and punctuation and hit send. He hoped that Julia would reply at some point soon, the feeling that someone might be ready to knock on his door at any point to haul him in to the police, or else do something even worse that he couldn't even imagine was deeply unsettling. When Garrett left the room he found his body was aching to climb into a bed that didn't stab him in the back with old springs and to use a shower that wasn't covered in six month old soap scum and limescale.

Garrett enjoyed the shower more so than he realised and part of him felt like he was washing away remnants on Garrett Langford which was a good thing in many ways. David was successful, charming and intelligent and was every bit the suave gentleman Garrett hadn't been. He climbed into bed feeling like he was, finally, moving forward and he awoke to no nightmares that night. In fact, Garrett slept soundly and didn't wake when the sunrise first crept into the flat as he would have done yesterday.

When the morning rolled around, Garrett awoke feeling better than he had in days. He felt stronger inside, a little more desensitised to the disgusting things he had had to do. The first thing he did was make his way to the office, which was a little trickier than usual due to the clothes and rubbish piling up, he would have to get around to that soon or risk letting his disguise slip. There were also a few clients that had emailed about jobs which he ought to work on.

When Garrett checked his email his heart leaped to see a response from Julia, it read:

Dear David,

I thank you for your email and would love to talk more about Robert, he was a great man and worthy of the tales told about him. Please do ask me anything, he would have loved that people were interested in his life.

Yours,

Julia Hanbury

Garrett wasted no time in sending his response:

Dear Julia,

Many thanks for your quick reply, I have a couple of questions but I'm not sure how much you might know or would be willing to help me. I heard a rumour that your husband had a twin brother, is there any truth to this? I'm hoping you might be able to tell me more about him.

I look forward to your response and wish you well,

David

Garrett hit the *send* button and left the computer. He sighed heavily as he looked around the flat that he had commandeered. Where to start? Garrett wondered. Cleaning the flat took longer than he had anticipated and the final area, which he had left until last, was the kitchen. As he opened to bin to empty it something felt off. He wasn't sure what it was, but he knew *something* was off. He put his hand begrudgingly into the bin and that's when it hit him. There was something missing. The gloves he wore when he drugged David into oblivion was missing. He hadn't even thought of the gloves since he had taken them off. Was this related to the break-in? Is that what the mysterious person had taken? Garrett refused to let this drag him down into the paranoia for fear of his hallucinations returning along with the insanity that he felt he was beginning to overcome. He was making progress and the idea of falling back into that mindset was not at all pleasant. He convinced himself that he must have thrown them away in a different bin or else, missed them among the rubbish; there was so much that it certainly wasn't impossible.

Without looking at it a moment longer than he needed, he pulled his hand quickly out of the bin and tied the bag and replaced it with a fresh one. A pile of dirty washing and another of full bin bags later, the flat was mostly clean. He breathed a sigh of relief. He was sure this would help him think more clearly. His mother's words echoed in his ears, *a cluttered house leads to a cluttered mind.* He'd never really understood the depth of how true that statement was until this moment.

By the time he had cleaned the house, there was another response from Julia waiting to be opened in his email, Garrett obliged:

Dear David,

I didn't realise anybody knew about Robert's brother; he was always very private when it came to family matters. It is true that he once had a brother, but they had long since ceased communication. It all started when Robert and his brother, Jake were growing up. There was a bit of a feud I'd call it. Their parents were not quite as fond of Jake and Robert was the golden boy. They wanted both of their kids to go to university and get a degree. But Jake had other ideas. He wanted to join the army but his parents outright refused.

So, he moved out at 16 and joined anyway. Robert always felt that it was Jake's fault for breaking up the family and that was why they never spoke to each other. I heard Jake was bitter and resentful but of course there are two sides to every story and I don't claim to know them both. A few years after Jake enlisted, he joined the SAS and the Secret Service so I was told. I'm not sure how much of it is true, mind you as, like I said, Robert and his brother rarely spoke so it could have just been wild conjecture and rumourmongering. After Robert died, I saw Jake at the funeral, we only spoke a few words together and mostly Jake spoke to his parents. I'm not sure whether they reconnected over his death or not. I'm afraid that's all I know about him. Funny, I was married to Robert for 15 years and everything I know about his twin brother can be condensed into one email. I'm not sure what you're expecting to find but I hope this brought you some clarity.

Best,

Julia

Garrett read the email twice over, turning the information over in his head. Jake. Jake. The contents made him feel slightly better. Although there was indeed a man speaking to him who potentially might know about his secret, it wasn't the ghost of a dead man named Robert. It was his twin brother, supposedly using his brother's name. Garrett concluded the only reason that he would use his brother's name was to protect his own identity seeing as almost nobody knew he even existed according to Julia. But that meant that Garrett had an advantage. Jake didn't know that Garrett knew who he was. All he had to do now was find out the connection between Jake and David. He was sure there must have been one or else he would not have approached him in the park or followed him down the street. Finally, he had the makings of a plan.

Chapter 11

Glaring at the slow ticking hands of the clock on the wall, watching the minutes drag painfully by, Jake Hanbury was sitting in a laboratory waiting room. It was just past one in the afternoon and he had been waiting since nine o'clock earlier that morning. The pair of gloves that he had stolen from David's flat was currently being tested for DNA. It was a rush job, paid for with cash, most of what was left from David's last payment. He had still heard nothing from him for days and Jake suspected something was gravely wrong; his infallible instincts serving him well. He wasn't quite sure why he cared so much about this man; he was just a client like many before him.

When he thought about it, Jake considered that maybe the notion of attempting to reconnect with parents (whether missing or disowned) was somewhat warming and made a nice change from the usual sort of requests he got as a private investigator. Jake considered that maybe this was the reason he wanted to solve the case. Having served in the military and the Secret Service for a long time, he was usually hardened to feeling pretty much anything.

Of course he couldn't go to the police, they would likely just say he had no evidence and they weren't in the business of wasting public money to investigate random people without any evidence to back it up. But those of sort of restraints did not apply to someone like Jake. Clearly nobody else knew what he did about the situation or it would be national news without a doubt. So it was down to Jake to figure out what had happened, how the dead Garrett Langford was involved and bring whoever the imposter was to justice. Which was exactly why he was sitting in the waiting room of the laboratory. With any luck, some DNA could be pulled off the gloves that might help piece together what happened to David and where he was right now. Many ideas came to mind and included such things as hostage, dead and missing.

It was almost two o'clock before a man in a white lab coat emerged from a door near the reception. The man made eye contact with Jake and moved towards him who stood up as he approached.

"Ok, Mr. Hanbury is it?" He spoke softly, checking the details on a clipboard which he read off. The man was young, maybe early thirties, thin and gangly, tall and tanned. He pushed his wavy hair off of his forehead and out of his eyes.

"That's me." Jake replied. His voice sounded a little crackly from the lack of use so he cleared his throat.

"I'm Dr. Pritchett, I work in the DNA testing centre out the back, would you follow me please?" Jake followed the man to a small office that only contained a desk, a small chair for a guest and two bookcases which were stuffed to the brim with textbooks and loose sheets of paper that overhung the edges making it look untidy and cluttered. The doctor closed the door behind him after they entered and sat in his own desk chair whilst Jake took the spare.

"Is there a problem, doctor?" He asked of the man in the

155

white coat.

"Not so much a problem as a question." He responded with a note of anxiety in his voice. Jake couldn't help but notice that the man spoke quietly, almost whispering like the conversation was a secret not be overheard.

"Fire away." Jake replied calmly. He could already tell the question was of a sensitive nature; nobody would take a person to a quiet room, close the door and lower their voice to ask a question that was perfectly normal and Jake prepared himself as such.

"Can I ask where you got this?" The doctor asked, taking from his overlarge pocket a plastic bag with the gloves inside.

"I'm sorry, no." Came Jake's reply in a calm, polite manner. He wasn't going to get into it with the doctor whose face turned away from him clearly stunted by Jake's rejection.

"Is this part of a crime?" The doctor asked.

"That's what I'm trying to figure out."

"I see. Well, we found some hair samples inside and it looks like it could be arm or hand hair and so we ran some tests. When we checked our database and it came back as a loose match." Dr Pritchett said in his low volume. Jake felt his pulse quicken.

"Whose was it?"

"A one Garrett Langford, recently pronounced dead, I'm sure you've seen the news." Jake's mind went spiralling into a haze of questions and possible conclusions.

"Are you sure?" He asked, though he already knew the answer.

"Most definitely, we checked it twice. But I do need to repeat it was a loose match. If you have any more samples we could refine it further but in its current state, that's all we can see." He said, shrugging, handing the bag back to Jake who tucked it into the large pocket of his coat. So a pair of latex gloves worn by Garrett, the man who recently committed suicide but was potentially a murder victim, turns up in David Ellison's rubbish bin in his own flat. Jake pulled out his trusty notebook and wrote down the latest development in what was quickly becoming a very deep plot. He was still struggling to understand where the overlap of David and Garrett began. How did they know each other? Why did both of their names keep cropping up together? These thoughts reeled through his mind and he kept rereading the notes he had already taken as he sat in his car, figuring out where to go next.

There was so much Jake didn't know that made all the facts feel like fiction. It was like trying to piece together a jigsaw without the picture to work from whilst only having half of the pieces available to him. What he needed was to examine Garrett's body. Maybe there was something that the pathologist missed and passed off because they, too didn't have all of the information. The only problem, and it was a big one, was figuring out how he would manage to examine the body when he couldn't tell anybody why he wanted to do so. For anyone other than Jake, this would feel all but impossible. Jake smiled slyly to himself and clicked his seatbelt in.

Only an hour later and he was standing in the morgue. It was cold and dark. He had of course seen many dead people during his service in the military, but he never enjoyed being around them; he always got an odd feeling that gave him the willies. He was not exactly supposed to be down here but a crisp £50 note in the hand of the security guard to take a long walk around the perimeter meant he had about 15 minutes of undisturbed silence to do a little more digging. To get his hands of the death record and to examine the body of Garrett Langford would require a lot of paperwork and clearance otherwise and even then, he doubted whether the police would allow him to be present. No, he had to do this himself and he had to do it quickly.

Jake pushed open the double doors leading to the autopsy room open and entered. It was even colder in here and that odd feeling pressed upon him even more causing goosebumps to erupt on his arms and the back of his neck and making the hairs to stand on end. There were three metal tables with giant lamps overhanging them in the middle of the room. The left two tables were covered with a blue sheet which was covering the body beneath it. The form of the corpse made the sheet stick out with small protrusions. As he breathed in, the sickly smell of blood and iron filled his nose along with a strong chemically scent that almost made him gag but he ignored this and walked further in making his way to the left hand table. He pulled a pair of latex gloves from a box on the wall and pulled them on over his hands. At the bottom of the sheet, he gingerly lifted one of the edges.

A grey foot poked out from underneath and the goosebumps rippled through him once more. He was staring at a paper tag which had a name inscribed upon it, *Jessica Ashley*. He gently re-covered the woman's foot with the blue sheet and moved over to the middle table. He repeated the same action on this table and another grey foot appeared. This one, however was bent at a crooked angle and he made an audible gasp as he saw a bone that was protruding through the flesh. The tag that hung from the broken foot was labelled, too. *Garrett Langford*.

Part of him was pleased that the body was still available for examination, the other part of him told him he was not going to enjoy this next task. He made his way up to the head of the sheet and pulled it back quickly, like ripping off a plaster. The body underneath was grey and covered in dark marks that he supposed were bruises. There were bloodless cuts and gashes over the body, primarily over the face which was badly wounded causing his features to look slightly warped. The torso was marked with a Y shape that was held together with stitches.

Jake tried not to stare at the face longer than he had to; the lifeless eyes were unsettling to look at and did nothing to make Jake feel better about what he was doing. At the end of the autopsy table was a note chart which Jake took and began to thumb through it, glancing at each page and taking in as much of the information on them as he could. He saw that it was marked as a potential homicide. Jake continued to hunt for a clue that might help him tie it all together.

The body was cold to the touch and Jake begrudged doing it but he didn't have time to be squeamish, he was already eating into his time. The stiff body was difficult to move but he made notes of any marks and scars that didn't appear to have come from the fall onto the motorway. There was a small scar on the man's left knee, and another just above it on the outside of the thigh. He checked the doctor's notes once more to see if this had been documented but found no record of it in the charts or in Garrett's prior history which accompanied the pathologist's findings in the file. That was all he could see. Feeling frustrated that nothing had jumped out at him, he had just began covering the body back up when he recalled a conversation with David that he had had on the phone just after he first made contact with him.

"I'm hoping you might be able to help me look for my parents.

159

I can pay well. They went missing on a hike a year ago and I've been searching for them ever since." David had told him. *"The police investigation has turned up nothing so the funding has been cut, they're relying on tip-offs now before they actively investigate. I would have hiked the trail myself to have a look but I'm still recovering from surgery. I tore my ACL in my left knee a while ago doing something stupid and now I'm still going through physiotherapy for it so I can't strain it too much."*

Jake wasn't quite certain why this conversation had come to him in this moment but he trusted his gut and knew it must be important somehow; his subconscious always picked up on things that his conscious mind might not have caught. He pulled out his phone and took a photo of the knee for his records and that's when a suspicious feeling crept into his stomach. He looked at the man's face again. It was familiar. Was this David Ellison? The tag was marked as Garrett Langford clear as day. He riffled through the notes once more and found some information about the possessions he was carrying on his person when he was admitted. It said quite plainly the man had a wallet and ID on him and that the ID had said Garrett Langford.

The feeling in his stomach nudged him again, hinting at something. He looked at the pale face again and studied it. This man was not Garrett Langford. The face, the scarring on his left knee. This had to be David and the moment he thought about it it was like he had known it all along. But there was no way to prove it. Jake paced on the spot for a moment as he processed the information. Then another idea crept into his mind. Maybe there was a way to prove it. He looked at the head once more and reached for a pair of thick, silver pliers on the silver tray beside him. He grimaced to himself as he put the pliers in the man's mouth and clamped them around one of his molars.

Jake had just made it out of the morgue when the security guard rounded the corner and resumed his post at the entrance. Jake, his hand clenched around another plastic bag that contained a single tooth, sped to his car door, yanked it open and sat down in the driver's seat. He threw the plastic bag containing the tooth onto the passenger seat, feeling disgusted by what he had just done, and pulled out his phone. He tapped some numbers into the keypad and waited for the dialling to stop.

"Dr Pritchett." The man's soft voice said.

"Hi, Dr Pritchett it's Jake Hanbury. I saw you about an hour ago."

"Mr Hanbury, yes, what can I do for you?" He asked in a friendly tone.

"I need another DNA test, a rush job if you'll take it, I have cash." Jake told him.

"Certainly, Mr Hanbury. Why don't you bring the specimen down and we'll see what we can do. At this time of day you might be looking at tomorrow to get the results, same fee as last time."

"I'll be with you shortly." Jake told the doctor and hung up the phone. If Dr Pritchett had asked questions about how he had obtained a pair of gloves, he was most definitely going to start asking questions about a tooth he had just pulled from a corpse that he had no business touching. But Jake had no choice. He needed answers and he had nowhere else to turn. There was a part of him that wondered to himself why he had not initially reported the imposter to the police when he himself had noticed it. But another voice rose inside him and answered the question as soon as he had considered it; it was a somewhat selfish reason, he knew that, but the £10,000 bonus for uncovering the truth about what had happened to David's parents was too good to pass up. If there was even a chance that David was still out there, Jake knew he had a better chance of finding him than the police did. He would figure it out any way he had to; of that he was certain.

Chapter 12

Feeling like he had just run a mile, his heart thrumming gently with the hint of excitement that only the thrill of success brought, Jake arrived at the laboratory once more, plastic bag containing a tooth in hand. Once inside, he approached the reception desk and asked to speak to Dr Pritchett. Just as he was about to take a seat in the all-too-familiar waiting room that he was beginning to like less and less the more time he spent there, the very doctor approached him with a concerned expression. In lieu of any explanation, Jake placed the bag into his hand. For a moment the man looked at it and then opened his mouth as if he were going to ask a question, looking slightly disgusted.

"Like I said on the phone, Mr Hanbury, I'll hopefully have some results for you tomorrow." He said and walked off into the back room beyond the doors marked for staff only. He knew he had some time to kill before he would get some results, so he took a moment to sit in his car once more and think about the developments in the case. Before he knew it, he was driving with no idea where he planned on going, passing over the wheel to his inner driver. But when he stopped some twenty minutes later, he looked out of his window and realised he had somehow driven himself to David's flat. He often did things like this, where he would almost shift into an auto-pilot mode. When this happened, it was usually his subconscious telling him something and he would be better off listening to it than trying to fight it.

Jake parked up and exited the vehicle. He found himself walking into the building once more and taking the lift up to David's floor. When got there, he noticed an old lady that lived in the flat next to David's struggling to carry several large shopping bags across the threshold.

"Would you like a hand, ma'am?" Jake asked politely. Already his mind was whirring into action. Years of training had made him quick on his feet and even quicker to think of plans. There was a point in his investigative training where he learnt how easy people were to manipulate. Of course the old lady beckoned him closer and gratefully accepted his help, just as he knew she would. Jake picked up the remaining bags which clinked and clattered as if they were full of glass jars and metal spoons and walked into her flat.

The layout was much the same as David's when he had made his silent visit to investigate the flat and hunt for him; spacious and open-plan. This lady's, however was cluttered far more so and was home to many pieces of décor that seemed not to match at all. There were plates and cups that were displayed on stands adorning pictures of different animals but there were also giant wooden sculptures that looked Balinese and wooden masks that wouldn't look out of place in the home of a witch doctor.

Jake followed the lady to kitchen, inhaling a strong scent of something like sherry or port, and set the bags on the floor as per her instructions. Then she turned slowly to him and offered him a cup of tea or coffee. Jake declined both but requested a glass of water; an excuse to stay longer than declining a drink would have allowed though, in truth, he wasn't thirsty at all. She handed him the drink and offered him a place to sit opposite to where she herself had just sat down. Jake obliged and began his interrogation.

"So how long have you lived here, Mrs...?" He began.

"Wilson. And I have lived here a long time," she replied with a wink, "about seven years now."

"Do you know many people around here, Mrs Wilson?" Jake asked with an air of nonchalance.

"Not many, I'll be fair with you. I don't really have a lot of friends since my husband passed." She admitted.

"I'm sorry to hear it." Jake replied. She waved off his apology.

"It was a while ago." She said simply.

"What about your neighbours, how are they? Jake asked. He was nearing the point of the conversation that was the reason he brought himself into the lady's home to begin with.

"They're ok. I don't really speak to them except perhaps David, next door." She gestured to her right, pointing to the wall she shared with David.

"What's he like?" Jake pressed.

"Quiet most of the time, but always happy to stop for a chat. Except he's been a bit off lately." She said, taking a sip from a glass of red wine that she'd just poured for herself.

"Off in what sort of way?"

"Well, up until almost a week ago every Monday he would drop by with a few bags of shopping, it's sort of an arrangement we've had for a while. But last week he just didn't show up. No reason, no excuse, nothing. He barely even looks at me now. I bet it was that man, controlling him or something." She said, her wrinkled lips pursed.

"That is indeed very odd behaviour. Who was this man, do you know him?" She shook her head firmly.

"Nope, never seen him before last week. I bumped into him and he barely had two words to say to me. Awfully rude if you ask me." She sniffed derisively.

"What day was this, ma'am?" He asked inquisitively.

"Maybe four days ago, I think. It was that Monday, maybe." Jake was once again thinking a few steps ahead. If there was another man here, Jake might be able to find him on the security footage and then locate him for questioning. Jake chugged the last of his water, noticing there was some sediment from God only knows what at the bottom. He grimaced slightly and tried not to think about it, he had consumed a lot worse things in the armed forces. Jake finished his conversation with the old lady and hurried to leave the flat. He turned toward the lift and rode it all the way down to the ground floor. When he got there, he went straight to the reception desk where there was a young man maybe early 20's manning the station in a full black suit with a red tie clipped to his crisp shirt. Jake approached the man with what he hoped was a warm smile on his face; an expression he wore far too infrequently.

"Good afternoon!" He exclaimed brightly, maybe too much. The man at the desk looked slightly put out by his overt friendliness. "I'm here to look at the security footage, something to do with a potential break-in." He added to the man who did not respond straight away. Immediately his expression relaxed and he took on a less-professional demeanour. Technically Jake hadn't lied at all. He was indeed there to look at the security footage and part of the reason was to look at the break-in.

"Finally, they said they'd be sending someone. I've got it on a USB stick all downloaded if that's good?" He replied.

"I'm also here to look at the same camera footage but from a couple of days earlier." Jake told him.

"Ok, sure. I'll take you to the security office you can access what you need to. I've got to be quick; I'm the only one on front of house today." He told Jake. The young man led him to a security office and opened the door, letting Jake step inside. The room was bare, the walls a slate grey. There was little furniture apart from a desk with neatly arranged paperwork on the edge of it and a computer monitor sitting squared and centre. A single chair was opposite it. On the wall there were several screens displaying footage from all over the flat block including the exterior of each individual flat within it.

"I hope this is alright? It's not exactly what you would call state of the art but I guess it gets the job done well enough; we don't have much trouble here." He told Jake who nodded politely in agreement even though he felt that it was inadequate for his needs. Jake took a seat at the desk as the young man left him alone in silence once again, returning to his post at reception.

Jake wasted no time in plugging the USB stick into the computer and opening up the footage. He found Mr Ellison's flat number on the list of displayed people. Jake checked around Friday's footage at 12:00pm and set the playback to six times normal speed. He watched as the lift pinged open and someone rushed out at six times faster than usual. They disappeared off camera and ten seconds later they re-appeared on camera. The person was walking toward him and he could see it was David Ellison. Jake slowed the footage down to normal speed but it didn't help; David would have had no idea he would be watched days later. He walked around the corner of the corridor and out of sight.

Jake shook his head slightly in frustration at not having found what he came here for so far when a thought occurred to him: surveillance cameras don't track movement in two directions only in one direction, or at least that is how they are designed to work. He checked over the rest of Friday's footage but apart from David going about his usual routine there was nobody else of interest that appeared on camera. So Jake moved on to Saturday of which he saw nothing of any interest once more. Finally, he checked out Sunday's footage. It was early hours and two men, whom Jake noticed looked remarkably similar, so much so that he might have thought the camera glitched had it not been for the fact they wore different clothes, stumbled out of the lift; their drunkenness was clearly apparent even from the grainy camera footage that Jake was currently sifting through. Both of the men looked as though they could be David but it was hard to tell on the ancient monitor. One of the men pulled keys out of his pocket and, with some difficulty, pushed one of them into the keyhole. They both half-fell, half-walked through the doorway and then the door closed behind them.

Jake noted down the timestamp of the footage for duplication when he had finished watching. He fast-forwarded once more until late morning when one man, looking haggard and hungover, trudged out of the door and into the lift. The man was wearing the same clothes as the night before which allowed Jake to deduce that this man must have been the visitor. Almost an hour later another man, far better dressed and looking less weathered than the first exited the flat and rode the lift down.

Jake once more fast forwarded through the rest of the day, keeping a focused eye on the door for any sign of movement. He noticed David returning alone later that evening and Garrett wasn't seen until the following morning where he was invited back in. Jake watched Garrett leave the flat that Monday morning and David departed soon after, leaving a note wedged into the door frame; Jake wished he knew what it said but maintained his attention on the security footage nonetheless. He watched as Garrett returned, reading the note that was left in the door. Soon after, David joined him in the flat and there was no more movement for hours on the camera except a few people that walked up and down the corridor, completely oblivious to whatever was going on just feet away from them, something Jake was trying to find out.

Jake continued to fast forward until 1am on Tuesday morning when, finally, he saw something that made him lean in closer to the screen. Garrett was exiting the flat but this time he looked panicked. He was dragging behind him a giant suitcase that he appeared to struggle with due to the weight of whatever was inside. This was very suspicious behaviour. Jake's hand began scrawling fast across the page of his notebook. Where would this visitor be going in the middle of the day in the same dirty clothes as the night before with a suitcase that was not his? David did not appear on the camera at all which only heightened the oddness of the scene playing out on the screen. Was this man stealing from David? The police report had said David did not notice anything missing from the flat. The man continued to drag the suitcase into the lift and left. It was late afternoon on a Monday and still David had not left the flat. Rubbing his chin in concentration, Jake copied down the time stamp once more and continued scrolling forward to see if he could find anything else that might help tie it all together.

There was a knock at the door to the security office and the young man from the reception poked his head in.

"I'm off now. Do you need anything before I go?" Jake shook his head and kept watching the screen as the door closed once more behind him and leaving alone once more.

The late evening sped into focus on the screen and Jake waited for the visitor to show up but he didn't. It was as though he knew he would be watched and had not returned since dragging that suitcase out of the flat. Or perhaps it was too heavy to carry around all day. He kept watching, waiting for someone else to arrive at the flat or for David to leave but neither happened. It wasn't until the early hours of Tuesday morning that the man finally returned. Jake's inner voice spoke to him once more and penetrated his conscious thought; was this the man that had something to do with David's absence? As far as he searched Jake never saw another person leave the flat before the event of the break-in began to play out in front of his eyes. The old lady from next door slowly hobbled toward David's front door, checked obviously around her and then pulled a key out from her pocket. Jake had no idea where or when she had gotten this key but it unlocked David's door without any problem and the old lady walked in. She was in the flat for no more than four minutes before she left and stood out the front, pulling an old flip-phone from her pocket and putting it to her ear. The lady chatted for a few minutes before replacing the phone in her pocket and heading back inside her own home. 90 minutes later the police arrived as did the visitor about 20 more minutes after that. The visitor spoke to the officer at the door and then gestured them inside as if he owned the place.

This must have been Garrett on the film. There could be no other excuse and clearly he had taken over David's identity, Jake thought to himself. If the police couldn't see anything wrong and the police report specifically mentioned speaking to David, he couldn't think of any other scenario that made sense. Jake scribbled more notes down in his notepad. He then copied all of the video files onto the USB stick that was still plugged into the computer and waited a while as it slowly copied over a gigabyte of video which took a long time on the ancient computer that whirred loudly as it struggled with the task. When the files were copied he pulled the USB stick from the computer and pocketed it. As he sat in the silence for a minute pondering it all over, a thought struck him.

He changed cameras to the lift and found the moment where the visitor entered it with the giant suitcase and began to track him across the hotel and down into the underground car park. In the very edge of the screen Jake could just make out the visitor loading, with difficulty, the suitcase into the boot of a BMW. There was a knock at the man's window and it looked to be the parking attendant who was quickly waved off. The BMW rounded the corner with speed and left the car park. Jake attempted to slow the video down to make a note of the number plate but the frame rate of the footage was so poor that each frame yielded only a blurry image of the bumpers and nothing of use.

Jake copied this file, too, onto the USB stick. At present, he had copies of many files that would all accompany the real evidence of Garrett's crimes. Without it, he would have nothing but suspicions and accusations. But he still didn't have absolute proof and part of him wondered whether he would ever get concrete evidence or if he would have to meet with him and get a confession himself.

But that was only one possible outcome. He knew this would likely be his only chance to view the footage so he didn't want to miss anything and had every intention of rewatching it back at a more convenient time. Jake paced the small room thinking it all over. David had invited a man back to his flat who left multiple times and then returned so clearly they must have been friends or acquaintances at the very least. Then David left and when he returned, he never set foot back outside the flat again. There was only one entrance to the flat so there could be no way that he left from any other door.

Considering Jake had met a man claiming to be David who was definitely not, he assumed that this was exactly what he was seeing on camera: someone pretending to the police to be David. Which mean that David was either still in the flat or... Or what? Jake thought.

It was at that moment his phone rang in his pocket and Jake pulled it out quickly and answered.

"Mr Hanbury? It's Dr Pritchett." Said the man on the other end.

"Dr Pritchett, I wasn't expecting you to call so soon, how can I help?"

"Yes we had some cancellations. I'll get right to it. I'm not sure if this means anything to you but the tooth you brought in came as a match." He said. Jake waited silently, wondering if it could be true.

"The tooth belongs to David Ellison, a man in his mid-twenties." Jake's heart almost stopped. He couldn't believe it. The body did not belong to Garrett Langford.

"Thank you, doctor." Jake said and hung up so he could

think. He had to find Garrett Langford. He had stolen David's identity and was living in this building, living David's life when he should be rotting in a cell. But if David was dead, how did his body get to the motorway? Of course the answer was simple, Jake thought as the question popped into his head. The suitcase. There was a reason it was heavy.

There was a sudden knock at the door and Jake approached it cautiously. He didn't want to be surprised by anyone he didn't know even if they did claim to be police officers or other internal security. He walked up to the door and opened it slowly only revealing his head so as not to startle whoever was on the other side.

It was one of those strange moments where time appeared to slow down and everything seemed clearer than normal as Jake saw two figures standing in front of him wearing dark clothing and sunglasses despite being inside a dimly lit building. Both of the men were at over six feet tall but they were both clearly overweight and unfit. Many thoughts raced through his head. If Garrett had killed David, who was to say he wouldn't hesitate to try and take out the man who might be the only one who was quickly discovering his secret? If he were taking on David's identity, that would mean he also had access to David's resources which Jake had personal knowledge to be seemingly endless.

"Can I help?" Jake asked cautiously.

"That depends. Are you Jake Hanbury?" They asked. Jake had not expected them to know his real name; he often used his brother's name for safety but clearly they were past that and he didn't want to give them any impression that he was intimidated by them, so he played along.

"Who's asking?" Jake replied coldly.

173

"I'm here to relay a message from David Ellison." The larger of the two replied with a slight lisp. Jake was suspicious.

"Are you now?" Jake asked in an almost bored voice. The man took off his sunglasses to reveal blue eyes. "Just a message, huh?" Jake asked; their posture was telling him something different.

The smaller man said nothing and stepped forwards still wearing the dark glasses even though there was no reason to do so inside, it was also dangerous as it prevented him from seeing anything properly such as a surprise attack. Their amateur behaviour was almost laughable. Jake doubted that the men had ever been in a fight before.

"I am Royce White and I'm working for Mr Ellison. He has informed us that you have been interfering and I'm here to tell you that you need to back off. Mr Ellison is a very influential man and has asked that we don't touch you and simply deliver you a warning. Stop looking." Jake fought hard to prevent himself from rolling his eyes. They must have been practicing their speech on the ride over to him. "He also said that if you so much as Google his name he will know, and we will be back in a less hospitable mood." Jake almost laughed. He didn't know quite what else to do. The way they stood there like tough CIA-style professionals was enough to tell him they were not a threat. Everything about them, from their dress sense to their voice screamed incompetence and it was as plain as day to see. The sunglasses inside were an awful idea, the suits, though nice-looking if not a bit cheap, were far too restrictive for any style of hand-to-hand combat. It was clear they had watched far too many movies and it made them stand out like a sore thumb. All of these things added up to make them look like nothing more than cosplayers at a sci-fi convention dressed as the Men in Black.

"Is that all?" Jake asked.

"That is all." Royce replied in his overdone scary man voice. "We are to give you one last warning, stop what you're doing or we will be back." He finished and then gave a nod to the man behind him who began walking towards hotel lobby exit. Royce was about to do the same when he stopped himself and turned back around to face Jake.

"By the way, did you notice that this building has an awful security system? Mr Ellison just hacked into it in less than five minutes." And then they both walked off leaving Jake in the doorway. He quickly shut the door and spun around. Sure enough the screens were all showing black images and the words *no data available* flashed repeatedly. Jake thanked his instincts as he held onto the USB stick in his pocket. He had almost everything he needed to bring Garrett Langford down. Up to this point, most of the evidence he had was not admissible in court as it was obtained illegally.

As he turned to leave, Jake noticed his wallet sitting on the floor beneath the chair he had just vacated. Figuring it must have fallen out of his pocket he bent down to retrieve it. Just as he was about to tuck it back into his pocket, he noticed a white piece of paper stuck to the back of it. He peeled it off and opened it up. It was a receipt but it wasn't his own. He recognised it immediately. It was the one other thing he had taken from David's flat the other day. It looked fresh and was dated Monday. He didn't quite know what made him take the receipt from the kitchen side but, as always, he trusted his gut instincts and pocketed it on his way out.

As Jake looked at it, he noticed something he didn't the first time. Beside the transaction amount, which was suspiciously large to begin with but not completely peculiar given the extent of David's wealth, there was a small sentence that said *ID verified by Passport.* Jake sat back down on the seat, turning it all over in his head. If he could prove to NationFirst that one of their accounts had been accessed fraudulently, then they themselves could contact the police and the investigation could go ahead with everything above board.

He looked to his left and noticed a small filing cabinet marked *CCTV HARD COPY* and smiled to himself; Garrett maybe smart enough to erase digital footage but he certainly would not have thought about the physical copies. Jake opened the cabinet and began to sift through the folders until he found what he was looking for; a folder marked with the date of David's death. Jake pulled out that file and sure enough, there was a disc with writing on the top which told him that the disc was not blank and had been filled recently with the damning evidence of Garrett's crimes.

He took the disc back to the computer and put it in the machine. When it loaded up he found the moment on Monday where David left his flat after Garrett had. He tracked him through the lift and noticed him move not towards the exit but to another door where, upon changing cameras, Jake noticed there was an on-site bar. David sat down at the bar alone for a moment before he was joined by a woman. He couldn't tell how old the woman was thanks to the grainy footage but he could see that she was older than David was. David chatted with her for quite some time, perhaps a business meeting or maybe a friend was Jake's guess.

After a while, David left the bar and Jake tracked him as he returned to his flat where he awaited a fate completely unknown at the hands of someone he clearly trusted. Jake copied this file, too onto the USB stick and ejected the disc. He replaced it back in the filing cabinet once more. So David had never been to the bank the day the transfer was made but someone had and had used David's own passport to verify his identity. Someone that must have looked somewhat similar to the photo, someone like Garrett. He jotted this last detail into his notebook and turned to leave the office once again.

Jake knew that if he wanted someone like Garrett to be convicted, it would take time and far more than circumstantial evidence alone. With David's money and resources, he would likely have access to some of the best criminal lawyers in the country. Still this footage had brought Jake one step closer towards revealing Garrett's true identity and hopefully preventing anyone else from being harmed in the future. If a man was willing to kill to steal an identity, he would more than likely be willing to kill to protect it. Jake wondered how long it would be until Garrett realised that hard copies of the footage existed and began to search for himself and the disc. He had a feeling that he would not have a lot of time before the suited men returned and how many more might be with them. He felt confident he could overpower the two of them, but four, five or more? Jake was good but he was only human and there was truth to the statement 'safety in numbers'. But now at least he had an idea of their next move.

Jake left the security room and made his way down to his car; he was not sure whether the men were watching for him personally or if they were just keeping the hotel on lockdown in case anyone came snooping around. Either way, Jake decided that the best thing to do right now would be to drive around aimlessly, losing his pursuers in the process and then head for NationFirst. With the security footage, he could confront Garrett directly and prove to him that there was no way out of this mess and that other copies existed just waiting to be found by the police.

He had to admit, as much as he hated Garrett for what he did, his tactics were very effective; using David's identity and faking his own death was something so elaborate and complex that Jake would never have thought of doing himself and it gave Jake some tiny sliver of respect for the man's cunning. He got into his car, buckled the seatbelt, and then began driving around on the off chance they were following him on foot or in a car outside. When Jake checked the rear-view mirror once again, he noticed, as he had guessed, the two men were following him a few cars back. However, once again they were displaying a comical lack of understanding when it came to reconnaissance; their bright orange Ford Focus stood out like nothing else among the white and black SUV's and estate cars. Jake shook his head and really did laugh this time. It only took him four turns to lose his pursuers who were too afraid to jump an orange light at a giant crossroad.

It was starting to get late and once the sun began to fall, he knew any hope they might have had of finding him would be gone completely; by now they probably realised their mistake and were blaming each other for it. He tried to imagine Garrett's fury as he realised how close he came to tailing an SAS soldier before realising too late that he was just like most criminals; seriously underprepared.

As Jake drove around, a sudden ringtone from his pocket brought him back into focus. Without checking who it was, he answered the phone and placed it on speakerphone.

"Jake speaking." He said calmly.

"Well, hello Mr. Hanbury." Came a voice from the other end

of the line, its tone spitting sarcasm. He knew instantly who this must be.

"Garrett." Jake replied in a cool tone; there was no one else he knew of that would talk to him like some evil mastermind from a James Bond movie.

"I'm glad you kept your phone on you; I really wasn't sure if I would be able to get a hold of you. It was a close call earlier." Jake rolled his eyes at Garrett's self-satisfied tone and replied,

"Your boys were certainly entertaining."

"But that didn't scare you, did it?" Garrett continued, "I'm calling because there is a bigger picture here and this is just one step towards the final goal." Jake laughed for real this time,

"Oh yeah? And what might that be?" He knew most likely Garrett wouldn't tell him anyway, but it was worth a shot.

"I can do so much good with this money. Think of all the people I can help, the homeless, the children." It was crazy listening to this man; he was clearly delusional. He had killed a man, he had lied and cheated his way to get his hands on some money and now he was kidding himself that it was for a better cause. Or maybe he wasn't, maybe he was just trying to convince Jake not to turn him in. Either way, Jake thought, if he could keep Garrett talking maybe he could get some clues as to where he was; there was no way Garrett would be returning to the flat with Jake on his trail.

"That's all well and good but you don't really think they are going to let you go now do you? This is not the kind of guilt that can be hidden away. There will be nothing for it, but to turn yourself in, if I found evidence against you, you can bet the police will find you. They're far more well equipped with man-power and money than I am."

"You know as well as I do that after a few months they'll

stop looking." Garrett retorted, dropping his calm voice.

"And how do you plan on staying hidden for that long?" Jake asked him, not really believing he would actually tell him anything of value. But Jake had the upper hand, his hands were clean in this and he had the evidence.

"Oh, I wouldn't worry about that." Garrett said with a sinister tone.

"Why would you? So long as the money is ok?" Jake asked, perhaps he could get Garrett angry; angry people always talked.

"Yes... The money is important." He paused for a second and then continued, "But all of this is irrelevant; no matter what happens between us, the money will still change lives not just mine!"

"There are better ways to help people than killing someone and stealing their life." Jake told him seriously.

"Well I think it's a little late for that, isn't it?" Garrett replied with an amused tone, it was odd to hear how humorous he sounded about everything.

"For you." Jake replied simply.

"For both of us; if I go down you're coming with me. If I can hack into a security office you can bet I've figured out your bank details. You can expect a nice hefty payment in your account for taking out the hit on David just like I asked." Garrett laughed.

Jake sucked in a sharp breath; he couldn't believe what he was hearing. He had actually hoped that Garrett would take the bait and reveal something, anything that might give them a lead to his location but this? This wasn't what Jake had anticipated at all. He knew exactly what Garrett's words meant. He was tying himself to Jake.

"We both know I had nothing to do with his death." Jake said, shocked. Garrett laughed again,

"Yes, I do. But when the police look through David's accounts if I'm arrested you know they're going to investigate any payments that might be construed as suspicious." Jake could feel himself growing angry again, how could he lie, kill, blackmail and feel nothing? This man was sick.

"You've lost your mind!" Jake shouted angrily, his voice reverberating around the car.

"Perhaps." Garrett replied calmly, "But think about it, I have nothing to lose this way. But if you turn me in now, I can promise you will be found guilty, too." There was silence on the line for a moment and Jake caught the sound of birds in the background, maybe seagulls.

"Where are you? Let's settle this." Jake asked him.

"We've already settled this. You've got yourself £50,000 from me for doing nothing. Take it and walk away and neither of us will regret it." He warned firmly. Jake did not like to be threatened.

"You know that's not going to happen." He shot back.

"This conversation has gone on long enough and I'm bored. If one siren reaches these docks, you can bet you'll be locked up long before I will." Garrett replied, seething. Aha. Docks. He was at the docks. Jake hung up the phone before he could say anything more. He was pretty sure Garrett didn't realise what he had said but he didn't want to give him the chance of figuring it out in a shouting match on the phone. The docks certainly narrowed down his location but not by much. He could be at hundreds of docks all across the country but something told him, his gut instinct maybe, that he wouldn't be too far away. It would look suspicious for him to go too far in case he needed to show face and continue his puppet show.

Jake drove the car around the city for a minute longer and then headed straight for NationFirst bank. He pulled up in the car park about 20 minutes before they were due to close; as far as he was concerned, his plan hadn't changed. He looked at the building in front of him and knew that this was his last chance to get some concrete evidence that Garrett had at least committed fraud. If Garrett said one word about David's death with his own name tied to the same sentence… He didn't want to think about it. But he had to be sure; he'd know when he saw the footage. He just hoped that Garrett wouldn't realise what had happened until after Jake returned with it.

He pulled up into the space directly out the front and walked into the bank calmly.

"We're closing shortly." The lady at the doors told him bluntly pointing at a sign on the wall telling people to come back tomorrow morning.

"I don't need banking services." Jake retorted quickly and she paused for a moment.

"What do you need help with then?"

"I'd like the manager please." He asked calmly though he did not feel it. She looked at him blankly for a moment but radioed for the bank manager who came out looking a little upset at being summoned so close to closing time.

"Good afternoon." The manager told him, "What can I do for you?" Jake knew that the man would not be as easy to fool as the one at the flat block. He couldn't pretend to be working for a security company this time. So he went with brutal honesty; it was his only option.

"I'd like to see the security footage from last Monday, if possible." The manager blinked stupidly for a second and then turned to the lady beside him.

"I'll deal with this situation. Would you please clean down the countertops?" The lady gave the manager a dirty look before turning away to continue with her job.

"And I'd like a giant lobster to tuck in to right now, but I don't have one." The manager sneered at him somewhat unnecessarily.

"You possibly have a huge lawsuit coming your way for fraud and if I don't see that footage there's going to be nothing I can do to stop it. So it's up to you." Jake knew this was a big leap. Giving ultimatums was notoriously risky but he was fighting against the clock.

The manager seemed to think for a minute. He looked torn between two terrible choices: let some stranger access their security footage or risk being the fall-guy of a lawsuit. He seemed to think that one option was better than the other, however, and allowed Jake to view the footage. In truth, he would probably be fired either way. Jake once more marvelled at how easy people were to manipulate; warn them that they could lose their job and people bend over backwards to help. It was kind of pathetic, he thought, treasuring a job so much that they will do anything to protect it yet this would be the same job they would curse every morning.

Jake followed the man out the back to a security room. This one was far better equipped than the hotel, thankfully. There were multiple high-resolution monitors with cameras covering every square inch of the bank. Jake wondered where they all were; he hadn't seen half the cameras he was viewing as he walked in. He settled down in front of one monitor then turned to the manager, who seemed like it would take a lot more than that to interest him.

"Which day do you want?" The man asked. Jake thought for a moment. If he could recognise Garrett's outfit, if he got close enough to one of the cameras, he was sure he could pick him out.

"Last Monday." Jake replied quickly and watched as the manager began flicking through the days until he found it. "Monday afternoon at around 3pm?" Jake suggested. The manager showed Jake the footage and left him to it, standing off to the side as he handed over the controls.

Jake watched it carefully; all the transactions that had taken place on Monday afternoon. Suddenly he saw what must have been Garrett's face appear on screen.

"Is this it? Can I get a copy?" He asked urgently. The manager looked over at him and then back to his monitor where Garrett was standing in line waiting to speak with one of the tellers. "Can you make me a copy?" He asked again impatiently. The manager sighed and went off to put a DVD in the machine for him while he continued looking through the footage until he found the moment where Garrett had handed over an ID in the form of a passport. He couldn't make out the name, however so when the manager returned, Jake quizzed him some more on the cameras.

"Do you have a camera here?" He asked pointing to the window at which Garrett was currently standing paused at. The manager took control of the mouse and clicked around before bringing up the camera at the tellers' window facing outward toward the customer. Jake watched the footage again; there was Garrett handing over the passport and he watched intently as the teller typed in something on her keyboard. Her eyes were firmly fixed on what she was doing, however, so he couldn't make out any details on the passport she was holding.

He could only assume that she was typing in one of their banking passwords which would allow Garrett to transfer the money from David's account.

"Can you zoom in?" Jake asked urgently, "I need to see everything." The manager did so without complaint this time. It took a couple of minutes to get an optimal shot but eventually they managed to zoom right in on the passport as it was shown to the teller, a fraction of a second before the back of the teller's head obstructed the camera. The name clearly state *David Ellison*.

"I need a copy of this." Jake demanded. The manager looked hesitant.

"I can't just give this to you." He replied, gesturing to the DVD he was holding. Of course he couldn't. However, there was a note in his voice that seemed to hint he was suggesting at something.

"Ok, what do you want?" Jake asked him, pressing on the hint. The manager seemed to think for a minute.

"Well I can't give this to you," he repeated, "the only way you can ever get this is if you somehow forced me to give it to you." The man said, his voice high and slow like he were explaining something incredibly simple to a five year old. But then it clicked. The man's demeanour had been hinting at it since Jake arrived and it was now past closing time. He looked exhausted, he was grumpy, and he had little life left in his voice. He wanted a fool-proof way to keep his job and also bag himself some time off work. If Jake threatened him to hand over the footage, then the manager hadn't technically done anything wrong, he had just complied for his own safety which Jake knew that bank staff were told to do so in the event of a robbery. Then he could take a couple of weeks off whilst he recovered from the supposed robbery and come back feeling refreshed. Unfortunately, it was all too common to see in the modern world of working. People over-exhausted, over-extended and over-worked, oftentimes for under-pay. He also knew there was a similar way to do so in the forces. One of his subordinates had been complaining about wanting to go home after being deployed to Afghanistan. Then, coincidentally, a few days later he broke his ankle and had to be discharged. There was nothing Jake could have done to prevent it, it was simply part of the job and some people just weren't cut out for it.

"What about when you report me to your higher-ups? I'll become a target." Jake asked of the manager.

"I'll be sure to make my descriptions vague. After all, you were in the security room and deleted the tapes of you being here, so it's really just based on my description, Janice out there barely even notices her colleagues let alone the customers so she won't be a problem." He promised. Jake could almost see the light spark in his eyes with the excitement of a few weeks off. Well, if Jake was going to sell the fake robbery, he'd better act his part. After all, he desperately needed the CCTV footage on the disc in the manager's hands and it didn't appear that there was any other way he could negotiate the trade-off.

"Give me your badge." He demanded without much enthusiasm. The manager handed it over with no fight. He could see that the man was pleased with himself. He probably already had the days off planned to spend with his family or girlfriend, Jake couldn't care less.

"Now hand over that disc." He said in a mock-aggressive voice. Jake almost felt embarrassed performing the fake robbery.

"Of course, please don't hurt me!" The manager half-yelled in his own, albeit terrible, performance. Jake winced at the volume as the manager handed over the disc.

"I was never here; destroy the security footage." He demanded of the manager who complied without a problem. He ejected the disc from the drive and handed it, too to Jake.

"Thank you for your cooperation." Jake said before leaving. The manager burst into laughter as soon as he was out of the room. The euphoria of his plan was clearly far too much to handle.

Jake rushed out of the building with his prize in hand, Janice nowhere to be seen. He moved quickly to his car and drove off with haste; if the manager was going to report the robbery he would do it straight away or it would look even more suspicious and Jake did not want to be at the scene when the police officers arrived to take statements.

As Jake left the area, he mulled over the damaging security footage that he now had in his possession of Garrett clearly committing fraud. On its own it would look just like David managing his own finances, but coupled with the footage from the hotel it would almost certainly be grounds for investigation; Garrett was wearing the same clothes both when he arrived and left the flat and also when he made his appearance at the bank. This was looking more and more unfortunate for him, but there were still some unanswered questions. Why did Garrett kill David Ellison? And why use his identity to go on a spending spree? There were too many questions and only way to get them. He needed to speak to Garrett and he was almost certain that Garrett wouldn't call again.

As Jake drove back towards the city centre, moving slowly

through traffic. He reflected upon the events at the bank. It didn't seem likely that the manager would hand over the information to the police like he had hoped and kick-start the investigation into Garrett Langford. He considered how else he could talk to the police without mentioning that he, according to the fabricated story, stole the security footage because that would almost certainly make it look like doctored evidence considering Garrett had threatened, and probably delivered, what would appear to be a large suspicious payment. If the police were to start digging into the case the first question they would ask him was why he was so involved in the case at all considering he was only hired by David and had no real, personal connection with the man. It wouldn't take very long to connect Garrett with Jake and even if he made an anonymous donation of evidence to Detective Brannon, it wouldn't stop them investigating himself. Even in the event that he managed to get off clean, Jake's reputation would be forever tarnished and so any police involvement would have be a last resort.

He resolved that his best course of action was to keep the story about the stolen security footage to himself and not mention anything about how he had discovered Garrett's identity. The police might be able to use their own contacts to uncover this and if they were able to do it without any input from Jake, so much the better for him.

He decided that it was probably best to cover his tracks. The truth about his involvement in the case sounded sketchy at best and in any case, the truth was a subjective ideology. The truth was the thing that could be proved the best in court, not what had occurred.

The truth that could be proven would be that he received

a pay-off from a man called Garrett Langford to kill David Ellison and then attempt to cover it up when the case became too hot. They would struggle to prove motive but Jake wouldn't put it past Garrett to fabricate a whole story that involved him possibly arguing with David about the amount he was being paid or something to that effect. The police would eat it up because they wanted cases closed; it was better for their budget and public image to be seen finding a culprit and locking them away.

The real truth, however seemed far more complex. Garrett had, for unknown reasons, killed a man in cold blood and stolen his identity. It was likely that he was also motivated by money at least to some contributing degree; David was a wealthy man, and it would not make sense to risk so much for so little reward.

The more Jake thought about how his involvement looked, the angrier he got. Part of him wished he had never started digging in the first place. Perhaps, Jake thought as he trawled his way through the traffic, headlights glaring at him from the other side of the road, he might be able to get through to Garrett, convince him of his wrongdoing. But to do that, he would need to find him and he only had a small clue to go on: seagulls and a dock.

He turned off the main road and headed down towards a private, underground car park, one he was sure was safe and unknown to the people who might be following him. He pulled up outside the building. Most of the spaces were empty, which made Jake feel even more at ease. The clearer the space, the easier it would be to spot approaching people. There were a few expensive cars parked up in the spaces including his own black Mercedes Sprinter van. He pulled up next to it and waited for a minute before getting out of his car, unlocking the van, and climbing inside the back.

Inside was a fully furnished home for his on-the-go work. He had fitted it to be as comfortable as possible for extended periods of time, including a small kitchenette and lounge area. He pulled out the dining table, that he transformed into his desk while he worked on cases and switched on his laptop. Once it was fully booted up, Jake got straight down to looking at the security footage yet again starting first with NationFirst bank.

As he had noted, the picture quality was such that Jake barely had to squint to make out the miniscule writing on the passport that Garrett had handed over and once more, he could clearly make out David's name. He pulled out his notepad again and cross-referenced the information he had made with the footage and continued watching. He replayed the same clip a dozen times until he had it memorised. Twelve steps to the booth window, 19 seconds before the passport was handed over.

Once he was sure he had gleaned every detail from the video he closed it down and loaded up the grainy footage from the hotel. First, the flat from the early hours of Sunday morning, then came the moment where Garrett left, follow soon after by David. When nothing else of interest happened on Sunday, Jake pulled up the footage from Monday morning and watched David invite Garrett back in to the flat. True to his notes, Garrett departed within hours of his arrival as did David to the bar soon after. Garrett returned a couple of hours later, shortly followed by his would-be victim. Jake paused the video as David entered his flat for the last time. This was the last minute of his life that could be seen and he would have had no idea that Garrett had already bled his finances and was prepared to kill him.

Jake documented the timeline down. First was the two of them turning up to the flat drunk in the early hours of Sunday morning. Later that day, Garrett left to go somewhere Jake didn't know as did David sometime later. Flicking back through the pages Jake pieced together that it was after this departure that the two of them met at the expensive restaurant at lunch. Skipping ahead to Monday, he saw Garrett leaving and, once more referencing his notes, he knew that Garrett had met D the drug dealer. He wasn't quite sure what had been purchased but it definitely wasn't over-the-counter painkillers. Scrawling on the timeline, Jake jotted down the next notable event which meant that Garrett left the flat with David's passport in hand and made a large, fraudulent transaction at NationFirst. He had then returned to the flat where he crammed David's body into the suitcase around 1am and left to dump it over the motorway.

Jake leant back on the seat and stared at the timeline he had drawn. It seemed almost cruel to trivialise a death in something as impersonal and detached as a ballpoint pen. Yet this was the reality of how quickly the events had transpired that ended David's life. He tore the piece of paper out of his notebook, took a photo of it to keep as a digital copy, then stored the original in a small box in which he had kept all the information he had gathered about David and his parents, previous criminal history on both men, the DNA testing reports from Dr Pritchett and all of the other bits he had managed to gather about the case. To this box, he also added the bank receipt that he had taken from David's flat.

Jake replaced the box in the drawer and closed the laptop

in front of him, rubbing his eyes wearily. It had been an exhausting day and he could feel the tiredness begin to wash over him where he sat, gnawing at his eyelids. He all but stumbled to the makeshift bed and within moments, he was asleep. Having always been a light sleeper thanks to his time in the military, he awoke countless times throughout the night to many completely ordinary sounds. The noise of a car starting caused him to sit bolt upright in his bed and stare at the mini cameras he had set up on his van that pointed outwards showing him his surroundings. In his line of work, Jake had made many enemies. He had ousted countless cheating spouses, lying businesspeople and umpteen thugs and criminals. He wouldn't put it past at least 60% of them to want revenge. Which was why he lived out the back of a van the majority of his time, keeping on the move every week.

He hadn't always dreamt of investigating for a living. After the military he swore to himself he would settle down, maybe even emigrate to somewhere that didn't rain five out of the seven days of the week. But when he started the odd job for the money, he found that it took up most of his days. He was devoted to it, it gave him drive and passion. The unsociable hours and prolonged trips away meant he struggled to maintain or even find a relationship, however. Even if he did manage it, he'd never be able to fully explain that his life was spent investigating fraud and theft and on this occasion murder. The part-time gig had grown into a full-time job and he actually cherished it, loved it even. He took as much pride in breaking open a case as detectives did, more so than some.

There were times where Jake thought about quitting the business entirely, but the problem remained that if by some miracle he ever decided to retire from being an investigator then what would happen? He would have nothing save for the clothes on his back. Not only that but the idea of retirement was something completely alien to him – at 39 years of age there were several decades ahead of him before he would even contemplate retiring.

Jake closed his eyes again and tried to focus on the positives of his life rather than dwelling on the negatives that often kept him awake. With a deep breath he pulled out his phone, dialled one of three numbers that were saved in his speed dial and waited for it to connect. The line barely rang twice.

"Hello?" Came the voice from the other end, tinged with sleep.

"Vincent? It's me, Jake."

There was no need to explain who 'me' was. He knew Vincent would understand but even so, they went through this every time he rang him at this hour of night. An ex-soldier like he, Vincent understood what Jake was going through more than anyone else in his life. Vincent had fought alongside him in Afghanistan some time ago and the two had been friends ever since. Vincent spoke with a thick Yorkshire accent. He was one of the few people Jake could trust in this world and he knew that when he visited his friend in the North, they would talk for hours on end about anything and everything in their lives.

"Tell me you're coming over." Vincent said wearily down the phone.

"I will," Jake confirmed, "soon." Vincent had always said that no matter what time it was, he should call if ever Jake needed anything, even just to offload his emotional baggage. That was the bond they had, a bond forged through gunfire and bombs, surrounded by enemies and with the understanding that at any day one of them might never make it back to base. It was hard times like those that exposed the true nature of a person. If you went into the army with an ego or a chip on your shoulder, you could be sure that nothing breaks a person down to their essence like the overarching knowledge that you might never make it home to your family. And these people you fought alongside had your back and would at any moment, jump onto a land mine to save their comrades; loyalty like that would never fade.

And so Jake talked. He talked about his life and his fears, he opened himself up in the rawest possible way, a way he wouldn't even feel comfortable telling a therapist. But an hour later an exhausted Jake thanked Vincent for taking his call.

"Don't you ever thank me. Say the word and I'll be glad to make up the spare bedroom. Call me whenever, ok?" Vincent told him sternly.

"Yeah, thanks. I'll see you." Jake replied and hung up. Laying back down on the bed, he closed his eyes again.

A powerful wind was howling through the air vents in the dark car park, rustling the bin bags and roaring wildly. There was something about the noise that appealed to Jake somehow, it was pleasant in a way and lulled him to sleep.

Chapter 13

On slow, bobbing water, Garrett Langford sat aboard the yacht that he had claimed from David along with his identity. The cursive writing along the side read *Serenity*. It was ironic. Garrett was feeling many emotions that night just before 1am, but serene was not among them. The feeling that overwhelmed him the most was fear. Fear that his threat to Jake Hanbury would not intimidate the man.

From what he had learned through hacking the man's phone whilst the bodyguards kept him talking, Jake was special forces and had been into some of the most hostile environments in the world. Garrett had some doubt that a somewhat hollow threat to tie him to a murder that he had nothing to do with would actually pan out the way he had hoped. But what choice did he have? When he spoke to the man, Jake had voiced a question that had been buzzing around Garrett's mind since he had killed David Ellison. What was it all for? Though he invented the reason on the spot, the idea that he could do some good with David's money was something he couldn't deny.

Garrett had absentmindedly pulled out his phone and part of him wondered why he had tuned in to watch a newscast that was just about to start. He couldn't remember even turning it on. As soon as he pointed his gaze toward the screen, he became somewhat aware that he was staring at his own picture that glared at him from a news channel. It was strange because up until this point, Garrett hadn't even considered what would happen if he actually were caught, only the overwhelming desire to not be caught. If they did catch him, all of his ill-gotten money could never provide enough evidence to clear his name nor garner sympathy from anyone after hearing the gory details about how he killed someone in cold blood for nothing more than cash. Whilst this was technically true in fact, he knew no one would listen to a word he said as he attempted to justify his actions.

The news anchor introduced a woman in a smart red dress who was giving a brief statement about who Garrett was before mentioning that the police still had no leads on the case but were appealing to the public for anyone who might have seen or heard anything that could be useful in solving who did this. Well, at least there was the smallest glimmer of good news; the police were still at a dead end. The news anchor returned to the screen and the topic changed to some burglary at a bank but Garrett paid it no attention and put his phone back in his pocket.

He had to do something. Something. But what? He stared out at the water through a tiny window below deck and wondered if he was dreaming and would wake up to find himself in his parents' house once more, late for work at his dead-end job with his awful boss. If this were any dream, he thought dully, it was definitely a nightmare. He cast his eyes over the dark waves that splashed calmly against the yacht, shimmering in the reflection of the lights that illuminated the dock. Part of him yearned to dive in and succumb to the darkness surrounding him at all sides but the need for survival, the primal driver that made him swerve into the path of chaos, ultimately enriching yet destroying his life, held him back.

The possibility of someone finding him on *Serenity* seemed so unlikely that Garrett felt safe there without the need for bodyguards. Inside, he wanted nothing more than to be free of all the lies but that would lead to him being severely punished for his crimes and that left running as the only choice left. As he sat in contemplation of his purpose in this new life he had stolen, thoughts came and went about how others would see him if they were to walk in on this moment.

His parents' faces swam to the forefront of his mind. He closed his eyes and prayed that he would find the strength to let them know what happened. Still, even if he could find the courage, there was no guarantee that they wouldn't warn the police just to watch him suffer after all the pain he'd caused them. What about his sisters? Would they forgive him? He would like to hope that they would but all he could think of was how disgusted they would be and how they would barely recognise the man he had become.

However, the fleeting thought of being caught and thrown in jail for what he had done was definitely better than the reality of it. His fate locked away in his mind was easier to forget than living a life in prison no matter how much he wished to be free of the guilt that was weighing him down like he was carrying an ever-growing kettlebell.

He stood up abruptly on the spot and paced nervously; this is where he would wait until daylight to leave the marina, he had decided that it was time to leave the country. If Jake was looking for him it would be a lot harder to do so in somewhere like France. He had specifically not booked a ticket so that he couldn't be traced and ambushed at the airport. He continually checked online to see that there were still seats available to buy and when it was time, he would take a taxi to Heathrow airport with just enough time to make the flight and purchase a ticket at the gate. If Jake were tracking him, he wouldn't have enough time to plan an ambush. If it were the police, which he felt pretty sure it wasn't, they would have already arrested him by now; they would be able to triangulate his position in minutes.

So Garrett waited and attempted to fall asleep. But it was hard to focus on such trivial things as sleep when a looming threat was overhanging like a blanket waiting to smother and suffocate him. He felt like he was in a race against time and the only choice he had left was to stay ahead of it or be crushed when it bulldozed its way through his life.

He nervously checked his phone again, partly hoping for another message from Jake with more evidence so that he had no choice but to focus absolutely on one decision to combat it, but none came. This left him feeling astray, unsure of what was the right thing to do in this situation, but of course there wasn't a Murderers Anonymous club he could pop into on a Tuesday night and ask the group for advice on how to deal with the very real threat of being exposed. He considered silently whether Jake's threat was real and if there was any chance of them working together to cover it all up, maybe involving a huge payoff. But that all came down to who could Garrett trust. What stopped Jake taking the payoff and handing him in as soon as he could call the police? Garrett continued to invent wild realities in his mind until just after 2am on Monday morning, having camped out on the vessel since he realised that Jake knew where he lived.

It was just past the hour when something broke him from

his reverie. Was it his imagination? Maybe it was the water sloshing against his yacht. But there was a noise from above. It sounded like light footsteps. There were many possible reasons for a noise to be audible from below deck, but in Garrett's mind, as unhinged and paranoid as it was in that moment, there could only be one.

Garrett leapt up from his seat and sprinted to the edge of the steps, listening intently for anything else. The steps he took were slow and deliberate and he moved as quiet as he could manage. He took hold of a large knife which he had left on a nearby counter top for self-defence. As silently as possible, he crept up the stairs with his back pressed against the side wall from where he kept watch over the lounge area. As soon as his head was above deck level, he could see that it was indeed Jake standing at the edge of the dock looking into his yacht.

"Hey Garret," Jake said without batting an eye, "I think we need to talk."

Garrett was caught off guard by how calm Jake sounded. It gave him pause to think whether this was yet another ruse or if perhaps he had come to visit in order to help Garrett. They both knew what had happened, but perhaps Jake could provide an explanation that would make it all okay. This thought didn't last long enough for Garrett to act upon it before he tucked the knife safely into his waistband behind his back, hoping Jake hadn't noticed; at least he'd have surprise on his side. Jake looked unperturbed by Garrett's presence whilst Garrett himself attempted to remain composed though his heart was pounding inside his chest.

"I think you owe me an explanation." Jake said softly. Garrett hesitated a while before he spoke.

"How did you even find me?" Garrett asked of the man in

front of him.

"You're not the only one who has friends that can track a mobile phone. Permission to come aboard, captain?" Jake said with an air of amusement.

"Hop in." Garrett said flatly feeling as though he probably would have come aboard no matter what he said. Jake looked slightly put out but barely waited a beat before clambering onto the boat. They both turned to look down toward the dock for a moment as Garrett spoke in the same flat tone.

"Are the police with you?" He asked, deflated.

"No. I wanted to clear everything up. You made it pretty clear that I would be on the same hook as you for something I didn't do if I went to them. I'm hoping we can talk." Garrett led Jake into the cabin of the ship. Having played many simulators and had flicked through a video or two online, he thought he could figure out how to drive the yacht. It really wasn't too hard to get the hang of it and so Garrett accelerated out of the dock. The engine revved and the water churned behind the yacht propelling it forward into the darkness. It was quiet and neither person spoke as Garrett angled the ship north and out towards the sea.

The farther out he drove, the choppier the water became and the wind picked up slightly, hitting the sides of the yacht, causing it to bob up and down. Jake, who hadn't spoken since they left had been holding on to the rails in the cockpit. His legs were steady and he barely moved as the yacht crashed over the waves. Garrett was once again left feeling overwhelmed by the presence of this man. Though he was nearly 40, the man was well-built like an oil-rig worker and legs as still as those of a practiced seaman. Garrett could see the veins bulging in Jake's forearms as he gripped the railing. The two were about the same height, but the way Jake seemed to tower over him was intimidating and made Garrett feel tiny.

Garrett drove for another half an hour until the land was no longer visible through the darkness or by the bright lights that shone from the yacht like a mobile lighthouse. He turned the wheel up toward the sky which caused the boat to rock, tipping away from him. He didn't know what he expected would happen next but it certainly wasn't for Jake to launch himself toward to the wheel and take control before Garrett rolled the vessel. It seemed there wasn't anything this man could not do. Garrett didn't protest and allowed him to steer the boat until he cut out the engine and turned to face him with a grim expression on his face.

"What do you want?" He finally spoke. Garrett wasn't sure what the real answer to that question was. He certainly didn't know what he wanted from Jake. He'd been following him around with bodyguards and tracking his phone calls behind his back for a day now but this was the first time they had met without any disguise or cover. It wouldn't have been a lie to say that Garrett desired him out of the picture, but he couldn't bare to be the driving force behind the loss of another life, not a life that had served his country even if this man did want to see him locked up and he knew, deep down, he would never use the knife that he had hidden away.

"I don't know... I want this to be over. I think you do too." Garrett said, breathing deeply and then releasing. The splashing waves around them was all that could be heard as they remained motionless and silent for what felt like ages before Jake finally opened his mouth, breaking the silence that had settled in.

"I have copies of all the evidence against you. I can put you down." He said plainly and with no air of a bluff. Garrett began to feel out manoeuvred by someone who had barely spoken three words to him since he arrived on the yacht.

"I'll play along if it means getting you off my back." Garrett rolled his eyes toward Jake's direction after saying this in somewhat sarcastic tones. Jake's mouth twitched slightly with the hint of a smirk.

"I think we can come to an arrangement." Jake told him. Garrett wasn't sure how much he was bluffing through his unreadable poker-face but called it regardless.

"How much?" He said, waiting for an extortionate number which Garrett would never agree to but would ultimately have no choice but to acquiesce.

"I don't want your... David's money." He replied viscously, spitting through his clenched teeth. The yacht gave a slight lurch on the water causing Garrett to stumble. Jake hadn't moved.

"What do you want then?" Garrett spat back at him though Jake didn't look nearly as intimidated as Garrett had when he had been snapped at.

"I don't want to be tied to you. I want a video confession stating that you set me up." Garrett was taken aback.

"Absolutely not. You know what would happen if that got released, I'd be in prison before you got home."

"You deserve to be. But no, I want it as insurance. I won't hand you in and I'll keep the video in case you change your mind to have it pinned on me."

"And what's to stop you handing me in after I give you it?" Garrett replied.

"My word." Jake said simply. Garrett almost scoffed audibly.

"Your word means nothing to me." He shot at Jake.

"That's not my problem. That's the only way this ends. If you don't agree to my terms, I'll hand you in." Jake threatened seriously. Garrett paced the cockpit and opened a cupboard door. From inside he withdrew two glass tumblers and a crystal bottle filled with amber liquid. Garrett slowly poured some into each glass, being careful to pour slowly with the bobbing of the yacht. Jake said nothing and merely watched the unsteady man before him. Garrett offered him one of the glasses.

"Whiskey?" Garrett asked. Jake took it from him and they both sipped at the drink as though they had all the time in the world. They could have been best friends out on the sea.

"Now you know full well that if you do hand me in, you'll be on the line, too." Garrett told him in a small voice, latching back on to the conversation he had abruptly ended. Garrett had attempted to sound impressive but his voice was faltering with the impending doom. He knew that Jake was right. If he didn't do as he said then it would be him locked away in prison with only the comfort of knowing Jake might be investigated to keep him warm in the cell.

"I don't care. First rule of politics; never negotiate with a gun to your head. Your whole plan rests on the police finding me guilty. What you don't realise is that I have more than CCTV footage of you. If I give the police what I have you'll be sent down, no question." Garrett's heart skipped a beat. But then he considered something. If that were absolutely true, then he would never have gotten on the boat to negotiate. This was exactly the question he posed to Jake.

"Why did you come out here then if you're so sure?" Jake thought a moment on this, taking another swig from his glass and draining it in one. He held out his glass for a top up and

Garrett obliged.

"Because I wanted to make you an offer that keeps us both happy. I don't want to be implicated no more than you do. I know how you feel, Garrett. I've been there, I've taken a man's life and I can tell you it doesn't get easier; you just get better at hiding it." For some reason these words seem to cut through Garrett like nothing else had before.

"I didn't mean to do it." Garrett admitted sheepishly. "I knew that David had money and yes I wanted some. But that's all it was meant to be. It was never supposed to go that far." Before he knew it and before he could do anything to prevent it from happening, Garrett sobbed. He sobbed harder than he ever had before and he felt that, to a certain extent, Jake did not judge him for it.

"I know. You were a desperate man and you made a mistake. But mistakes have consequences Garrett. If you don't do as I say there's going to be one hell of a consequence coming your way."

Garrett sat down in the chair opposite to Jake in front of the controls. He rested his head on his hands and cradled his face to think. In this moment he knew it wasn't just himself who was going to get screwed if he didn't agree but also Jake, an innocent man just doing his duty.

"I need some air." Garrett heaved and stumbled out onto the deck of the boat gasping in lungfuls of salty air, the rocking of the boat doing nothing to help him. The wind was cold and bit at his cheeks and exposed skin. He could feel it blustering through his hair and whistling in his ears making them tingle. With each breath he tried to determine what his next move should be.

He knew that he couldn't go to prison. Not now, not ever. If

David's family ever reconnected and saw him they would tear him apart limb by limb and leave nothing but a red puddle on the floor where Garrett used to be.

"You're looking awful over there." Jake shouted over the wind as he joined him on the wet decking of the yacht which glistened under the lights mounted around it like stars.

"I've been better." Garrett called back in a feeble voice. Jake was standing next to him hardly swaying whilst Garrett was pulled back and forth on the turbulent water that rocked the yacht heavily.

"David's parents abandoned him, you know?" He told Jake in a sombre voice. "What if they decide to reconcile?"

"David's parents have been missing for over a year." Jake corrected him. Garrett's mouth fell open and he tasted the salt on his tongue as the overspray from the sea kissed his face.

"He never told me that." Garrett said through his teeth. Jake was looking at him with confusion but Garrett's mind was spinning too fast for him to decipher what he meant. He didn't know whether to feel anger or pity because if David hadn't told him about the parents, then perhaps he'd lied about other things as well...

"What happened?" Garrett asked cautiously.

"They went hiking one day and at some point, they went missing and never returned. Nobody found out what became of them... Except me. I was going to tell David that day I met you in the park. They're dead. They slipped off the edge of the cliff whilst they were at the back on the hiking group and nobody noticed." Jake leant over the edge of the yacht staring into the foamy water below. He exhaled a long sigh.

"I've had enough of this job. I can't be the bearer of bad news anymore. In some perverse way I'm kind of grateful that he's dead. Now I don't have to give him the gut-wrenching truth that his folks died. It's not nice being the only one to break the news. I never know what to do or what to say because there's nothing I *can* do or say that would ever heal that kind of wound." Jake barked a bitter laugh that was devoid of any humour, "And then I get to ask for payment." He shook his head splattering water droplets around him from his hair that was now soaked.

"If I could take back what I did I would," Garrett told him remorsefully, "but that's not going to fix the pain I've caused." Garrett's voice was strained as he tried to speak over the noise of the sea. The fresh air helped him feel a little better but the constant bobbing was starting to make him feel queasy again.

"Do you mind if I go back down?" He said to Jake.

"Sure, sure." Jake mumbled without looking at him and his attention was already back on the waves.

"I thought there was more you were going to tell me." Garrett tried to say but he stumbled backwards and lost his footing. He slipped on the wet decking and the boat lurched at the same time and he smashed into Jake, swiping out his legs from underneath him. The knife in his waistband slipped free and clattered over the edge of the boat and out of sight.

Jake tumbled over the edge of the boat and plummeted down into the black water below. The sloshing and churning of the water swept Jake beneath the surface and when Garrett had managed to regain his footing he could not see any hint of the man.

"Jake!" He screamed to the black water. "Dammit." He cursed under his breath as he moved cautiously towards the edge of the boat. Once he reached the spot where Jake vanished, he peered over into the water expecting to see him struggling but there was nothing.

"Hey, Jake. Are you ok?" Still nothing, not even a ripple in sight or a flailing limb. Garrett waited for another few seconds before turning to make sure nobody else had seen him fall overboard. Of course in the pitch black there was no one around and they were completely alone. An intruding thought crossed Garrett's mind. If Jake was gone there was no threat. He'd admitted it himself, there was no police waiting for him.

Garrett's heart raced sending adrenaline coursing through him. With the water so turbulent there was surely no way he could survive for long and he couldn't see Jake resurfacing. Then a voice inside him told him to drive away and leave the man to succumb to a cold, watery end. It was a dark, intrusive thought. The voice that he hadn't heard since considering what to with David's body a week ago when he had found him dead.

A week. That's all it had been. Garrett could hardly believe that eight days ago he was working his terrible job, watching movies on the sofa with his parents. If someone had told him then that this would be his future a week later he would never have believed it. He would have told the crazy person that there was no way he could do those sorts of things; he simply didn't have it in him. But here he was. He did do it and what's more there was a part of him that knew, deep down he would do it again if he had to. The voice told him to drive away once more, to pretend like all this never happened and to get on with his life as he had planned to before Jake had barged his way into his life.

Garrett walked slowly towards the helm of the boat in a daze as though sleepwalking through a haze of self-denial. In the back of his mind he knew if nothing had been done about Jake then there would always be someone chasing after him which meant, for now, he was safe from being captured.

It wasn't until he got closer to the wheel did he see a glimpse of something in the water. Garrett spun around so fast it made him dizzy. It was Jake in the water, not 10 feet away, struggling against the current that was pulling him under once more. If Garrett left and through some miracle Jake survived, he would have no more second thoughts about handing him in and there would certainly be no chance at negotiation. So he did what he knew he must and tugged a life ring from the edge of the boat and threw it with all his might at Jake.

Through scrabbling fingertips Jake caught the life ring and hauled it over himself with extreme effort. Pulling with all his strength, Garrett tugged at the rope. It burned his hands and his fingers screamed in protest but he didn't stop, he couldn't leave a man in the water who knew his secret. He pulled some more and eventually, Jake was near enough to pull onto the deck.

Garrett grabbed the man by the back of his jacket and hauled him onto the deck. He was sopping wet and coughing hard. It was clear he had almost no energy left and was fighting for every breath. He couldn't talk and could barely move. He needed help and fast.

Without thinking or without even trying to fight it, Garrett's hands reached out and his fingers closed around Jake's throat. Slowly they tightened until he heard Jake gurgling as he tried to speak, his fingers feebly scratching at Garrett's hands.

There was no thought process behind it, it wasn't grounded in anger or hatred. There was only the primal, instinctual need to survive, to be the one that prevailed in this fight. Jake wanted to bring him down he knew that, but he was given an opportunity right now to be free of that fear that had driven him mad for days. He knew the police would never figure it out on their own; if they were calling for public witnesses they were already prepared to close the investigation.

All these thoughts crossed his mind as Garrett closed his eyes, tears running down his face, pretending it was not him who was doing it. He could hear a man screaming but he didn't know where it was coming from until he opened his eyes and realised the screaming was coming from himself; the man before him had stopped moving.

Garrett dropped Jake's body to the deck, his hands shaking uncontrollably. The voice inside was screaming at him now in a familiar tone he couldn't control but was forced to obey. It was telling him he had no other option. But now he was faced with a different choice. What to do with Jake.

Sprinting below deck without even stopping to think about it, he found rope and kettle bells in the on-board gym and lugged them up the deck, huffing and sweating as he did so though his clothes were already sodden. Part of him was hoping that Jake would be standing up, maybe coughing but alive and well. But as he knew was the case, he wasn't. He was lying in the same position that Garrett had left him in. He tried not to think about what he was about to do and let the voice in his head guide him. Garrett looked around frantically once more for any sign of movement. It felt like any moment a chopper would beam a search light at him and all would be exposed. But here in the darkness, surrounded by nothing but black water and sea spray, nobody came. No lifeboat or police chopper interrupted him.

Garrett untangled the rope, picking at the knots and kinks

then began to link it around the man's wrist, neck and ankles. He then looped several kettlebells to it with the rope and knotted it tightly. He gave it a strong tug and checked the knots once more. They were secure. Garrett quickly fumbled in the man's pocket and withdrew his phone. He opened the email app and typed in his own email address in the recipient line and then copied in David's, too. In the body of the email he wrote:

Garrett, I have to tell you the truth. I killed you. I know I don't seem like the type but the guilt has gotten to me too much that I have to confess my sins. I know I never seemed like the religious type but God can find you in the darkest of places and I hope he has found you, too. I hope you can forgive me for the heinous way I made your death look like a suicide in that degrading way. It was wrong and all I can do is hope that one day you will forgive me.

Jake

It was poorly written, Garrett knew that but in that moment it was the best he could do. He just had to hope that it would do the trick. In the event of Garrett's capture, he would be put on trial for murder, but he would attempt to maintain David's identity as long as possible, even pinning the murder on Jake. He had to be cunning about it in order for it to work and the plan seemed to fall into line in his head as Garrett thought quickly.

If he could use this fabricated evidence to prove that the body did belong to Garrett and that it wasn't a suicide but murder at Jake's hands, he may not ever need to admit to stealing David's identity at all. He could go about his life keeping up the façade.

All he needed to survive the trial was reasonable doubt. Reasonable doubt that he might not have done what the prosecutors would tell the jury that he had and he was sure his lawyers would be grateful for this piece of evidence, something to latch on to. He knew from his own court hearing, hearsay testimony was not usually admissible unless in extenuating circumstances such as not being able to find the person who made it. Garrett knew for sure that they would never be able to find Jake. He would be sat on the bottom of the sea for a long time.

With the overspray lashing at his face, Garrett slipped and stumbled on the deck as he dragged the weighted body to the railings at the edge of the boat. He stood there panting for a moment, gazing out as far the lights would allow him. Listening to the waves as they crashed and curled was deafening. He could hardly imagine what the life of a seaman must be like, to work in worse waters than those he currently stared at.

Garrett bent over Jake's body and hoisted him with all his strength over the railings until he was balanced around his midriff, kettlebells hanging over both sides keeping him in limbo. Garrett froze as the flashbacks hit him like one of the waves. He was on the bridge again with the car headlights flashing through the trees. He could feel the adrenaline pumping again but he didn't let it take control.

He steadied his breath and attempted to calm his mind. This was ok. It was going to be fine because the voice in his head was telling him so. It *guaranteed* it. So Garrett did the only thing that made logical sense. With heavy feelings of déjà vu, Garrett placed both hands underneath the man's legs and hoisted them upwards, tipping Jake and the kettlebells into the water. Though it should have made a loud noise as Jake was dragged into the ocean, it was silent amongst the crashing waves. Jake's body sank within seconds. Garrett expected to see a lingering moment that happened almost as if in slow motion like a movie. But there was no slow motion or sad music as Jake sank. There was a brief reflection of the light on Jake's wet face and then he gone, a prisoner to the ocean.

Garrett leant over the railing panting hard. His heart beat pounded loudly in his ears and hammered through his body. He couldn't believe he'd done it. Part of him felt terrified but most of him felt relieved and he was sickened by it. But just like David, it had been an accident, he hadn't intended to kill Jake. Until he did. He knew that ultimately, he had killed Jake but did he not just help him on the way to his inevitable destination? Garrett wanted to believe that with every ounce of his being. He was not a killer. Of course, the police would say otherwise but thanks to Jake's unfortunate end, Garrett didn't have to worry about that anymore. He was safe. He was free, there would be nobody to say otherwise.

He knew that what he had done was wrong but, in the end, he ultimately couldn't afford to have someone know too much and be walking free; it would drive him crazy wondering if they were going to turn on him. What if the person was hit by a car and had a sudden urge to divulge all of their worldly secrets on their deathbed? That just wouldn't do.

"Ok. Ok." Garrett said to himself in an effort to bring down his blood pressure that was thumping through every vein. He wiped the sweat and sea water out of his eyes and off his brows. It was done, there was no point thinking about it any longer.

Fighting hard to remain upright on the swaying boat, he plodded into the cockpit once more. The warmth hit him like he had just walked up to a fire pit. It made him shiver. He removed the red jacket that he had been wearing and hung it on one of the coat hooks by the door where it dripped a small puddle onto the floor.

He picked up the glass of whiskey that he had barely touched from the sideboard and downed the contents. He then refilled it once more and did the same. Garrett shook his head to clear his mind, splattering the cabin in tiny droplets of water. He faced the command console and turned the key. The yacht barely made a noise as it started and Garrett kept his eyes focused on the GPS which pointed him south, back towards the dock. He didn't even turn around when he pushed the accelerator forward. Garrett knew he was leaving behind a person but what it really felt like he was leaving behind was an anchor, a liability that would only pull him under into the crushing depths with him.

The boat started to build up speed. The wind howled around the windows of the cockpit and the salty beads of water dripped down his face, but he remained firmly planted in the cockpit. He had sobered up from his adrenaline and felt more alive than ever before. He didn't have to worry about Jake anymore. All that mattered was getting back onto dry land unscathed where he could be rid of the fear that was plaguing him.

The boat flew over the surface of the sea in a hurry. It wasn't long before he approached the coastline. He knew there was already some slim chance someone could have heard or seen him, it would be the only thing they could report to the police, but in the darkness, he doubted they would have seen enough to warrant a phone call. The only loose end he could consider were the two bodyguards he had hired. However he had been thoughtful in his approach to hiring them. He told them only his name, David Ellison and that they were to intimidate and follow a man called Jake Hanbury.

Based on his minor interaction with them, he doubted very much that they were clever enough to put the whole thing together. Garrett already didn't miss the fear he felt when he realised how close Jake came to ruining everything just because he couldn't mind his own business. He breathed a sigh of relief as he docked the yacht and tied it up. It felt like such a weight had been lifted off of his shoulders almost like he had been reborn and had just woken up. He was back in the real world and he didn't have to worry about prison or that man any longer. Now all that mattered was making sure no one linked him to what he had done so he could continue living with himself, even if nobody else knew.

Garrett thought about his steps to ensure every loose end was covered. He felt fairly certain that David was taken care of, although he admitted it went awry for a while. But Jake was more spontaneous. He was caught off guard and surprises caused mistakes. Mistakes sent people to prison.

He was sure that Jake had not sold him out, he had made that fairly clear. From his investigative work and everything he could dig up on Jake, he had no immediate family that would notice him missing for a long time and by the time they did there would be nothing left of him to find except a skeleton which even Garrett didn't know the exact location of. Lastly, he had covered himself in the incredibly unlikely event of his capture for David's murder. An email from Jake asking for forgiveness for killing him, providing Garrett with enough reasonable doubt to hopefully give him a not guilty verdict in a jury trial. He felt reasonably pleased, all things considered. And now he felt confident he could portray David with conviction without the overhanging doubt and fear crippling his every waking moment. He breathed deeply and let it out in a big sigh feeling cool, clean air filled his lungs. He was free at last.

Chapter 14

Relief and a sense of calm washed through Garrett as he walked to his car. He moved slowly and deliberately savouring every step, casting his eyes around the docks as he did so. There were boats of all sizes moving gently on the surface of the water. The biggest of which was a 60-foot-long yacht which looked like it must have cost upward of ten million. Garrett wondered idly what the owner did to afford such an impressive piece of machinery. He walked past a shop that was currently closed as it was gone 3am. It was a fishing and tackle shop. There were a few buckets outside that contained dead bait which clearly the owner thought was not worth bringing inside. Garrett doubted someone that owned a 60-foot yacht would be that interested in stealing a tub of bait.

Garrett continued to amble down the marina enjoying the salty, fresh air as he inhaled though the cold still nipped at his cheeks. It was a nice kind of cold, it grounded him and it wasn't nearly as bad on the land as it was on the yacht. He approached the BMW which was parked out of sight on a nearby road and unlocked it, not paying a thought to the suitcase that he hadn't moved from the boot. He climbed in and started the car, watching the headlamps spew its light over the ground in front as they flicked on automatically. The headlights illuminated the ground and Garrett simply sat for a moment, perfectly still. He hadn't felt still in what could've been years though the reality was far shorter than that.

It was an odd thing that he did next as he reached for the knobs and dials around the touch screen. He turned on the radio, something he hadn't done in a long time. It wasn't anything particularly upbeat or heavy, it was a slow, soft ballad. The sound filled the car and as Garrett pulled off the side of the road, he found he was humming along contentedly, drumming his fingers gently on the wheel. The was barely a car that passed him on the way back into the city and there was no rain or wind as he drove. The calmness of the usually busy tarmac was peaceful and soothing. Through everything that had transpired that night, an amazing sense of inner peace filled him and the knot in his stomach was all but untied. Thinking about how he had felt on that wretched boat, which he intended to leave exactly where it was for a long time, he was surprised that he could have felt so serene. The irony of this thought made him smile his first, genuine smile since taking on David's identity.

As he neared the city the buildings on either side of him grew bigger and bigger and soon there was no grass to be seen or water that sloshed and ran down the ditches. There were traffic lights and roundabouts with posters and signs. There were shops and billboards that shone neon-bright, slicing through the darkness and stabbing his eyes with its glaring light. Though intimidating for non-city dwellers, townies like Garrett found the overbearing sights somewhat comforting. The roads became wider with more lanes and footbridges appeared above him. The city that was, at this moment, so calm seemed so busy and alive with all-hours gambling and drinking adverts, yet there was almost nobody on the roads. The intimidating skyscrapers were visible towering over the other buildings on the horizon that were lit up in the darkness thanks to the city glow. Each and every way he looked was plastered with buildings and shops.

Garrett turned off onto a slow road that was lined with residential houses, Victorian-era style. There were speed bumps in the road that made the car wobble and Garret, who was still humming along to the music that leaked out of the speakers paid them no attention. He continued to drive down the road and turned left at the junction, the sound of his indicator cutting through the music like a metronome at quarter speed.

Pulling into a 30-speed road, the streetlights flashed over his eyes one by one like someone turning a light on and then off again repeatedly as he passed underneath them. The light cut onto the passenger seat as Garrett continued to hum quietly along to the music.

Blue lights flashed rapidly in his rear-view mirror and Garrett stopped humming. As they got brighter and brighter, Garrett felt his hands grip the wheel tighter but did not change his driving speed. As it drew nearer, he could make out that it was an ambulance and it pulled out into the lane next to him and overtook him, speeding along down the road. Garrett's grip loosened on the steering wheel, and he turned the volume of the music up a few notches feeling himself melt back into the rhythm.

It was 4:30am and the flat block reared into sight. Garrett steered the car towards the underground parking and was greeted by an elderly man in a black, formal suit and fedora, the same one that usually worked the night shift.

"Good morning, sir." The old man greeted him with a smile.

"And to yourself!" Garrett told him warmly and for the first time he really did feel like it was a good morning. The old man tipped his hat and waved him through, giving access to the parking spots. Garrett located his own and reversed the car in. He put his hand up once more to the parking official as he walked into the building. He greeted the man at the reception with a cheery greeting and asked how his weekend had been.

"Jolly lovely, thank you, sir. I hope yours was good, also?" The man was clearly adopting an over-the-top demeanour like a British stereotype in an American TV show for some reason, but Garrett appreciated the sentiment all the same. Garrett told him he had had a good weekend, too and then made his way toward the lift.

The doors pinged open and he stepped in, pressing the number 13 which illuminated under his touch. The doors closed and the lift moved. The radio was playing in the lift and music trickled out of it but Garrett wasn't listening. He was looking at his reflection in the mirror of the lift. He looked weathered and ill as though he were recovering from a particularly nasty flu. His eyes were slightly blackened and he needed a shave. His skin was speckled with small white spots from the dried-on salty water of the sea and his hair was still damp. Garrett must have looked odd to the man at the reception desk, but he hadn't made it obvious if he had.

The doors pinged open once more and Garrett exited the lift. He moved slowly toward the front door of his flat. He pulled the keys out of his pocket and unlocked it. He was grateful for the clean and tidy flat that welcomed him and thanked his past-self for having the forethought to clean up. He was barely aware what his feet were doing or where they were

219

taking him yet he didn't much care. He could feel an aching tiredness sweeping over him. Garrett dropped his keys on the kitchen island and kicked his shoes off noticing his damp socks leaving faint footprints on the wooden floor. He felt himself walking down the corridor, opening the bathroom door and stripping off. He turned the shower on hot and climbed in feeling the warm water cascade down his back and wash over his face. He looked down and could see the bits of dirt swirling down the plug hole. It was so calm and quiet that he almost fell asleep right there in the warm embrace of the water. He washed as quickly as his exhausted body would allow him and dried himself with the same level of haste. Garrett brushed his teeth and quickly shaved away the stubble on his face. He then looked once more at his reflection in the mirror. It was definitely an improvement. He left the bathroom with his towel wrapped tightly around his waist.

The sun was just peeking over the horizon displaying a generous yellow glow that would be waking up the nation's early risers and businesspeople. He imagined the look on his old boss' face waking up at this time. Garrett's mouth hitched up slightly, the shadow of a smile on his face. He closed the blinds, blocking out the light that was creeping into the flat and made his way to the bed. The room was just warm enough to be comfortable yet cool enough to sleep with the duvet tucked under his chin. He dropped his towel on the floor and climbed into bed; it welcomed him graciously. It took only seconds for sleep to tranquilise him.

Chapter 15

Dreaming peacefully, the way he hadn't experienced in years, Garrett awoke almost 14 hours later, somewhere around 5pm. The familiar dream-like smog took a moment to dissipate and when it did, the room swam into focus. He chugged from a fresh bottle of water under the bedside table and exhaled a long sigh. He sat up and propped himself up against the thick pillows on which he'd slept. He rubbed his eyes wearily noting that his body felt stiff.

He got out of bed and proceeded to the kitchen. His legs were sore and his head felt foggy. Opening the fridge, he pulled out some bacon and quickly began to fry it in a pan. The whole room filled with the scent and Garrett's mouth began to water. He buttered two pieces of bread and sandwiched the crispy bacon between it. He didn't realise quite how hungry he was until he was eating; he couldn't recall the last time he had some actual food that wasn't eaten in a rush but now that he had found his appetite, he could barely stop. Garrett made another three more sandwiches and ate until he couldn't fit any more in his stomach.

Garrett returned to the bedroom, walked into the closet and dressed himself in a smart, casual set of chinos and shirt, adorning another of his new, expensive watches to his wrist.

He checked out his reflection in the mirror before he left and felt as though David's style suited him perfectly.

A knock at his front door startled Garrett and he slowly made his way to the front door, tugged at the sleeves of his shirt and straightened his jumper. He answered the door and there was an old lady staring back at him with her wiry grey hair. Her clothes, however looked expensive and her bag had some designer label on. Garrett thought she looked familiar but for a moment couldn't place her face. She had a name tag hanging about her neck attached to a lanyard. It looked like an executive badge, but he couldn't make out from what company. The name on the tag read *Barbara Wilson*.

"Hello David," she smiled, "I was just hoping to talk to you for a moment if that's alright?" That's when Garrett realised where he had seen her. It was the day of David's death. He'd gotten into the lift with her, and she tried to talk to him but he left before they struck up a conversation.

Before waiting for an answer, the old lady had entered the room and Garrett had no choice but to close the door behind her. He felt a small pang of worry in the pit of his stomach but squashed it down with a heavy breath in and then out. He smiled at the lady and gestured her to the sofa where she sat comfortably among the cushions, placing her handbag on the floor beside her feet.

"What can I do for you?" Garrett asked politely taking a seat opposite her in a matching armchair. She wringed her fingers for a moment looking as though she didn't particularly feel like saying what was on her mind.

"Is everything alright?" Garrett pressed. The lady looked at him nervously which, in turn, made Garrett feel a little nervous, too.

"Yes. Well, no. I'm not sure" Barbara babbled. "It's just lately you haven't been speaking to me very much, it's like you've forgotten who I am and it… It just hurts to feel invisible. You used to help me with my shopping every Monday and now…" She trailed off, saying all of this very fast as though she were concerned if she stopped for a moment, she may not finish her sentence. Garrett felt the little knot in his stomach loosen.

"I'm sorry," he said to her in what he had hoped was a sympathetic voice. "I've been a little distracted lately."

"Was it that man?" She asked, an edge of sympathy on her voice, too. Garrett clung to the excuse like a lifeline.

"It was. I really don't feel comfortable talking about it. He wasn't very nice, but it's all over now. I'm still happy to help. Please forgive me." Garrett said a little pompously. She smiled widely at him.

"Of course, I'm sorry I shouldn't have said anything. There was just one more thing." Barbara offered.

"Please."

"Well… About a week ago I know you had a break-in," she began, and Garrett's stomach knotted up once more, "and I felt awful because I hadn't said anything but… It was me. David I'm so sorry." She wiped a tear away that welled in her eye and Garrett felt a small amount pity for the old lady but it was mostly overshadowed by confusion.

"Why did you do it? How did you do it?" Garrett asked eagerly, predominantly to understand where his security needed updating.

"Please forgive me, I didn't take anything; I would never! I was just so upset that I used the spare key you gave me and went to come and find you but nobody was in. As soon as I realised, I felt awful and I called security to report it because

I wanted to inconvenience you, which I admit was petty and wrong. I didn't mean to cause any fuss or harm, really I didn't." Barbara was now crying heavily, and Garrett offered her a tissue from a box on the coffee table between them.

Garrett was silent for a moment. He was both horrified and relieved. There most definitely had been a break-in and at the time, Garrett could hardly think through the anxiety of what that meant and how it might affect him later down the line. But this also meant that the break-in may not have meant the end of his life and perhaps he could now move past it and begin to leave fear behind, something he was more than keen to do. He also needed to change the locks first thing in the morning. In a way, Garrett felt pleased that he did not stop Barbara from coming into the flat, or else he may not have ever found out that she was the one who broke in and he would live with the knowledge that someone else may know about his secret.

"I'm not upset." Garrett settled on, "I get it, but you need to understand that it was a huge betrayal of trust and I do have to ask for that key back." He felt this was a perfectly reasonable request to make of a neighbour that broke into his flat whilst he wasn't there with the sole purpose of yelling at him for hurting her feelings.

"Yes, of course." She said and picked her bag up off the floor. She unzipped it and plunged her hand into the inside pocket and rummaged around and withdrew a set of keys on a ring. She flicked through the keys and fumbled for a moment, detaching a silver one from it. She handed the key to Garrett. He took it from her and put it in his pocket.

"I'm so sorry, I hope I can earn your trust back." Barbara's voice broke a little when she spoke.

"I'm sure you will. I'm always here if you need anything, ok?" He told her with another smile. This one was sincere. In truth, the lady seemed alright. A little nosy, maybe and a bit needy, but he didn't mind her and she certainly seemed better than the old neighbours he had grown up with. Perhaps it was because they now had something in common; wealth. Barbara stood up and he escorted her back to the front door. She patted him on the shoulder affectionately, like a grandmother saying goodbye to her grandkids.

"I'll see you." She said and she hobbled down the corridor to her own flat. She took one last look at him from the doorway and vanished inside with a small smile. Garrett huffed out another sigh and went back inside.

He couldn't believe what he had heard. The old lady had broken in to his flat, but of course she had a key which was why there was no sign of forced entry. He wondered who else might have a key but was firm that he would not be giving any out himself when the locks were changed. Garrett moved to the office where he searched the internet for a locksmith in the local area. There were a few that were poorly rated but when he found one with over four stars, he scrawled the number down on a piece of paper and tore it off.

Heading back to the kitchen, Garrett plucked his phone from the countertop, having not even used it since he came back in last night. He punched the number in and dialled it. After a few rings a man picked up.

"Afternoon, Gordon's locksmith, how can I help?" The voice was gravelly like a smoker.

"Good afternoon, I need a lock changed in my flat as soon as humanly possible."

"Right-o. I can do tomorrow morning, just had a cancellation." He grunted. He had a thick country accent and dragged out the end of his words like a farmer.

"Perfect, I'll be in all morning just pop by when you can." Garrett replied eagerly. He gave the man the address, which was noted on a recent letter that Garrett found tucked away in a drawer, and ended the call.

It was then that Garrett recalled a card he was given from the officer that investigated the break-in advising him to make contact if he had any further information that could be of use. He considered for a moment before deciding it was probably best to have the case closed. He found the card in the back of his wallet and called the number written across it.

"Sergeant Allison Brown." Answered the lady on the end of the phone within seconds of it ringing.

"Hi there, it's David Ellison calling. You recently investigated a possible break-in at my flat."

"Yes, is everything alright, Mr. Ellison?" She asked him with a crisp voice.

"More than alright, Sergeant. You asked me to call if I had anything else to add at all that might be of use. It turns out, my neighbour was the culprit and I had no idea until she confessed just now." He sighed as though this was mildly infuriating but altogether not a problem.

"I see," She replied sounding a little irritated, "if you could give me their name and address, we'll send a couple of officers down right away." She promised.

"No, really we've wasted quite enough of your time. There's no need, she's elderly and I've already spoken to her about it. She was just upset and went looking for me." He replied. He found he was gesturing with his hands rather a lot as if he were not in fact talking to a police officer, something he had been fearing all week, but perhaps an old friend.

"Are you sure, Mr. Ellison? We're more than happy to make a visit."

"Honestly, there's no need. I'm having the locks changed tomorrow; she used a key that I forgot she had and, besides, there was nothing taken and no damage. I'll give her the cold shoulder for a bit and that'll be more than enough. Thank you, though. I just wanted to update you." He laughed exhaustively, internally grateful that he was becoming better at holding conversations posing as David than he was at the beginning.

"That's alright, thanks for calling. I'll make sure the case has been closed and just be careful who you give keys to. Bye for now." And the line dropped off.

Garrett shook his head, he felt her last words were awfully passive-aggressive. Garrett double-tapped his phone and checked the time. It was almost 7pm. He felt good. In fact, he felt great.

Epilogue

David Ellison, previously known as Garrett Langford around five years ago, was pacing a hole in the white tiled flooring of a villa in Son Vida, Mallorca. The bedroom was vast and bright. The white walls reflected the dazzling sun that poured through the windows of the upper floor. A gigantic bed took up almost half the wall.

He was currently on hold, his phone in hand, waiting for the operator to pick up the line. He had been waiting for almost twenty minutes and could feel the frustration bubbling beneath his skin but he attempted to remain calm. Feeling the cloying heat sticking his short-sleeved, cream shirt to his skin, he wafted it gently but it did nothing to cool him off. He crossed the length of the room, past the wall-mounted television to the glass table in front of the floor-length window. David picked up a small remote control and pushed the button hard. The air-conditioning unit above the bed whirred into action, spewing its delightfully cold breeze into the room. David sighed gratefully as he stood under it, letting the cool air lick his face. He flapped the cold into his shirt as the line finally connected once more.

"I'm so sorry for the delay, Mr Ellison," came the bright voice of a lady through the phone, "we only have a seat in Business Class available in the morning, will that be alright?" Her voice had a note of pleading in it.

"No," David exclaimed feeling frustrated and hot which only added to his annoyance, "I want a First Class ticket and it has to be tonight. I don't care what the price is, I need to be in London tonight." The line was silent for a moment before the lady spoke once again.

"I understand, Mr Ellison, please bear with me and I'll talk to my manager and see what we can do."

"No, no, no!" David shouted, but it was too late. The phone began to blare out old timey music as he was placed on hold yet again. Breathing hard, David walked over to the window. The sun looked like it was beginning to set but had no plans to lower its intense heat. The golden light of the sun bleached everything in warm yellow. The vast hills that surrounded the villa were covered in tall trees and small clusters of buildings were nestled within them. The view was truly spectacular and there was little better to wake up to than the glorious weather and picturesque scenery of Son Vida. He had been staying here on and off for the past year, taking time off between his work to enjoy the delights that Spanish culture had to offer.

To enjoy the cool water of a glistening swimming pool and relaxing in the modern villa, that he had recently splashed an eye-watering six figure sum on to refurbish it, really made his life feel whole. Or it would be if the irritating woman would find his seat on the flight. Hadn't he made it expressly clear that no sum was too high? David huffed out a big sigh.

"Mr Ellison?" The lady from the airline spoke after a few minutes.

"Yes?" David replied eagerly.

"We have managed to book the seat, but it will cost 7,653 Euro and 87 Cents. Is this suitable?"

"Yes, yes it's fine." David replied a little snappishly. And once he had confirmed the payment and received his email booking confirmation, he hung up the phone feeling a little more relieved than he had when he started it.

Muttering to himself, David filled a small carry-on suitcase with essentials, knowing he had plenty of clothes and amenities at his flat in Mayfair, and zipped it closed. Feeling a lot cooler with the air-conditioning unit blasting, he reluctantly switched it off and carried the suitcase down the giant staircase that rose from the centre of the hall. Downstairs, he switched off the same cooling units and headed out the front door into the gigantic driveway. The heat of the evening hit him, making him feel like he had stepped inside of an oven. As he breathed in, the hot air whipped down his throat.

The taxi he had ordered via an app was waiting for him outside the double gates that enclosed his property. Wheeling his suitcase up the paved drive, he buzzed the gate open and climbed in the back seat, grateful for the cool air that greeted him inside.

"Palma de Mallorca, por favor." David said to the driver. He needed the airport soon or he would miss his flight. He had a party to get to and, though he was never a fan of crowded spaces, part of him felt excited to be around his friends.

When he arrived, David was ushered into the First Class seating area almost immediately and was approached by a server who offered him drinks. Ordering a tall glass of orange juice, he settled himself comfortably into the small cabin that he had all to himself. He often travelled First Class whenever he used trains or air transport. The luxury of money really had made a difference to his life and had aided him in almost everything he did. David still got blown away by the difference in the treatment he received when he flashed a pricey watch or expensive ticket.

Kicking his feet up on the recliner seat, David was swiftly handed his drink and a menu from which he could order food. Not feeling particularly hungry, he put it to the side and watched the woman leave.

The plane rumbled to life some 40 minutes later and, with the tv on set to some action movie he had been wanting to see for some time, he began to relax.

The plane ride was a comfortable six hours during which time, David had enjoyed a tempting chocolatey dessert that had called him from the menu he had set aside.

He arrived in Heathrow airport to a dark sky and a cold chill on the air that caused goosebumps to erupt on his exposed arms; he really should have changed on the plane but having spent little time in London recently, he had acclimated to the warmth of Mallorca and often forgot how different the weather really was.

The airport was surprisingly busy for the evening, but David walked with a brisk pace through the small crowds and he was through customs in no time, noting the way an envious security officer eyed his Rolex that glinted on his wrist with a look of supreme jealousy.

As he had hoped, his driver was waiting for him outside. Fighting his way through the small throng of people that were congregating around one of the entrances, David pushed his way through the people, feeling a great sense of belonging as he approached the black BMW with dark tinted windows.

"Ah, it's gorgeous!" David exclaimed with excitement to Harris, the driver he had hired for the last week who had picked up his brand-new car only days ago and had been keeping it safe at his flat.

"I'm so jealous, it drives like a dream. The pull is just..."
Harris trailed off as he struggled to find a word that could
sum up the feelings he was harbouring for the vehicle. Harris'
brown eyes swept over the contours of the car. He was an
older man than David, in his late thirties but had been a private
driver for the wealthy for years and came highly recommended
online.

"Thank you so much for handling the pick up and whatnot,
I would've come back sooner but I had some stuff to sort out."
David told him, feeling excited to climb in and take it for a
spin.

"Don't even worry, honestly I'm just glad I got to drive it,
you'll love it." He promised.

"Do you want a lift home?" David offered.

"No, I've got a ride, a friend's waiting for me down the road.
You're suit's in the boot." Harris added pointing to the car.
David gave Harris a firm handshake and thanked him for being
so flexible and helping out at such short notice then bade him
goodbye. He put the suitcase in the boot and put the suit jacket
on over his shirt, grateful that he had at least had the sense to
wear full-length trousers that didn't clash with the jacket.

David sat in the driver's seat and spent a moment playing
with the knobs and dials of the electric car. He wished he
had the time to take it for a quick drive but time was wearing
on and his friends would undoubtedly be waiting for him; he
would give it a full test-run tomorrow.

Only half an hour later, David was sipping from a cold glass
bottle at a bar in the heart of London. He was surrounded
by some friends he had made after attending a premier of a
long-awaited movie. David had been asked to work on the
social media posts for the movie and he had been given an

incredible opportunity to attend the first showing to cast and crew though he really was neither. The movie was thrilling but he had signed a non-disclosure agreement and couldn't talk about it to anyone for some months except the other people in attendance. During the after-party he had struck up a conversation with some of the editors and they talked for hours, laughing and joking, swapping stories in the euphoria of the night. That had really drawn him into the world of movies. He knew he was never going to be an actor, director or producer but his love for movies stemmed from just that - watching them, as he always had.

He finished up his drink and got another at the bar and began to sip that one, too. One of his friends began to talk about the time that David had tried his hand at movie editing for a trailer that was planning to be released, and he wasn't half bad.

"I'm not going to lie, I would watch that!" Jason exclaimed tipping his own beer toward David.

"Wait, wait, wait," Shana could be heard saying over the chatter of the group of six that was currently celebrating the movie's resounding success at the box office, a party that David had been invited to due to his ongoing friendship with the crew. "I haven't heard of this, what happened?"

"David put together a mock-up of the trailer." Jason repeated.

"How did it go?" Shana implored buzzing with excitement and the alcohol in her own glass.

"It was okay, I think," David said shrugging his shoulders even though the sentiment in his heart was that he was proud of what he had accomplished even if nobody else was. "I mean, I was given a few scenes from the movie to work with and showed them to Jason here."

"I don't think it went as well as you thought," Jason said, laughing before turning to the group, "He had his final edit done about two hours before we were supposed to watch it and we all thought he was going to die of a heart attack when I looked at it." Jason, who was the lead editor for the movie, was messing with him again and David felt humbled to be friends with people of such talent.

David laughed along with everyone else because he could remember the feelings of dread that Jason was describing about how tense the situation had been for him and how much he didn't want everyone else to watch it. He remembered feeling like he would get fired even though it wasn't his job, but he had survived, barely. After the clip was over and they all gathered around him to discuss his work. David still couldn't believe that it wasn't half bad even if Jason did make comments during the whole thing in a jovial, light-hearted way. But it worked out in the end and he got some good experience.

"I'm glad you guys had fun," Shana responded, "but in all seriousness, David I heard there's an opportunity in the editing room, it's super junior, probably just making coffee for the main guys but it could turn in to something; you should go for it!"

"I'll pass," David responded. "I don't even think I want to do anything with making movies."

"Why?" Jason asked confused, "You love this stuff!"

"Not anymore," David said looking down at his beer and becoming a bit serious. He wasn't sure how much he wanted to tell everyone but they were friends, after all, most of them really close friends. Just not the kind that wouldn't judge him for coming clean about something from his past that had kept him up at night ever since.

"Okay, I do love it but I just don't think I could deal with the stress of overheads, like this wise-ass right here," he joked, gesturing in a mock-subtle way to Jason much to the delight of his friends who laughed raucously, "I like being my own boss." He laughed.

As the night continued to wear on and the empty bottles began to stack up, midnight soon arrived and not long after, the pub's landlord was calling for everyone's last order. David drained the last of his beer and put £50 on the bar beside him. The group stood up, stretched and began to walk out toward their cars. David followed the rest of the crew ahead of him while Jason grabbed a hold of Shana's arm and pulled her ahead for a quick goodbye kiss. He had forgotten that they had recently become an item until that moment, and they canoodled a little before going into their respective cars. He was just glad that he hadn't lingered or he'd have had to listen to Shana telling Jason how much she loved him and hear them going all gooey; he didn't want to be around that.

As everyone drove off into the night David began to make his way back home. He climbed into the brand-new BMW, inhaling the new-car smell that always made him feel good. He was aware that he was probably over the limit, but he figured as long as he drove slowly and paid attention, he would be home within fifteen minutes and he could sleep the rest of it off. He started the engine and backed out of the parking space, using his reversing camera to guide him. He watched and waved at the three cars ahead of him as his friends pulled out of the car park and drove away.

Once he was on the road himself, he felt the drinks really starting to hit him hard and he really should have called a taxi but that would mean leaving his car where it was at the pub and he wasn't sure if he wanted to park it there overnight, being brand new. Undoubtedly he'd end up with a ticket, too and the whole thing would be a hassle. He knew that alcohol was against his new policy of being safe at all times but he felt that he deserved a drink after working so hard recently. As David began to swerve slightly on the road, he quickly overcompensated and yanked the wheel in the opposite direction.

It all happened so fast. He could barely even see what was happening but before he knew it the front of his car was mounting a kerb, blowing out a tyre. As he swore loudly, he tried to correct himself but found he couldn't quite make out through the haze of his inebriation which way was the road and which way was the railing up ahead. Before he could think to stop, the nose of his brand-new car ploughed into a streetlamp which buckled and fell into the road with a resounding *crash*.

The airbags deployed with such force that when it made contact with his face, he felt like he'd been punched straight in the eye. He sat there, swaying in the drivers seat for a moment before he decided to get out of the car and assess the damage. He stumbled out of the vehicle and fell into the road, feeling the knee of his suit trousers rip and the tarmac graze the skin beneath. He just managed to right himself when his eyes fell upon the damage he'd caused.

The entire front of his car had crumpled and the bonnet had broken the windshield with the force of the impact. He glared through his drunken haze and noticed a steady stream of steam rising from the bay of the engine. He walked, or rather stumbled, to the front of the car and his heart dropped into his stomach when he saw that there was a man laying on the floor under the front wheel, trapped by the weight of the car. That's when the realisation struck him. His wheel hadn't hit a kerb at all, it had hit a person and David didn't see them. He rushed over to the man and attempted to lift the wheel off of his leg. It did nothing at all and the car didn't move; if anything it clamped down even more as the man let out a terrible scream.

"Oh my god, please don't die," David pleaded as he began weeping over the man. "I'm sorry; I didn't mean for this to happen." He quickly pulled out his phone and called 999.

"Emergency, which service do you require? Fire, police or ambulance?" The operator asked instantly. David didn't know what to say. His head was spinning and he could barely think straight.

"My car just crashed into someone!" He all but screamed. The words blurted out of his mouth before David had realised it.

"Okay sir I'm sending an ambulance now but can you tell me-." The operator began but was cut off by the sound of the man trapped under the car when he screamed in pain, "sir, can you tell me where you are?" David started babbling something incoherent and was told to calm down and look for a street sign.

"Wimpole Street." David stuttered.

"Alright sir, the ambulance has been dispatched and we've sent officers to your location. Try not to move the victim; we don't know how bad his injuries are yet and he'll need to be assessed." David listened to what she said and tried his hardest not to move the man but it was harder than he anticipated when the guy screamed and cried to get his leg free.

Before long, multiple officers arrived on scene and began taking statements from David and everyone else who had just arrived including bystanders who had pooled around them to video it. He really did not feel like he was that drunk, especially after sobering up in the cool air and with the panic flooding through his system. The last thing David wanted right now was to be arrested but before he could even try and come up with a plan an officer came over to him and produced a breathalyser. He shoved it into David's mouth and ordered him to blow hard until he was told to stop. David did so and just as he felt like he was about to pass out, the machine beeped loudly and it was withdrawn from between his lips. He gasped a little for air as the officer read out the results.

"You have failed the test, you are under arrest for driving under the influence and dangerous driving." The officer said. David could not believe it. He was about to get arrested because he didn't want to cancel his night out with his friends and refused the sensible idea of calling a taxi and just leaving his car behind at the pub. He barely heard the officers recite him his rights and merely nodded when they asked him if he understood. All he wanted to do was go home and sleep this off but that was not an option anymore. His mind started racing with thoughts of how much time he would serve in prison if convicted, especially after David had caused someone severe injury. What if they had to have their leg amputated? How much would they sue him for?

He tried asking everyone what would happen next but no one seemed willing to answer him so David decided it best to say nothing until he had a lawyer present. He'd been in contact with a lawyer for the last couple of years whose name was Adrian Wellman, a titan of the legal world and charged exactly what was expected for a man of such calibre.

"I'd like to call my lawyer." David with cuffed hands behind his back said to the officer that was holding him lightly on the shoulder.

"I think that would be an excellent idea." The officer uncuffed him and allowed him to make a phone call to Adrian who picked up on the first ring.

"David, what's wrong?" Adrian sounded panicked and David could hear the sound of papers shuffling in the background.

"I've been arrested, I hit a man with my car. I've had a drink -."

"Don't say anything else until I get there. Hear me, David? Not a word to anyone. I'll meet you at the station."

"Yes." David replied quietly before hanging up, he heard how slurred his own speech sounded and attempted to say nothing.

David was guided into the back of the police car and the last thing he saw was the paramedics loading the man into the back of their ambulance and speed off in the middle of blue flashing lights. The drive was quiet and the officers never spoke to each other or to him which was good because David was afraid of what he might end up saying if they grilled him hard; he wasn't in any shape to be thinking quickly or to be cunning with his answers. He had a lot of dark secrets. One badly placed answer could dredge up the name Garrett, a name he hadn't spoken in many years, and that absolutely could not happen. He had to play this as apologetic and remorseful as he could manage and he might, with Adrian's help be put on community service or have to pay a fine and everything about his past would remain hidden.

The police cruiser pulled up to the station and he was slowly frog-marched up to the desk for processing. He gave his name,

David Ellison when he was asked. He was then told to empty his pockets and into a small tray and he did so, feeling lost without his mobile phone and wallet. They then told him to surrender his hands for finger printing which he obliged to, not that they really gave him much choice. After they took his prints, he was once again frog-marched into another room where he was given a sign to hold up. He was told to stand next to a height chart and then a camera flashed blindingly, dazzling David's eyes as they took his front and side profile mug shot. After this, they took him to another room where they did yet another breathalyser test.

Again, nearly passing out, David blew a 0.48 which meant he was definitely well over the legal limit and his stomach dropped again when he heard this though he was hardly surprised; his vision was still swimming and he only caught half the words that he was told. He cursed himself silently and was taken back out of the room to wait in a holding cell whilst they processed him.

Around twenty minutes went by and he was called into an interrogation room and handcuffed to a chair. Beside him was Adrian, he could tell before he had even entered the room because they wore the same cologne; something David had noticed when they had first met. Adrian was accompanied by his legal assistant, a young woman who seemed like she would be more at home in the business end of a nightclub than working as a lawyer's assistant but David was too far gone to pay her much attention.

"Hello, David." Adrian started, "I'm sorry that you're having such a bad night but we'll try to make this as painless as possible. Now tell me exactly what happened." Adrian, ever the man of business, doing away with any small talk or comforting words, jumped straight into it.

"Ok." And David recounted the story of exactly what happened from drinking in the bar to getting in his car and crashing it into the lamp post and then finding the man trapped under his wheel. When he was finished, Adrian went silent for a moment and told him to wait whilst he went to speak to the officers in charge. He was gone for about 15 minutes and when he returned he was wearing a look of pure fear.

"David... They're saying... You're fingerprints. They're saying your prints match someone on a case a long time ago. You're coming up in the system as a man previously thought of to be dead." Adrian's voice was lifeless as if he couldn't believe what he was saying and he wasn't the only one. The assistant was silent, her mouth hanging open with a look of bewilderment on her face whilst David was focused on not throwing up. His stomach seemed to knot so tight that it made him feel sick. No, please don't say the name, David thought with panic coursing through him.

"Garrett Langford." Adrian said the name softly, almost a whisper and David could feel his heart racing as the name pounded in his ears. It was like he could hear it echoing loudly as if someone had shouted it in an empty hall. It couldn't be, it simply couldn't. Garrett had been gone for five years. He was David, he knew that completely and utterly. He'd taken on his identity and life and had embodied him with every fibre of his being and now here he was, sat in an interrogation room waiting to hear about what would happen to him next. Surely he was dreaming or hallucinating. Yes, maybe he was so drunk he was making the whole thing up.

"I have 10 minutes before they come in to question you

and your answers need to be absolutely perfect." Adrian said forgoing the niceties once again. David just nodded shortly, realising that there was no way his mind could make up something so real and so terrifying; it paralysed him and rendered him almost completely unable to talk.

"David, who the hell is Garrett Langford and what does he have to with you?" When David didn't answer, Adrian told him that he had to say something and that the police sounded like they were picking up an old case and piecing things together.

"I... I'm - " Too late. The door opened and two people walked in. The first was a burly man in a police officer's uniform and the other was a lady, mid-fifties in a crisp pant suit. She was most definitely the one in charge. She was holding a case file in one hand and a cup of coffee in the other. She sat down slowly as if she were about to discuss meal prepping whilst David was starting to sweat in his chair.

"Officer, please remove the handcuffs I doubt this gentleman is going to give us any trouble, will you?" She added looking directly to David with a sweet smile that didn't reach her eyes. He glanced at his lawyer who nodded in encouragement.

"No." David said in a small voice and was all he could manage.

"Now, gentlemen. Mr Ellison will not be giving us anymore trouble as he is going to tell me everything I need to know." She said as she sipped her coffee and opened the file as if it were an interesting novel.

"Do you know how I know that?" She didn't wait for an answer. "Because I think you have some answers for us and those answers are going to determine how long you'll spend in prison, Mr Ellison." She hit each of the last six words with a small slap of the table to reinforce her point. Or maybe it was for intimidation purposes and if that were the case, it worked. David's heart almost skipped a beat. He remained silent whilst the handcuffs were being taken off.

"Mr Ellison, tell me do you know of a person name Garrett Langford?" Detective Brannon asked in a polite voice that sent a shiver down his spine. David hesitated for a moment.

"It sounds familiar." He said making no commitment. There was of course no way they would find Garrett Langford, he thought to himself, thanks to his incredible forethought on that awful night. He remembered stating how he wished to be cremated. This was one of the absolutely crucial elements of his plan and it was something he had seen on television once before. It was a documentary. The investigator was attempting to solve a murder that had happened some time ago and it was proving particularly difficult as the body that he wished to exhume had been cremated so no new evidence could be gleaned from the body and the old evidence was insufficient as they had no idea the death was even a murder until after the cremation.

"Here's the thing," Detective Brannon replied, "I think you know a lot more about Mr Langford than you're letting on. So this is what I'm going to do for you, I will give you five minutes to confer with your lawyer and when I come back, I'm going to ask you the same question. I do hope you'll have a longer answer to give me for your sake, Mr Ellison." Detective Brannon rose slowly from her chair; David couldn't tell whether this was an intimidation tactic also, the calm demeanour to make him think she had everything worked out and was just waiting for him to crack. When she left the room, Adrian turned to him after telling his assistant to go home for the night as there was nothing she could do for him right now.

This did not make David feel better.

"David, I cannot ask you if you did something bad because if you tell me you did I have a duty to the courts to report it and pierce the veil of attorney-client privilege. What I do want to ask is are you vulnerable? Are they going to find something if they keep digging?" His tone was serious and heavy with worry and concern. But there was no way David could tell him what he did.

"No." David said without even thinking about it, "Adrian I didn't do anything to Garrett Langford, I promise you that." Lying like that was so easy to David now and just came as second nature. He'd introduced himself hundreds of times over the years and each one made the lie a little bit easier to believe. Once upon a time he would have quivered and perspired as the lies struggled to come out as he even uttered David's name. That that was the old David - that was Garrett. David was strong and smart, he was cunning and intelligent and would never let anyone over the giant wall he had built around himself.

By the way the detective had spoken, he was also certain that nobody had heard of what happened to that nosy private investigator, Jake Hanbury; he would never be interfering in anyone's life again. He was but a pile of bones swimming eternally at the bottom of the ocean. Garrett Langford was a ghost and David Ellison was free.

But then Detective Brannon's voice echoed in the room once more, this time calling his name. Adrian gave him an encouraging pat on the shoulder before leaving to join her. David rose from his chair, his palms sweaty and his heart racing and paced nervously on the spot, something he hadn't done in years. He hated the way the name 'Garrett' dredged up the worst parts of him like the pacing, the sweating and the insecurity.

"Mr Ellison, I hope you've had a chance to confer with your lawyer. Now, I want you to answer me this question, do you know of a person by the name of Garrett Langford?" David cleared his throat before answering.

"Yes, I know who he is." Detective Brannon's eyes widened in surprise.

"Can you tell me what your relationship with Mr. Langford was?"

David licked his lips nervously; the alcohol was inhibiting his ability to lie comfortably, and he could still feel the after-effects of inebriation. He could sense that his secret was getting closer and closer to being uncovered and when it surfaced it would never be hidden again. The detective was smart, he could already tell that by the way she spoke and the way she moved. Her body language exhibited all the tell-tale signs of a powerful person. She would find out sooner or later and, deep down in the pit of his stomach, at the core of his consciousness, David knew that. But Adrian had warned him not to say anything even if it meant taking the fall for Garrett.

"We were acquaintances." He said finally and slowly.

"In what capacity were you acquaintances?" She pushed, her voice a little more strained than before. But it was at this moment that an idea struck David so he leant over to this lawyer and whispered in his ear low enough that nobody else could hear.

"Can I get an immunity deal?" He asked. David could see the look of excitement cross Adrian's face who cleared his throat and relayed the request to the detective.

"I can't make any promises, Mr Ellison," the detective told

them, "but I will take your request into consideration; it all depends on the quality of your information. Now, can you tell me anything else about Mr Langford?" David shook his head firmly.

"No, I don't want to say anything without the deal." Detective Brannon barked a short, humourless laugh.

"I don't negotiate in bad faith." She said sternly.

"If you haven't got enough evidence to charge my client, he is free to go."

"We have enough to keep you here for at least a DUI and several other charges." Detective Brannon insisted. "Your client could end up in prison as it is." There was something about the word 'could' that made both David and Adrian excited.

"Could, for something minor. You know as well as I do he'll get a fine and probation. You want more, you give more. If he testifies what he might or might not know about the death of Garrett Langford, he'll need an iron-clad immunity deal." Concluded Adrian, nodding.

"Yes." She replied smoothly. "I don't want you charged with a DUI. I want to solve the case that's been sitting on my desk for the last five years. I need to know what happened to Mr Langford and you are the only potential lead we have had in a very long time. So I'll repeat one last time. What happened to Mr Langford?" Her voice raised louder and David could see, with some satisfaction, she was getting annoyed.

"Once I see that immunity deal signed and sealed in front of me, I will tell you everything that I know. And you can rest assured you will be able to close your case." David replied coolly, inventing wildly on the spot. He only hoped that the detective would not be able to decline the possibility of solving what was probably her longest open case. She might even get a promotion, David mused silently. He could almost see the cogs working in her mind. Eventually she gave in.

"Alright, Mr Ellison," she all but spat, "If you can solve my case and only if your testimony is solid enough to do so, you will have your immunity deal. You have my word."

"I don't know you," David replied, "your word does not hold any value to me." David suppressed a flashback of him saying something identical on a yacht to a long-dead man. "Show me the deal and I will talk."

The detective hesitated for a beat before finally getting up and leaving the room once more. It would be some time before she returned and David started to wonder how long he would be here. The hours ticked by slowly and David had watched the clock almost exclusively the whole time, Adrian promising he would return when the deal was ready to be signed. There were soft footsteps that approached the doorway and David's head snapped up to face them. It was the police officer that had entered the interrogation room with Detective Brannon when he was first brought in and handcuffed to the chair.

"Coffee?" The man asked simply. His tone was polite, he didn't particularly seem bothered what David was being questioned for or maybe he didn't really know.

"Please. Milk, two sugars." David replied. He wasn't really a coffee man; water would have been preferable but he wanted to make absolutely sure that he was as sober as he could possibly be before he divulged any of his information. David sat back down on the chair, tapping his foot slowly with the ticking of the clock for almost ten minutes before the officer returned and placed a paper cup of coffee on the table in front of him. He thanked the officer who left without a word a moment later. David stirred it with a wooden skewer that was poking out the top and thought about what he would say to the detective when she returned. He wanted to make sure his story was as believable as possible. What was more, hadn't he prepared himself for this eventuality?

It was fair to say he had not anticipated being charged with other crimes at the same time but the plan would, with any luck, play out as he had expected it to if he stuck to his story and did not deviate from it. One thing he could not do was get angry. It was such a common tactic in the police force because it worked, getting someone upset would almost always make them blurt something out that they hadn't intended to and this could not be the case with David if he wanted to avoid spending the rest of his life behind bars.

At just gone eight in the morning, Detective Brannon finally returned with Adrian on her heels. He walked with a little spring in his step, looking almost overjoyed by the expression on his face.

"I've checked it and it's good. So long as your testimony solves the case all charges against you will be dropped and you'll be free to go. But do read it yourself and be sure you know what you're signing."

"All charges?" David repeated hopefully. It was Detective Brannon who answered his question.

"Yes, including the DUI for tonight. You'll get a driving ban off the record but we don't get brownie points for a DUI."

"The police force will look far better solving a murder case than arresting a man who crashed into a lamppost." Adrian summed up for him rather unnecessarily.

"What about the man that I hurt?" David asked in a low tone, leaning in on the remorse in his voice.

"He's fine. Not even a broken bone, just a few bruises." The detective said in a light voice, almost as surprised by the information as David was, "Your car ended up riding up the lamp post and the gentleman's leg got caught in the wheel well. He was very lucky, and so are you; it could have been a lot worse. He might try to sue you but from I've heard, you'll likely still be rich come the end of it." She finished matter-of-factly.

Detective Brannon put the folder on the table that she was holding and slid it across the table to David, who opened it and quickly read over its contents. There was a lot of legal jargon, a lot of *heretofore's* and *henceforth's* but he got the general gist of it. The part he read over twice was near the end:

Should the signor fulfil and meet the terms of this Immunity Deal, there can be, in no uncertain terms, any charges or punishment of any sort whatever for the testimony surrendered no matter the contents. This document is valid and will be respected in all courts of the England and Wales legal system. The bearer of this document, along with the signor named on Page 1 both agree to be bound by these terms and understand they will take immediate effect after it has been signed.

He read it once more just to be absolutely certain and then he nodded to the detective who handed him a fancy ballpoint pen. Satisfied, he signed it with a flourish, feeling his heart flutter slightly, then passed the pen and the paperwork back to the detective.

"Now," she said, wasting no time at all, "are you ready to talk?"

"I am." He replied simply.

Detective Brannon leaned back in the chair when she sat down, studying the man seated in front of her who looked a little pale and sickly. It was clear to Garrett that Detective

Brannon had been through a lot - the dark circles under her eyes attested to that - but he doubted whether she realised just how much.

"Alright," she said finally, "what happened to Garrett Langford?" David exhaled slowly.

"I met him in a bar a long time ago... We were both working a similar job and got talking about computer stuff." He went on to explain everything in detail, Adrian sitting quietly in the corner of the room taking notes on an electronic tablet. His story was mostly true to the real events that had transpired. Except he told it from David's point of view. Leaving out all the parts that tied him to an intimate relation with Garrett, which would not have made his story more believable, he explained how he had met him once again at a restaurant and hoped he would see him again. In David's fictional story that he recounted to the detective, that was the last time he saw the man.

"And then I got a call from a man named Jake Hanbury. He asked to meet me on my boat. He was a private detective, ex-military, I'm sure you'll find him on a database of some sort. I had initially hired him to help locate my missing parents but it turned out that they had unfortunately died." David attempted to shift his expression into one of grief but he wasn't sure that he had managed it; he could barely feel his face, in fact most of him felt numb thanks mostly to the knot in his stomach that still would not loosen.

"Of course..." Detective Brannon whispered to herself. "I saw him. He came to speak to me just days after the death of Mr Langford." David could almost see the cartoon style lightbulb flash over her head as she put together the fake story he was feeding her.

"Then what you might not know is what he told me." David continued to make up. "We spent many hours together as I funded the hunt for my parents and you'll see evidence of that in my bank statements. But I believe I told him something about not liking Garrett and he must have thought that I wanted him dead." Detective Brannon seemed fixated on David's story and she was focused on every word. "When he came to me he admitted to me everything he had done. What he did to Garrett. He swore me to secrecy and told me if I ever told anyone I would end up his next victim. I don't know for sure why he did it, maybe he was unhinged or felt some sense of loyalty to me, I can't say for certain. But he told me exactly how he did it, with the drugs and making it appear to be self-inflicted. He even sent an email to Garrett detailing it all and, for some reason, copied me into it, maybe to scare me – I don't know. If you trace the point of origin I'm sure you'll see that it came from a device registered to him." Detective Brannon's face seemed to glow with the grim excitement of solving a case and her words came out fast.

"Where is it, the email?" David could almost feel the eagerness emanating from her.

"I have a digital copy on a USB stick which I keep attached to my keys, and I have made duplicate copies both digital and physical, but the original is saved in my inbox. If you get me access to a computer, I'll show you."

"Fetch Mr Ellison's personal effects." She barked at the officer standing guard at the door almost as soon as David had finished his sentence. The officer nodded his head once and stomped away heavy-footed. Nobody uttered a word whilst they waited for the officer to return and when he did, he was holding a plastic bag that contained a wallet, keys, phone, chewing gum, and a small selection of coins. Adrian did not wait to be invited to inspect the items but the detective did not protest.

"May I?" She asked, turning back to David with her fingers poised over the opening of the bag like a child deciding which to grab in a bucket of Halloween candy. David nodded and Detective Brannon withdrew the set of keys which, true to his word, had hanging from it a red USB stick. She unhooked it from the rest and turned it over in her fingers as if she were inspecting it for flaws.

"Is there anything else on here?" She asked quietly, more to herself than anyone else in the room.

"You're welcome to check it, it's mainly a collection of all the evidence I have about my parents' last known whereabouts. Please do not delete any of the files it's all I have." Detective Brannon gave a sharp nod of her head. She pulled a phone from her pocket and tapped quickly on the keyboard. David wondered for a moment who she might be talking to but his question was answered within minutes when she was delivered a laptop by a tall, lanky man with a greasy face who set it down in front of her and left the room. She pulled the laptop closer, opened it up and then turned it slightly toward David.

"You may log in and show me the email but do it slowly." She warned him with a serious expression on her face. David did as he was told and as soon as he brought up the email, Detective Brannon took the laptop from him.

"I need to speak to a digital analyst, anyone that can verify Mr Ellison's story." She said to no-one in particular. It seemed that the officer who brought in David's belongings knew he was being spoken to and once more left the room, pulling a phone from his pocket as he did so to make a call that David wouldn't be able to hear.

"In the meantime, I'm going to have to take you back to the holding cell but if your story is accurate, I'll petition for your immediate release." She said. The notes of excitement in her voice made it clear that she was either unaware or unbothered that she had been on the clock since at least last night. David nodded, considering she might not even have a family or a pet waiting for her at home and part of that idea resonated with him though he fought not to feel it; this was someone who would gladly lock him away and he could not feel empathy for someone who worked against him.

"I understand." He said in a hollow voice.

"We'll get this sorted out as quickly as possible, Mr Ellison." She promised though he felt it was more for her own gain than his.

Adrian looked over at David with a worried expression yet squeezed his shoulder reassuringly before following the detective out of the room. David sat alone in the room for a moment, lost in thought, trying to process everything that had just happened, trying to make sure he remembered all the finer details of the story he had created in case he needed to recount them again. Looking down, he realised he hadn't drank much of his coffee and, figuring it might be a while before he was given another drink, he chugged the lukewarm liquid, set the empty cup back down on the table and waited for someone to escort him back to his cell.

Finally, just as he considered that they might have forgotten about him, another officer, a lady that he didn't recognise took him back. He sat on the edge of what was supposed to be a bed but was really just a blue mat barely thicker than an inch.

Soon he was lying down and before he knew it, a banging on the cell door awoke him from a poor sleep but he could not tell quite how long it had been. His eyes were bleary and he felt groggy and thirsty.

"Mr Ellison, you're wanted for questioning. Detective Brannon insisted that you were ok without cuffs but if you make any sudden moves, I will not hesitate to restrain you and put them on you. Do you understand?" The man's gruff voice echoed in the empty cell and was much too loud for David's pounding head that he now realised was the symptom of a particularly nasty hangover the likes he hadn't had in some time being teetotal.

"Ok." Was all his hoarse, dry voice could manage. There was silence for a moment and the door lock clicked open and the officer behind it pulled the door wide. David stood, feeling a stiff resistance in his joints and a pain in his lower back that definitely hadn't been there the day before, and followed the officer to the same room he vacated hours ago. Once more he took a seat and Adrian entered the room just after and took sat beside him.

"How are you doing?" He asked immediately. He sounded tired and looked it, too. He couldn't imagine how many hours Adrian had been awake but he was grateful for his presence and expertise in this difficult time.

"I'm ok. Did they tell you anything?" David replied and Adrian smiled wearily.

"I think it's good news but Detective Brannon will be along in a moment and she'll give you the run down." David felt his heart skip a beat. Could his quick thinking really get him out of this? Just as Adrian had predicted, the fierce-looking lady walked in just then followed by two other police officers. She had removed her blazer and was holding a fresh cup of coffee. The smell wafted into David's face and he felt a yearning to ask for a sip.

"I'm afraid there has been a problem." She said in a would-be unfortunate manner but David detected the lick of a satisfied smirk playing about the corners of her mouth which made his arms erupt in goosebumps.

"What sort of problem?" David said, barely above a whisper.

"I'm afraid you're under arrest for murder." She said matter-of-factly, blowing on her coffee as she stirred it with a wooden skewer.

"What?" Blurted Adrian.

"This man is not David Ellison. This here is Garrett Langford, the man we presumed dead five years ago."

"Detective, I think you need to take a step back and reassess your evidence. My client has been more than cooperative up until this point, but he is not going to sit here and take this defamation. We have an immunity deal, no charges." The detective glared at them both.

"I'm afraid the deal is off the table." Detective Brannon replied curtly.

"Absolutely not, this deal is signed!" Adrian said heatedly jabbing a finger at the folder on the table between them.

"This deal is only valid, and I made this expressly clear before it was signed, if and only if, his testimony solves the Garrett Langford murder. Which he didn't considering he is Garrett Langford and thus, he cannot have solved the murder." The detective looked at Adrian smugly.

"Your client is in violation of section 3 paragraph 27 subsection F which states that 'knowingly providing false information results in the immediate loss of all benefits, privileges and immunity afforded in this Immunity Deal.' It's right here, in black and white." She added, opening the folder and withdrawing the paperwork. She flicked through to the correct page where she poked a thick finger at the section she was referencing.

David stared at her confused and flabbergasted, unsure what to say or do next. Adrian, too, seemed stunned but recovered quickly.

"What kind of planet do you live on? What you're saying is ludicrous." But of course it wasn't ludicrous. Not to Detective Brannon. Not to David, or as he had been denying for so long, Garrett. He began to feel numbness sweep over him making him feel like he was going to pass out at any moment. His ears were ringing with the detective's words. Garrett was barely even aware of the whispering (or was it shouting?) around him. He distantly heard the names Garrett, David, Jake. Jake? How could she know about Jake? She couldn't, surely. The numbness became a pit in his stomach, an empty void like a black hole that threatened to suck him in and implode.

"Well I think it's pretty evident what happened, Mr Ellison, or should I say Mr Langford, when you connect the dots." She said condescendingly. It was only then Garrett realised she knew and could see through the whole ruse. And then his worst fear became a reality. It was happening, she started to detail it all to him. Exactly as it happened. It was like he was back there five years ago, replaying the events in his mind like they happened just yesterday. Yesterday, when he was absolutely and completely David Ellison.

"You see, after you were admitted to our fine establishment we took your prints. It turns out that Garrett, what am I saying, *you* have a criminal record. An ASBO from when you were

just a kid and the prints matched up perfectly. At first we thought it was a mistake but we ran them again and it kept telling us the same thing. So when we finally accepted that you were indeed alive, we had to find out exactly who we buried -
"

"Cremated." Garrett jumped in quickly. It had just occurred to him that there was no way they could tie him to a murder considering there was no body now to identify or pull evidence from.

"No, Mr Langford. Buried. You see, although you had expressed your will to be cremated in that wonderfully crafted suicide note, it is not legally binding. Your parents, when they saw your body, very impressive finding a lookalike by the way, agreed to have you buried on the advice of the police in case the body needed to be exhumed at some time later on."

She continued to talk as Adrian furiously tried to interrupt her but Garrett just let her talk. He already knew what she was going to say because he had lived it and knew it all to be true, it was all coming back to him now. The anger started to well up inside him. The injustice of it all.

"We traced back five years ago back to where it all began, and contacted your flat complex and requested CCTV logs for the week you turned up dead. We have you on video, entering the building with another man. David Ellison, the owner of said flat. However when you left and came back some time later, we never saw a second person exiting the building. What we did see was you pulling along a suitcase, a suitcase we now have reason to believe hid Mr. Ellison's body. Once we had video footage, we asked them to supply your vehicle details and they were only too happy to oblige." The detective took a seat opposite him and interlocked her fingers, staring into

Garrett's face. "We were able to contact the car manufacturers. Did you know that vehicles with a built-in satellite navigation system can be traced?" Garrett said nothing. He did know this but did not know that the police were able to request the logs from the manufacturers. He felt sweat begin to bead on his forehead. Not even Adrian could say anything at this point. The detective stood up and took a step closer to him, he could smell the coffee on her breath.

"We have you, Mr Langford." It felt like ice was running through his veins. This couldn't be happening. Not again. This is what he had been afraid of most. Being caught and everything he had done to assume David Ellison's identity would be for nothing.

"We also contacted NationFirst who were only too happy to supply all bank transaction records to which I credit the speed of the justice system for signing a warrant that made it all possible. It also appears that Mr Ellison opened a new account and deposited a large sum of money on the day that he died. But the funny thing is, he never left the flat complex that day, but you did."

"How on earth can you be sure that the body belongs to David Ellison and that the man before me is not in fact he?" Adrian jumped in.

"When we began to suspect it might be, we had an expedited DNA test via dental records which confirmed it." She told him, a real smile appearing on her face showing slightly yellowed teeth.

"And lastly, the cherry on the cake if you'll forgive the use of an overused expression, we have also have evidence that suggests you also killed another man by the name of Jake Hanbury. The email that he supposedly sent to Garrett, or rather, *you* – god, this gets confusing," she rubbed her temples with her fingertips, "was traced thanks to the wonder of technology. Now I don't understand a thing about technology, I have trouble even accessing my emails. But our IT analysts, now they're fantastic. They were able to trace the sent location of this email and do you happen to know where it originated?" Of course he did. But he wasn't going to do her job for her and she seemed to be building to something that was making her voice quiver with excitement. Maybe she could see her promotion just peeking around the corner, smell the extra cash that it would give her.

"Why don't you tell me?" He said in a flat, emotionless voice. It was more of a statement really than a question. The sweat had permeated his shirt by now and he could feel it trickling down his spine, he could barely see through the stars that were popping in his vision. Maybe he was falling or floating, he couldn't tell.

"It came from just north of Margate, funny enough exactly where Mr Ellison moors a private boat. I've never been a boat person, myself; I get seasick. But there you are." She walked around the other side of the table, sat down directly in front of him this time, only inches away and continued. He barely heard her; all he could think about was a cold, dark cell that would be his home for a very long time, he could feel his heart thrashing in his chest.

"We are in touch with the mooring company right now who actually keep CCTV footage for 10 years, apparently it's for insurance purposes but I, for one, am very pleased. I think I know what I'm going to find. I think I'm going to see Jake Hanbury boarding this boat with you but I don't think I'm going to see him come back, does that sound about accurate?"

"My client is not answering anything without evidence." Adrian said sternly though it didn't make a whole lot of difference because it was true. The detective smiled an evil grin.

"Oh this is going to be good. Once I have this evidence I'm going to get a judge to sign a warrant to access the computer logs of that vessel on that night and I'm going to see exactly where you went. Which will then lead me, no doubt, to Jake's body and you will face charges for double murder, obstruction of justice, identity theft, fraud and a thousand other things including what happened last night." Detective Brannon concluded with a grandiose slam of her hand on the table, he saw a bit of spit fly from her mouth.

Garrett felt his knees buckle and he slumped down in the chair. Adrian was up in a second, trying to catch him as he fell. It took a few minutes for Garrett to compose himself. When he finally looked up, the detective was gone but her words still rang in his ears. Double murder. Jake Hanbury. The boat. The panic attack that had hit him earlier, the overwhelming feeling of dread. He was going to prison for a very long time, there was no escape from it.

When Detective Eileen Brannon had resumed her role as lead detective after a two-year absence, she would have had no idea that the first case she would be investigating would be the only one she hadn't been able to solve. Garrett Langford, the man who had killed David Ellison, had somehow slipped through the cracks for five years posing as him every single day, hiding in plain sight.

The detective was confident that she knew what she was going to find when she accessed the CCTV footage from the mooring company. And she was right. Garrett was left alone in the interrogation room for another two hours before the detective returned, she was holding a laptop out like she was presenting him a gift. Garrett felt his stomach sink even farther if that were even possible. All he could think about was the numbness in his body and the blankness of his mind. But there was something else, a small hole in his chest. Almost a slight weightlessness to him that he hadn't felt in a very long time, was this the guilt and the pressure slowly falling away?

She placed the laptop in front of him and stood by the side of the table, her fingers resting on the lid waiting to open it like a chest full of gold and jewels.

"I think we should all take a break and let's watch what I just received from the mooring company." She said with a flash of teeth. The only emotion Garrett felt wash over him was an all-consuming emptiness. Before he could say a word the screen sprang into life and a video with dates and times embedded into the frame of the footage began to play.

It was a dark night, there were tiny flecks of dirt and bugs passing over the lens of the camera. The infrared lighting illuminated a boatyard which covered two berths, one of which was empty. The other had a fancy yacht docked in it. The name of the yacht was *Serenity*, it was clearly David's boat. The video played for a moment and the yacht bobbed ever so gently on the calm water. The time was 02:03am. Garrett watched as a man walked onto the screen, not looking at the camera, instead he walked up to the yacht and looked over the edge toward the cabin, presumably checking something. At 02:04 another man, clearly Garrett, appeared on the footage emerging from the cabin and walked towards the man leering at him from the dock.

At this point there were four officers huddled around the

laptop watching intently, Detective Brannon stood off to the side keeping her attention on David and Adrian alone having presumably seen the video already. The footage continued for another three minutes or so until the man was invited onto the deck of the yacht and both people on the screen turned, their faces clearly visible on the camera. Garrett knew that any minute he would see his past-self driving off toward the open sea with Jake Hanbury on board. Though he knew it was him, he couldn't quite remember it this way; it was as if there holes in his memory.

The video suddenly cut out and Detective Brannon closed the laptop lid. Garrett could feel his world crumbling around him and he knew that there was no way out now. The evidence was conclusive, he had been caught on camera with Jake Hanbury which was the last time he was seen alive. Adrian sat quietly by his side, attempting to offer him support in some way but Garrett pushed him away, unwilling to take the reassuring hand on his shoulder. This was his problem to deal with, no one else's and now he had to face the facts that he was going to prison. No one could make that feel better and, in a way, he knew he deserved it.

"I also have one more video to show you, this one is particularly interesting." Detective Brannon said, breaking the silence that fallen in the room since the video had stopped. Her sudden voice made him jump but he remained quiet as she opened the laptop once more, located another video file and loaded it up. When she hit play he saw it was the same camera but the time stamp had changed to 03:34 and there was no yacht docked in the same space *Serenity* had vacated. At 03:35 a white yacht crept into focus as it made its way back. Garrett knew that he would be the only person to disembark but he was still forced to watch it play out in front of Adrian, Detective Brannon and the other officers.

This time when the video ended, there was an audible gasp from the group. Garrett had been caught on camera again, alone as he knew he would be. The evidence against him was damning and there was no doubt of what had transpired on the open waters and knew it would play out the exact same way to a jury. Garrett could feel the tears welling up in his eyes but he refused to give the detective the satisfaction of seeing them fall. Part of his tears came from fear but another part he was sure was relief. Relief from living a lie for so long. It was really over.

"I need a moment to confer with my client." Adrian said in a low voice. Detective Brannon smiled and nodded her head. She motioned for the officers to follow her out of the room and they obliged.

Adrian sat down next to Garrett and took his hand in between his own, grasping them firmly. He could see the fear and uncertainty in Garrett's eyes and knew that he had to be honest with his client.

"David... Garrett, I've been a lawyer for a long time and I know the law inside out. I can argue for a lighter jail sentence if you confess. The evidence is overwhelming, but I'm advising you as your lawyer and also your friend. You don't want this to go to trial. A jury will put you away for the rest of your life." Garrett was silent for a moment before he finally nodded his head. Adrian squeezed his hand and gave him a small smile.

"I'll make the arrangements, we'll get the detective in and you can make your confession."

"Am I going to die in prison?" Garrett asked. It felt stupid to say it. He felt like a child asking his parents if they were mad because he broke an ornament.

"Not if I can help it but I have to be blunt with you, it doesn't look good. I'm not here to judge you for anything you've done, I'm just here to advise and to fight for you, that's all." Somehow this made Garrett feel a little bit better.

"Ok. I'm ready to confess." He replied with a small sense of inner peace filling the void in his stomach. Adrian left the room and returned with the detective who sat down and propped up a video camera. She pressed a button and a red light appeared in the corner of the screen that faced him. He looked dishevelled and unkempt, a hollow look on his sunken face. There were bags under his eyes which were bloodshot.

"Your lawyer tells me you want to confess. I have this camera set up to record it all to be used as evidence. Do you understand?" Garrett made a small but obvious nod. When he started talking, he found he couldn't stop. The darkness inside him that had grown for five years, the heinous things he had done, the people he had hurt and lied to all hit him with full force but he kept talking nonetheless. As he admitted to each crime, it felt like a small piece of the darkness fell away from his soul. He knew he would never be whole again, that he would never see his family again; he'd hurt them too much. But he was at peace and when the red light went out he found he couldn't talk anymore.

The voice that had spewed nothing but lies every waking second of the last five years had had enough of talking. And Garrett Langford never spoke a word again, not when they hauled him off to prison, not when he was handed a life without parole sentence, not even when his father came to visit him in prison for the first and only time some fifteen years later to tell him that his mother had passed away.

Television screens across the nation broadcast the news that Garrett Langford died in prison sometime in his early forties from a heart attack that claimed him in the middle of the night. The reaction from the general public was not unexpected; thousands of people posted on social media of their happiness that one more evil soul had been wiped from the planet. Though there was a minority that seemed to feel only pity that such a person could be led astray and wished his family peace as they processed the death. The news was huge and came as a shock to prison officials who noted that he seemed to be healthy the day before and insisted that there was nothing they could have done to prevent it. His funeral consisted of one person, Detective Eileen Brannon who had become the Commissioner of Police. She had simply tipped her head as he was lowered into the ground, ready for the earth to greet him. There were no friends or family around him to wish him peace as he departed from this life; in their minds, the Garrett they knew had died long ago and the person in the coffin that had been sent down for double murder was nothing more than a lookalike of the man they once knew and loved.